IVAN SERGEYEVICH TURGENEV was born in Orel in 1818. He was educated first at home, later at the universities of Moscow and St. Petersburg. In 1839 he studied at the University of Berlin where he acquired the Western values for which he was much criticized in Russia throughout his life. In 1843 he successfully published *Parasha*—a tale in verse. His infatuation with the famous singer Mme. Viardot caused his mother to cut off his allowance, and he lived as a Bohemian until her death in 1850 made him a rich man. In 1852 Turgenev abandoned poetry and the drama; thereafter he devoted himself wholly to fiction. His first successful novel, *A Sportsman's Sketches* (1852), contrasted appealing peasants and unpleasant masters. The next decade produced *Rudin* (1856), *A Nest of Gentlefolk* (1858), *On the Eve* (1860), *First Love* (1860), and *Fathers and Sons* (1862)—all of which drew critics' applause. The radical press, however, initiated strong and continuing criticism of the "nihilist" Bazarov in *Fathers and Sons*. Deeply offended, Turgenev left Russia for France, where he became an intimate of Flaubert and the French literary world. His novels *Smoke* (1867) and *Virgin Soil* (1877) show the depth of his bitterness and his loss of touch with contemporary Russia. However, his last visit to Russia (1880) marked a triumphant homecoming. He died in 1883, at Bougival, near Paris.

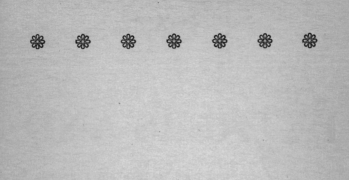

Ivan Turgenev

FATHERS AND SONS

A NEW TRANSLATION BY
George Reavy

WITH A FOREWORD BY
Alan Hodge

A SIGNET CLASSIC
NEW AMERICAN LIBRARY

SIGNET CLASSIC TRADEMARK REG. U.S. PAT. OFF. AND FOREIGN COUNTRIES
REGISTERED TRADEMARK—MARCA REGISTRADA
HECHO EN CHICAGO, U.S.A.

SIGNET, SIGNET CLASSIC, MENTOR, ONYX, PLUME, MERIDIAN AND
NAL BOOKS are published by NAL PENGUIN INC.,
1633 Broadway, New York, New York 10019

16 17 18 19 20 21 22 23 24

Foreword

FOR Western readers Turgenev is the most engaging of the great Russian novelists. Open any of his novels, and from the first chapter one's sympathy and curiosity are aroused. Take the beginning of *Fathers and Sons*. A middle-aged landowner is affectionately waiting to welcome his son, freshly down from the University. In very few words Turgenev conveys the amiable but ineffectual charm of Nicholas Kirsanov. This is done not so much by the summary of his life, all to the point though that is, as by the lightly drawn contrast between Nicholas in his dusty overcoat and his foppish and pretentious valet.

As Nicholas waits on the porch, lost in the warm glow of reverie, a plump gaudy chicken struts by on sturdy yellow legs, eyed with hostility by a marauding cat. Is this just a telling stroke in the picture of a rural posting-house—the sort of realistic item Defoe might have thought of? Or is not Nicholas himself a kind of plump gaudy chicken, upon whom hostile fate is about to spring? The book is full of these significant touches in which a bird or a pot of gooseberry jam, a piece of furniture or the cut of a coat—all the adjuncts and surroundings of everyday life—are brought out of the background to suggest the colour of a mood and the shape of expectations to come. When young Arcady Kirsanov arrives, we very soon see who will play the rôle of marauding cat. It is Arcady's formidable college-friend whom he worships and from whom he takes all his opinions, Bazarov the Nihilist. But though we know, or rather guess, that conflict will break out between Nicholas and young Arcady, we have only this neat and light hint to go on. Turgenev never underlines, never over-emphasizes. The plump gaudy chicken struts out of the story, having for the space of one sentence become almost a symbol.

If there is one supreme gift in the novelist's art, it is the capacity for drawing his story out of the very natures of his characters, letting the situation unfold and develop as the various and frequently contrasting sides of their personalities are revealed. This gift Turgenev possesses to the highest degree. Every character in his books, whatever his faults, has the attractive quality of humanity, and it is out of the human contrariety of his people that the story grows. It has been said of Turgenev that he never provides a plot. In the sense in which Trollope builds up his plots, step by step, according to a careful dramatic schedule, this is certainly true. By comparison Turgenev is episodic; seemingly casually, he assembles one telling scene after another. Each one is a portrait of moods and feelings at a moment in time, compounded of memories and of hopes, of conflict and of harmony—between the characters, and within themselves. The scenes are so vivid, and their succession so unerringly presented, that one is left with the impression of knowing every significant detail of the lives of Turgenev's creation. Through his imaginative insight, the slightest characters appear in the round, and the most ordinary incidents acquire their full emotional importance.

It was this mastery of impressionistic realism, in psychology and in background as well, that won for Turgenev his enthusiastic following in France. Flaubert was perhaps his closest friend, Maupassant his most brilliant disciple. Towards the end of his days, Turgenev became practically an honorary Frenchman of letters. All his life he had been a "Westerner," as the Russians defined it. Largely he was so by temperament, but there were other motives. His tyrannical mother kept a firm grip on the family estates; living on them, with her in charge, was never a pleasure for long. For a large part of his life, also, Turgenev was deeply attached to Mme. Viardot, the opera singer—and, curiously enough, to her husband and children too. There were few years when he did not spend many months in her company. But for all his ties with the West, Russia is always the essential subject of his books. In his political outlook—and long before Communist days no Russian author was without one—he was a liberal, an advocate of emancipation of the serfs and, in Tsarist terms, altogether a man of "advanced" views. In his own country his "Westernism" and his liberalism brought him many critics. But never had Turgenev to face such a storm of criticism as was provoked by *Fathers and Sons*. The reason for this was wholly the novel revolutionary figure of Bazarov.

Before and after Turgenev's day, Russian fiction has been full of delightful characters who plan great projects they will never accomplish, of brilliant talkers incapable of managing even their own private lives. Turgenev's own Rudin, in the novel of that name, is one of the most impressive of these "superfluous men"—to use Turgenev's own phrase. To them, Bazarov stands in complete contrast. In a sense he is the literary ancestor of the hard-shelled, self-possessed commissars celebrated in so many early Soviet films and novels. For Bazarov is the rejector of all current beliefs and illusions; only after they have been swept aside, he is convinced, can a new and better world be built. In Turgenev's eyes, Bazarov was the most profoundly sympathetic of his creations—and we shall see in a moment how often and how skilfully he engages the reader's feelings on Bazarov's side. But to the young intelligentsia of Petersburg and Moscow, Bazarov seemed an uncouth caricature of all they stood for. And by the diehards he was considered to epitomize the crudity of would-be revolutionaries. Turgenev was horrified to find himself congratulated by crusty old believers in serfdom, whose friendship he did not welcome, and bitterly reproached by the young reformers, whose views he largely shared.

The dust of this controversy has long since settled—at least for English readers. But its violence is a proof of how brilliantly Turgenev held the scales in the conflict of *Fathers and Sons*. He remained convinced that Bazarov was the most striking of all his characters, and for a long time he kept a diary in which he entered with relish the sort of iconoclastic opinions that Bazarov would have expressed on all sorts of general subjects. But here we need to remind ourselves that Turgenev compiled similar dossiers, though less thoroughly, for most of his characters; and that his supreme interest lay in people, not in opinions. *Fathers and Sons* is not a study in the doctrine of Nihilism, or even a simple story of conflict between parents and children. Its drama lies in the impact on all its characters of one extraordinarily gifted, impatient and caustic man. Bazarov alone is the agent who utterly changes the tenor of existence in the household of the Kirsanovs; in the life of the brilliant, beautiful and cold-hearted Mme Odintsov, with whom he falls in love, and finally in the wonderfully characterized home of his own tedious but adoring parents. The genius of the novel lies in the delicately even balance kept between the rights and wrongs of all parties to the drama. For though Bazarov may be a destroyer, so much that he attacks is false and sham and worthy of destruction.

The Kirsanov household, for instance, is full of fine feelings and good intentions. But their estate is hopelessly mismanaged. What useful purpose in the world do the two elder Kirsanovs serve? Nicholas, for all his liberalism, keeps a former peasant girl for a mistress, like any old-fashioned feudatory, and his brother, Paul, is a touchy dandified romantic, doting on long-lost love. Yet when the conflict finally breaks out between the older and younger generations, one's sympathies go to the old people: it is the old who possess tolerance, good manners, and the desire to understand. On the other hand, while he has been on the estate, Bazarov has succeeded in making Nicholas's mistress, the shy and lovely Fenichka, feel at ease with "the gentry" for the first time in her life; and he has been most kind and attentive towards her baby. . . . In this debate there is no end to the oscillation of rights and wrongs. If Bazarov in Chapter X seems a lout in comparison with Paul Kirsanov, how neatly the tables are turned in Chapter XXIV. There, in a superbly grotesque duel, it is Paul's behaviour that is ridiculous and absurd.

Neat shifts of emphasis, intricate changes of feeling—the story abounds in them. Nothing could be finer, to take another example, than the hardly perceptible stages by which young Arcady Kirsanov begins to doubt some of his friend's judgments, then to question them, and finally to quarrel with him. A simple process, one might suppose, of disillusionment with theories, once they have started to come into conflict with the loyalties of love. But the most straightforward themes in Turgenev have subtle complexities. Arcady's change of mind could not take place without the transfer of his worship to Katya. He would not have fallen back upon Katya had he not imagined himself under the spell of her elder sister, Mme Odintsov. And would he have thought himself in love with her, but for his desire to follow Bazarov's example in everything?

Bazarov's own end is tragic and ironical. Mme Odintsov is delighted to discuss with him everything under the sun.

He is tremendously moved and impressed by the emancipated brilliance of her mind. Has he at last found someone with whom he can really and truly share the great future that lies before him? But Mme Odintsov has the timidity of an intellectual flirt; she is thoroughly frightened by the violence of the passion she arouses in him. Had she been able to respond, he would not have gone sulking off to his father's small village, nor in an idle and disgruntled moment have undertaken to perform an autopsy, cut himself, caught typhus and pitifully died.

By a magnificent piece of alchemy in these last pages, Turgenev manages to convince one that though Bazarov's great talents have been wasted, and his life almost fruitless, here was a personality possessed of fascinating stimulation. Arcady may marry his Katya, and Nicholas at last his Fenichka, but are not these happy endings in a way Bazarov's achievement? And will not the most important thing in the lives of the Kirsanovs, as of everyone else in the book, always be to have known Bazarov? That, at least, is the answer Turgenev would have given to those who accused him of letting the old order of humanity triumph and, in Bazarov's death, of stifling the new.

Alan Hodge

Father and Sons

I

"WELL, Peter, any sign of them yet?" This was the question addressed on the 20th of May, 1859, to his servant—a young and lusty fellow with whitish down on his chin and with small dim eyes—by a gentleman of just over forty years of age, in a dusty overcoat and check trousers, as he emerged hatless on the low steps of a posting-station on the X highway.

Everything about the valet—his single turquoise earring, his pomaded hair of various shades and his studied gestures—proclaimed him a representative of a modern and more perfect age; and, as he stared superciliously down the road, he vouchsafed a reply, "No-o, there's no sign of them."

"No sign of them?" his master queried.

"Not a sign," the valet repeated.

His master gave vent to a sigh and sat down on a bench. While he is sitting there, with his legs tucked under him and gazing pensively around, let us introduce him to our readers.

His name was Nicholas Petrovich Kirsanov. Within ten miles of the posting-station he owned a fair estate—a "farm" as he now called it, having divided his land and rented it out to his former serfs. His father, who had seen service as a general in the War of 1812, had been a half-literate, coarse, but not bad sort of Russian; as a commander, first of a brigade and then of a division, he had led a strenuous life, but had spent most of his time in the provinces where, by virtue of his rank, he had wielded quite an appreciable influence. Nicholas Petrovich, like his brother Paul (of whom we shall speak later), was born in the south of Russia and brought up at home until the age of fourteen in an environment of inexpensive tutors, garrulous and obsequious adjutants, and other such regimental and staff personages. His mother, who came of the Kolyazin family and in her youth had been called *Agathe* and later, when she married a general, Agafokleia Kuzminishna Kirsanov, belonged to

11

the species of "commanding matrons"; she wore brightly
coloured caps and gaudy silk dresses, was invariably the first
to put her lips to the cross at mass, and was in the habit of
holding forth loudly and at length upon having her children
kiss her hand in the morning and bestowing a blessing on
them at bedtime—in short, she ruled the roost. Although
not distinguished for courage—he had even been dubbed
"poltroon"—Nicholas Petrovich was under an obligation,
as was his brother Paul, to join the army; but having broken
a leg on the very day that he heard the news of his success in
obtaining a commission, he spent a couple of months in bed
and retained a slight limp for the remainder of his life. Giving him up as a bad job, his father let him take up a civilian
occupation. As soon as Nicholas had reached the age of
eighteen, he took him to Petersburg and registered him at
the University. By that time, his brother Paul had got his
commission in a Guards regiment. The two young men
started their life together, in the same apartment, under the
distant tutelage of Ilya Kolyazin, an official of standing who
was a cousin on their mother's side. Their father rejoined his
division and also his wife; every now and then, he dispatched
to his sons a few large sheets of greyish paper scribbled over
in an ornate clerkly handwriting. At the bottom, these sheets
were decoratively inscribed with the words, "Peter Kirsanov,
Major-General," painstakingly ringed by an ornamental
scrawl. In 1835 Nicholas Petrovich took his degree. In the
same year, General Kirsanov, who had been retired from the
service as a result of an incident at a military parade he had
commanded, arrived in Petersburg with his wife, intending
to settle there. But he suddenly died of an apoplectic stroke
when he was on the point of renting a house in the vicinity
of the Tavrichesky Gardens and had put his name down for
the English Club. His wife soon followed him: she could not
get accustomed to a dull life in the capital; the boredom of
living in retirement had proved too much for her.

In the meantime, to his parents' great annoyance while
they were still alive, Nicholas Petrovich had fallen in love
with the daughter of an official by the name of Prepoloven-
sky, his former landlord. She was a pretty and, as they say,
"cultured" girl, who was addicted to reading serious articles
in the Science section of the *Gazettes*. He married her as
soon as the period of mourning was over and, having
resigned from the Ministry of Pensions in which his father's

influence had procured him a post, lived very happily with his Masha, first in a cottage near the Lesnoy Institute, then in a small but attractive apartment in town, with a clean staircase and a chilly drawing-room. Finally he withdrew to the country, where he settled for good and where his son, Arcady, was born. The young married couple lived very happily and tranquilly: they were almost inseparable, they read to one another, played piano duets and sang together; she planted flowers and kept a poultry-yard, while he sometimes went out hunting and busied himself with the management of the estate. In the meantime, Arcady grew and grew—also very happily and tranquilly. Ten years passed like a dream. In 1847 Kirsanov's wife died. He hardly survived the shock and went grey within a few weeks; then he decided to go abroad for a change . . . but it was 1848, the year of revolutions. Reluctantly he returned to the country and, after a prolonged period of inactivity, set about "reforming" his estate. In 1855 he took his son to the University: he spent three years with him in Petersburg, avoiding social engagements and trying his hardest to strike up an acquaintance with his son's young friends. He had been unable to spend the last winter in Petersburg—and so we meet him, in the month of May, 1859, a grizzled, slightly bent, stoutish, elderly gentleman, waiting for the arrival of his son who, as he himself had once done, had just taken his degree.

Out of a feeling of respect or, perhaps, because he wished to escape his master's scrutiny, the valet strolled under the gateway and lit his pipe. Nicholas Petrovich let drop his head and began to examine the rickety steps of the porch: with an air of dignity, a plump, gaudy chicken was strutting on them, stamping firmly about on its sturdy yellow legs; a filthy cat was eyeing him with hostility as it sprawled posturing on the banisters. The sun was blazing: a smell of freshly baked rye bread was wafted from a shadowy passage in the posting-house. Nicholas Petrovich had surrendered himself to his reverie. "His son . . . a graduate . . . his Arcady . . ." Such were the thoughts ceaselessly spinning in his head; he made an effort to divert his mind to other things, but the very same thoughts came flooding back. He remembered his late wife . . . "She did not live to see this day," he whispered mournfully. . . . A bulky blue pigeon settled on the roadway and waddled off hastily to quench its thirst in a pool next to the well. Nicholas Petrovich directed his attention to it just as a rumble of approaching wheels began to impinge upon his ears. . . .

"Looks as if they're coming," the valet reported, darting out of the gateway.

Nicholas Petrovich jumped up and fixed his gaze on the highway. A tarantass came into view, drawn by three stage-horses; in the tarantass the band of a student's cap gleamed for an instant, and then he caught sight of a dear and famil-iar face. . . .

"Arcady! Arcady!" Kirsanov shouted, waving his hands and running forward. . . . A few seconds later, he was already pressing his lips on the young bachelor's beardless, dusty and sun-tanned cheeks.

II

"LET me dust myself, daddy!" Arcady exclaimed in a ring-ing, youthful voice, which the journey had made slightly husky, as he cheerfully returned his father's embraces. "I shall only soil you."

"No matter, no matter," Nicholas Petrovich kept repeat-ing with an affectionate smile as, first of all, he slapped his son's coat a couple of times, and then his own. "Let me look at you, let me see you," he added, standing back. Then he hurried off towards the posting-station, reiterating as he went: "Quick there, quick, bring out the horses."

Nicholas Petrovich appeared more excited than his son; he looked a little flurried and overcome with shyness. Arcady stopped him.

"Daddy," he cried, "allow me to introduce my great friend Bazarov, about whom I have written so often. Very kindly he has consented to stay with us."

Nicholas Petrovich spun quickly round and, going up to a tall man in a longish, loose-fitting country overcoat with tassels, who had just climbed out of the tarantass, he warmly gripped the red, ungloved hand, which his son's friend had been in no hurry to extend to him.

"I am heartily glad," he began, "and grateful, too, for

your good intention in wishing to visit us; I hope . . . May I ask your name and patronymic?"

"Eugene Vassilich," Bazarov replied in a drawling but virile voice and, throwing back the collar of his coat, showed his full face to Nicholas Petrovich. The face was long and gaunt, with a broad forehead, a nose flat above but tapering below, large greenish eyes and bushy whiskers of a sandy colour—the whole animated with a serene smile and expressive of self-assurance and intelligence.

"I trust, my dear Eugene Vassilich," Nicholas Petrovich went on, "that your stay with us will not bore you."

Bazarov's thin lips gave a slight twitch; but he made no reply and merely touched his cap. His fine dark hair, which grew long and thick, failed to conceal the bulges on his large skull.

"Well? What shall we do, Arcady?" Nicholas Petrovich began again, turning to his son. "Shall we have the horses harnessed at once? Or would you prefer to rest here first?"

"We'll rest at home, daddy. Tell them to get the horses ready."

"Immediately, immediately!" his father exclaimed. "Hey, Peter, did you hear that? Get on with it. Look lively."

Peter, as an up-to-date servant, had not ventured to approach the young master to kiss his hand, but had merely bowed from a distance; now he vanished once more through the gateway.

"I have my barouche here, and there is also a fresh relay of horses available for your tarantass," Nicholas Petrovich put in fussily, while Arcady gulped some water from an iron mug which the station-master's wife had brought, and Bazarov, puffing at his pipe, went up to the coachman who had unharnessed the horses. "There is only room for two in my barouche, and I don't know how your friend . . ."

"He'll manage in the tarantass," Arcady interrupted in an undertone. "Please don't be so ceremonious with him. He's a grand fellow and very simple at heart—you'll see for yourself."

Nicholas Petrovich's coachman led out the horses.

"Get on with it, you bush-beard!" Bazarov exclaimed, addressing the coachman.

"D'ye hear, Mityuha," interjected another coachman, who was standing nearby with his hands thrust into the back openings of his sheepskin coat, "d'ye hear what that gentleman was after calling you? 'Bush-beard,' that's what he said."

Mityuha merely gave a pull at his cap and started to drag the reins from the sweating shaft-horse.

"Look lively, lively, my lads. Now come along and lend a hand," Nicholas Petrovich shouted. "I'll see to it you get money for vodka!"

Within a few minutes the horses were harnessed; the Kirsanovs got into their barouche; Peter clambered up on the box; Bazarov leapt into the tarantass, pressed his head against the leather cushion—and both vehicles drove away.

III

"HERE you are, a graduate now, and back in the fold," Nicholas Petrovich said, patting Arcady now on the shoulder, now on the knee. "Home at last!"

"And how is Uncle Paul? Is he keeping well?" inquired Arcady who, despite a sincere and child-like feeling of elation, was anxious to switch the conversation as soon as possible from an emotional level to one of ordinary conversation.

"He's well enough. He wished to come and meet you, but for some reason changed his mind."

"And have you been long waiting for me?" Arcady asked.

"About five hours."

"How kind of you, daddy!"

Quickly turning round, Arcady gave his father a smacking kiss on the cheek. Nicholas Petrovich uttered a subdued laugh.

"You should just see the horse I've got waiting for you!" he began. "You'll see. And we've also had fresh wall-paper put in your room."

"And is there a room for Bazarov?"

"We'll find him one, too."

"Please, daddy, do be very kind to him. I can't tell you how much I esteem his friendship."

"You became acquainted recently?"

"Yes, recently."

"That explains why I did not meet him in the winter. What does he do?"

"The natural sciences are his main subject. But he knows everything. Next year he intends to take his final medical exam."

"Ah! So he's in the medical faculty," Nicholas Petrovich remarked and then paused. "Peter," he added, pointing, "are those our peasants driving along there?"

Peter glanced in the direction his master had indicated. Several carts, drawn by unbridled horses, were rolling at a good pace along the narrow by-road. Each cart held one or two peasants, wearing sheepskin coats flapping wide open.

"That's correct, sir," Peter replied.

"Where are they going? To town?"

"To town most likely. To the gin-shop," he added superciliously, with a slight nod at the driver as if expecting him to confirm this. But the latter did not move an eyelid: a peasant of the old school, he disapproved of the modern outlook.

"The peasants are giving me a lot of worry this year," Nicholas Petrovich went on, addressing his son. "They won't pay their rent. What am I to do with them?"

"And the hired labourers? Are you satisfied with them?"

"Yes," Arcady's father squeezed through his teeth. "But the trouble is they are being led astray; they are not doing their best yet. They only smash the tools. However, in their ploughing they did tolerably well. There should be enough flour when the corn's threshed. Have you become interested in farming now?"

"How unfortunate to have no shade here," Arcady remarked, without replying to the question.

"I had a large awning put up on the north side, over the terrace," Nicholas Petrovich answered. "Now we can even dine in the open air."

"That will make the house look like a summer cottage. . . . However, that doesn't matter very much. The air here is magnificent. How fragrant it is! I do believe the air smells sweeter here than anywhere else in the world! And these skies . . ."

Arcady suddenly paused, glanced quickly back, and relapsed into silence.

"Of course," Nicholas Petrovich remarked, "you were

born here; in these parts everything must seem very special to you."

"But, daddy, what does it matter where a man was born!"

"And yet . . ."

"No, it doesn't matter at all."

Nicholas Petrovich glanced sideways at his son: the barouche rolled on for another half a mile before they resumed their conversation.

"I don't remember if I ever wrote and told you," Nicholas Petrovich began, "about the death of Yegorovna—your nanny."

"You don't mean that she's dead? Poor old soul! And is Prokofyich still alive?"

"Yes, and he hasn't altered a bit. He grumbles as much as ever. On the whole, you won't find many changes at Maryino."

"Have you still got the same steward?"

"That's one of the few things I have changed. I decided that I would not keep any of the former house-serfs about the place once they were liberated, or at least, that I would not entrust them with any jobs involving responsibility." (Arcady glanced significantly at Peter.) *"Il est libre en effet,"* Nicholas Petrovich remarked in an undertone, "but he's merely a valet. My new steward is a man from town; he seems an efficient sort of person. I pay him a salary of two hundred and fifty roubles a year. However," he added, rubbing his forehead and eyebrows with his hand, "though I told you that you would find no changes at Maryino . . . that is not quite correct. I think it my duty to warn you that . . ."

He hesitated for an instant and then went on to speak in French.

"A strict moralist would judge my frankness improper, but, firstly, this thing cannot be concealed and, secondly, as you know very well, I have always had principles of my own as to the relations between father and son. You would be within your rights, of course, to condemn me. At my age . . . In short, that . . . that girl, of whom you have probably heard already . . ."

"Fenichka?" Arcady asked in a clear voice.

His father blushed.

"Please don't mention her name aloud. . . . Well, yes . . . she is now living with me. I have taken her into the house

. . . we had a couple of small rooms to spare. However, we can change all that."

"But why should you, daddy, if I may ask?"

"Your friend will be staying with us now. . . . It might be embarrassing."

"Please don't worry about Bazarov. He is above prejudice."

"It's off my chest, at least," Nicholas Petrovich said. "The rooms in the wing are not so comfortable, that's the trouble."

"But, daddy, you seem to be apologizing," Arcady interjected. "Are you ashamed?"

"Of course I should be ashamed," Nicholas Petrovich replied, getting redder and redder.

"Enough, daddy, enough, I entreat you!" Arcady exclaimed, smiling affectionately. "Why apologize?" His heart filled with a feeling of indulgent tenderness for his kind and sensitive father, mingled with a secret sense of superiority. "Do please stop it now," he repeated, involuntarily enjoying the awareness of his own advanced and emancipated state.

Nicholas Petrovich glanced at him through the fingers of the hand with which he continued to rub his forehead, and felt his heart twinge. . . . But immediately he took all the blame on himself.

"Look! Our fields already," he said after a long pause.

"And isn't that our forest over there?" Arcady inquired.

"Yes. But I have just sold it. It will be cut down this year."

"Why did you sell it?"

"I needed the money; and besides, those lands were part of the peasants' share."

"Of the peasants who won't pay rent?"

"That's their affair; anyway—they will pay me one day."

"I'm sorry about the forest," Arcady remarked, staring round him.

The locality through which they were driving could not be described as picturesque. On all sides, fields upon fields spread as far as the horizon, now sloping gently up, now sloping gently down; scattered here and there, copses could be seen, and winding ravines planted with sparse, stunted bushes, which reminded the traveller of the way they had been indicated on the old maps of Catherine the Great's reign. They also came on streams whose banks had been hollowed out, minute ponds with rickety dykes, hamlets with squat little huts beneath sombre thatched roofs which were only partially intact, tumbledown threshing barns with wattled walls and doorways gaping on abandoned threshing floors, and churches, sometimes of brick with peeling plaster and sometimes of wood with crosses awry and graveyards gone to wrack and ruin. Arcady felt his heart gradually contract. As though to confirm this pattern of neglect, the peasants whom they met on the way looked miserable and their nags wretched; like ragged beggars, the roadside willows stood with their bark ripped off and their branches broken; emaciated cows, shaggy and gnawn with hunger, were plucking greedily at the grass in the ditches. They looked as if they had just escaped from the dread and deadly claws of some wild animal—and, on this beautiful spring day, the heartrending plight of these enfeebled animals evoked the white spectre of a joyless and endless winter, its blizzards, frosts and snows. . . . "No," Arcady mused, "there is no prosperity here. There is no abundance and no hard work; this country simply cannot remain as it is, it will have to be transformed. . . . But how can that be achieved? How should one go about it? . . ."

Such were Arcady's reflections. . . . While he meditated, spring claimed its own. Everything round him glittered gold and green; in the soft breath of a warm breeze everything stirred gently, all things—the trees, the bushes and the grasses; on every side larks trilled endlessly and ecstatically; the plovers called, weaving in flight over the low-lying meadows or skipping from stump to stump in silence; the rooks strutted about, beautifully and blackly outlined against the tender green background of the as yet short spring corn; darting into the rye, which was already slightly tinged with white, they let their heads be seen now and then among its smoky waves. Arcady stared and stared until his thoughts grew dim and, finally, faded. . . . Throwing off his student's greatcoat, he glanced at his father so brightly and boyishly that the latter embraced him once again.

"It's no distance now," Nicholas Petrovich remarked. "Once we reach the top of the hill, the house will be in sight. We shall have a glorious time of it, Arcady; you can help me to manage the estate if that doesn't bore you. We must draw closer, we must get to know each other better, don't you think?"

"Certainly," Arcady replied. "But what a marvellous day!"

"Especially for your arrival, my dear. Yes, spring is at its glorious zenith. Incidentally, I agree with Pushkin—do you remember those lines in *Eugene Onegin?*

> How sad your coming is to me,
> O spring, O spring, the time of love!
> What——"

"Arcady!" Bazarov shouted from the tarantass. "Will you send a match over? I have none left for my pipe."

Nicholas Petrovich fell silent. Arcady, who had begun to listen to the recitation not without surprise and a certain sympathy, hastened to produce a silver match-box from his pocket and to send it over with Peter.

"Would you like a cigar?" Bazarov shouted again.

"Send it over," Arcady called back.

Peter ran back to the barouche and, together with the match-box, handed him a black cigar, which Arcady instantly lit, diffusing such a potent and acrid smell of cheap tobacco that his father, who was no smoker, was obliged to turn away his nose—but this he did very discreetly for fear of offending his son.

A quarter of an hour later, both vehicles pulled up in front of the porch of a newly built wooden house, coated with grey paint and topped by a red iron-sheeted roof. This was Maryino, known also as the "New Suburb" or, as the peasants had dubbed it, the "Will-o'-the-wisp Farm."

IV

No throng of servants swarmed from the house to greet the gentlemen; only a girl of about twelve came down the steps, followed by a lad very like Peter, wearing a grey livery jacket with white crested buttons; he was Paul Petrovich's valet. Silently he opened the door of the barouche and then undid the leather apron of the tarantass. Followed by his son and Bazarov, Nicholas Petrovich passed through the dim and almost bare reception room, behind the door of which they caught a glimpse of a young woman's face, and into the drawing-room, which was furnished in the latest style.

"You're at home now!" Nicholas Petrovich exclaimed, taking off his cap and tossing back his hair. "What you now need is supper and rest."

"Actually, a bite to eat would not be a bad idea," Bazarov remarked, stretching himself and sinking down on the sofa.

"Yes, indeed, we must have supper served. The supper quickly!" Nicholas Petrovich exclaimed, stamping his feet for no apparent reason. "Ah, here comes Prokofyich!"

A man of about sixty years of age, white-haired, lean and swarthy, in a brown tailed coat with brass buttons and a pink handkerchief, entered the room. He grinned, went up to kiss Arcady's hand and, having bowed to the guest, retreated to the door and put his hands behind his back.

"Here he is, Prokofyich," Nicholas Petrovich began. "He has arrived at last. . . . Well? How do you find him?"

"Looking his best," the old servitor replied, grinning once again. Then knitting his thick brows, he inquired significantly: "Do you wish me to lay the table, sir?"

"Yes, yes, please. But, Eugene Vassilich, wouldn't you like to retire to your room first?"

"No thank you, I have no need. But will you be so good as to have my luggage taken there, and this little garment too?" he added, pulling off his travelling coat.

"Certainly. Prokofyich, will you see to the gentleman's coat?" With a look of slight perplexity on his face, Prokofyich picked up Bazarov's "little garment" and, holding it with both hands high above his head, tiptoed out of the room. "Now what about you, Arcady? Do you wish to retire for a moment?"

"Yes, I must tidy myself," Arcady replied. He was about to direct his steps to the door when, at that instant, in came a man of medium height, dressed in an English suit of dark material, a fashionable cravat, and patent-leather shoes. It was Paul Petrovich Kirsanov. His appearance suggested that he might be forty-five: his grey, close-trimmed hair shone dark as silver; his bilious, unwrinkled face, whose lines were unusually symmetrical and clean-cut as though carved by a fine, light chisel, bore the traces of exceptional good looks: his black, glowing, almond-shaped eyes were particularly

attractive. The whole mien of Arcady's uncle, elegant and
well-bred in appearance, had preserved a youthful upright-
ness and a certain soaring quality which usually tends to
disappear when a man turns thirty.

From his pocket Paul Petrovich drew one of his graceful
hands, with long pink nails—a hand whose grace was further enhanced by a snowy-white cuff, linked together by a
single large opal. He extended it to his nephew. Having
achieved a preliminary European hand-shake, he kissed his
nephew thrice in the Russian fashion, that is to say, he
brushed his cheeks thrice with his scented moustaches, exclaiming, "Welcome home!"

Nicholas Petrovich introduced him to Bazarov: Paul
Petrovich gave a slight inclination with his flexible body and
a slight smile, but failed to offer his hand and in fact put
it back in his pocket.

"I was beginning to think you would not arrive to-day,"
he said in a pleasant voice, graciously swaying his body,
twitching his shoulders and displaying his fine, white teeth.
"Did anything happen on the way?"

"Nothing happened," Arcady replied. "We just took it
easy. But, as a result, we are now as hungry as wolves. Will
you tell Prokofyich to hurry up, father? I shall be back in
a second."

"Wait, I'll go with you," Bazarov suddenly exclaimed,
leaping up from the sofa. The young men went out.

"Who is he?" Paul Petrovich inquired.

"A friend of Arcady's and, according to him, a very
intelligent fellow."

"Is he staying with us?"

"Yes."

"That hairy creature?"

"Yes, he is."

Paul Petrovich drummed with his finger-nails on the table.
"I find that Arcady *s'est dégourdi*," he remarked. "I'm
so glad he's back."

There was little conversation at supper. Bazarov, in
particular, almost failed to utter a word, but ate a great
deal. Nicholas Petrovich related various incidents of his
"farmer's life," as he called it, discussed the imminent government reforms, the committees and the deputies, the need
for more farm machinery, and other matters of the sort.
Paul Petrovich slowly paced up and down the dining-room

(he never supped), taking an occasional sip of red wine, and, more rarely, uttering some remark or, rather, some exclamation, such as "Ah! Aha! H'm!" Arcady gave them news of Petersburg, but experienced a slight embarrassment—the embarrassment a young man is liable to suffer when he has just emerged from adolescence and then finds himself in a place where the company is still accustomed to regard him as a child. Drawling his sentences unnecessarily, he avoided addressing his father as "daddy," and once, though with an effort, called him "father"; with excessive assurance he poured out rather more wine than he really wanted, and drank it all. Prokofyich could not take his eyes off him and kept chewing his lips. After supper, the company immediately dispersed.

"What an eccentric uncle you have!" Bazarov exclaimed, as he sat in a dressing-gown near Arcady's bed and sucked a short-stemmed pipe. "Just think, what elegance for the country! And as for his nails—why, they're only fit for an exhibition!"

"You don't realize, of course," Arcady replied, "he was a society lion in his day. One day I shall tell his story. He was as handsome as they make them, and a regular Don Juan."

"That explains it! It's for the sake of old times, then! There are no hearts to captivate here, so much the worse. I just couldn't take my eyes off him: what wonderful collars he wears, they might be made of granite, and he shaves his chin so smoothly. Don't you find him funny, Arcady?"

"Perhaps. But he has really a very good heart."

"He's archaic! But your father's fine. A pity he has a weakness for reciting verse; it's unlikely that he understands much about estate management, but he must be a kind-hearted man."

"My father has a heart of gold."

"Have you noticed he tends to be a little shy?"

Arcady nodded his head, as though he himself were exempt from shyness.

"They simply amaze me, these old romantics!" Bazarov went on. "They excite their nervous systems to the point of irritation . . . well, and that upsets their balance. However, good night! In my room I have an English washstand, but the door of the room won't shut. Nevertheless, it's a thing to be encouraged: English washstands spell progress!"

When Bazarov had gone, a feeling of joy swept over

Arcady. It was sweet to fall asleep in one's own home, in a familiar bed, under a quilt embroidered by loving hands—those of his nanny, perhaps. Oh, those fond, kindly, indefatigable hands! Arcady remembered his nanny—Yegorovna—and sighed, wishing her eternal peace. . . . He said no prayers for himself.

Both he and Bazarov dozed off immediately, but it was a long time before some of the other inhabitants of the house could fall asleep. His son's return had excited Nicholas Petrovich. He did not snuff out the candles before getting into bed and, propping his head with his hand, remained plunged in thought for a long while. His brother sat up far past midnight in his study, in a roomy armchair in front of the fireplace where a few embers still glowed faintly. Paul Petrovich did not bother to undress but only changed his patent-leather shoes for a pair of heelless Turkish slippers. In his hands he held the last issue of *Galignani,* but did not read it; he stared fixedly into the fireplace where, dying and kindling again, a pale blue flame flickered. . . . God alone knows where his thoughts were roaming, but they did not roam only into the past; his face wore a grim and tense expression, and this does not happen when one's thoughts are absorbed merely in recollections. Meanwhile, a young woman, dressed in a warm, pale blue knitted jumper and white kerchief, was sitting on a large chest in a small back room; it was Fenichka, and alternatively she listened, dozed or stared at a door which was wide open—a door through which a child's cot could be seen and the steady breathing of a slumbering infant was audible.

V

NEXT morning Bazarov was the first to wake and be out of the house. "H'm!" he thought, gazing round. "This is hardly an attractive spot." When Nicholas Petrovich had redistributed his lands among the peasantry, he had been obliged to include in his new domain some nine acres of entirely flat and barren fields. Here he had built a new manor house and sunk two wells; but the young trees were tardy, the pond proved shallow, and the water from the wells tasted rather brackish. Only an arbour, contrived of lilac and accacia, had sprouted properly; there tea or dinner was sometimes served. A few minutes sufficed for Bazarov to walk all the garden paths, inspect the cattle sheds and the stables, and to come upon two servant lads with whom he at once struck up acquaintance. With them he set off in search of frogs to a small marsh less than a mile distant from the manor.

"What's the frogs for, master?" one of the lads inquired.

"I'll tell you," Bazarov replied. Though he never indulged common-folk and treated them offhandedly, yet he had the special gift of inspiring their confidence. "I'll split a frog open and see what's going on inside. Except for the fact that we walk about on our hind legs, we are very like these frogs, and that will help me to learn what is going on inside us too."

"But what's it for?"

"To prevent me from making mistakes when you feel sick and I have to doctor you."

"Are you a doctor then?"

"Yes."

"Vaska, d'ye hear that? The master says you and me are like them frogs. Funny, isn't it?"

"They scare me, them frogs," remarked Vaska, a boy of seven, with flaxen hair, bare feet, and a grey cossack coat with a high collar.

"Why be scared? They don't bite, do they?"

"Go on, scramble in, you philosophers," Bazarov said.

In the meantime, Nicholas Petrovich had also wakened and called on Arcady, whom he found already dressed. Father and son went out together and stopped under the awning of the terrace; set among a profusion of lilac bouquets, a samovar was already steaming on the table close to the banisters. A young girl came out—the same as had greeted the travellers at the porch on the previous day— and piped out:

"The young lady, Fedosya Nicolaievna, is not very well, and can't come. She ordered me to ask you if you would be pleased to pour out the tea yourselves or will you have Dunyasha sent for."

"I'll attend to it," Nicholas Petrovich interjected hastily.

"How do you like your tea, Arcady? With cream or a slice of lemon?"

"With cream," Arcady replied and, after a short pause, pointedly said: "Daddy!"

Nicholas Petrovich glanced at his son with an air of embarrassment.

"What is it?" he asked.

Arcady dropped his eyes.

"Pardon me, daddy, if my question strikes you as out of place," he began, "but the frankness with which you spoke yesterday encourages me to be as frank. . . . You won't be angry? . . ."

"Go on."

"You give me the courage to ask you. . . . Is it because I . . . is it because I am here that Fenichka has not come to pour out the tea?"

Nicholas Petrovich turned his face slightly to one side.

"Perhaps," he said at last. "She supposes . . . she feels ashamed. . . ."

Arcady cast a quick glance at his father.

"A great pity if she does feel ashamed. In the first place, you know my views" (Arcady found great pleasure in uttering these words), "and in the second—would I ever dream of upsetting your life by so much as a hairbreadth? Besides, I am convinced that you could not have made a more suitable choice; the fact that you allow her to live with you under the same roof implies that she deserves to do so: in any case, it's not for a son to judge his father, least of all for me, and especially a father like you, who has never restricted my freedom in any way."

Arcady's voice quavered at first. He felt that he was being magnanimous, but at the same time he realized that he was lecturing his father; but the sound of his own speeches has an intoxicating effect on any orator, and Arcady uttered his concluding words firmly and even with emphasis.

"Thank you, Arcady," Nicholas Petrovich replied in a hollow voice, while his fingers danced again over his eyebrows and forehead. "Your assumptions are quite justified. Of course, if the girl were unworthy . . . It is no passing lust of mine. I don't find it easy to talk to you about it; but as you will understand, it was difficult for her to come here, in your presence, especially on the first morning you are here."

"In that case, I'll go and find her myself!" Arcady exclaimed, as a fresh wave of generous sentiments broke over him and he jumped up from the chair. "I shall make it clear to her that she has no cause to feel ashamed because of me."

Nicholas Petrovich also stood up.

"Arcady," he began, "do me a favour . . . how can you . . . there . . . I did not warn you . . ."

But without heeding him, Arcady left the terrace at a run. Nicholas Petrovich stared after him and then, in great confusion, relapsed into his chair. His heart was pounding. . . . It would be difficult to say whether, at that instant, he pictured to himself the inevitable peculiarity of his future relations with his son, whether he realized that Arcady might have shown greater respect for him by ignoring this affair altogether, or whether he was reproaching himself for his weakness; all these feelings stirred within him or, rather, he sensed them—and very indistinctly at that. In the meantime, his face remained flushed and his heart kept beating fast.

There was a sound of hurried steps as Arcady came back to the terrace. "We have made friends, daddy!" he exclaimed with an expression of affectionate and good-natured triumph on his face. "Fenichka is really not feeling too well, but she will come later. But you didn't tell me that I had a brother. If I'd known, I would have kissed him quite as fondly yesterday as I did just now."

Nicholas Petrovich tried to say something, he tried to stand up and open his arms. . . . Arcady threw himself on his neck.

"What's this? Embracing again?" Paul Petrovich's voice sounded behind them.

Both father and son were equally glad at his coming that moment; there are touching situations from which one is nevertheless anxious to escape as soon as possible.

"Are you surprised?" his brother gaily asked. "After an age of waiting, Arcady is with us again. . . . I didn't have my fill of him yesterday."

"I'm not in the least surprised," Paul Petrovich remarked. "I wouldn't mind embracing him myself."

Arcady went up to his uncle and once again felt his perfumed moustaches brush his cheeks. Paul Petrovich sat down at table. He was wearing an elegant morning coat of English cut; a smoking-cap graced his head. This cap and a small, carelessly knotted cravat were the only hint that he led a more relaxed life in the country; but the stiff collar of his shirt, which was indeed not white but striped as befitted morning wear, was cutting as inexorably as ever into his clean-shaven chin.

"Where is your new friend?" he inquired of Arcady.

"He's gone out; he usually gets up early and goes exploring. The main thing is not to fuss over him: he can't stand ceremony."

"Yes, that's obvious," Paul Petrovich retorted, beginning hastily to butter his bread. "Will he be staying with us long?"

"That depends. He's stopped here on his way to his father's."

"And where does his father live?"

"In our province, about fifty miles from here. He owns a smallish estate. He used to be a regimental doctor."

"Tut, tut, tut, tut. . . . And I kept asking myself where I had heard that name before. Bazarov? . . . Nicholas, do you remember? Wasn't there a surgeon of the name of Bazarov in our father's division?"

"I believe there was."

"So there was, so there was. And that surgeon is his father. H'm!" Paul Petrovich allowed his moustaches to twitch. "Well, and what exactly is Mr. Bazarov himself?" he inquired with deliberation.

"What is Bazarov?" Arcady smiled. "Would you really like me, uncle, to tell you exactly what he is?"

"Do me the favour, my dear nephew."

"He is a Nihilist."

"What?" Nicholas Petrovich gasped, while his brother poised his knife in the air with a piece of butter on the tip of the blade, and froze into immobility.

"He is a Nihilist," Arcady repeated.

"A Nihilist," his father said slowly. "As far as I can judge, that must be a word derived from the Latin *nihil—nothing;* the term must therefore signify a man who . . . will admit nothing?"

"Better still—a man who will respect nothing," Paul Petrovich interjected, and then resumed his buttering.

"Who looks at everything critically," Arcady remarked.

"And what is the difference?" his uncle inquired.

"There is a difference. A Nihilist is a man who admits no established authorities, who takes no principles for granted, however much they may be respected."

"Well then? Is that a good thing?" his uncle interrupted.

"That depends on the circumstances, uncle. It's good in some cases and very bad in others."

"So that's how it is. Well, I can see this is not our cup of tea. We men of an older generation assume that, without princ*eeples*" (Paul Petrovich pronounced this word softly in the French manner; Arcady, on the contrary, pronounced it principle, stressing the first syllable), "without prin-*ceeples*, taken as you say on trust, one cannot move a step, one cannot even breathe. *Vous avez changé tout célà.* May God grant you health and a general's rank, but we can only admire you from a distance, gentlemen. . . . Nihil . . . What did you call it?"

"Nihilists," Arcady said distinctly.

"Yes. Formerly we had the Hegelians, and now the Nihilists. We'll see how you will manage to survive in a void, a vacuum. And now, Nicholas Petrovich, will you please ring the bell? It's time for my cocoa."

His brother rang the bell and shouted, "Dunyasha!" But, in place of Dunyasha, Fenichka herself appeared on the terrace. She was a young woman of about twenty-three, white-skinned and soft, with dark hair and dark eyes, red, childishly pouting lips, and small delicate hands. She was wearing a neat cotton dress; a new, pale blue scarf rested lightly on her rounded shoulders. She was carrying a large cup of cocoa and, as she set it down in front of Paul Petro-vich, she blushed violently of a sudden: the hot blood gushed in a crimson wave beneath the delicate skin of her pretty face. She dropped her eyes and stopped near the table, leaning on it slightly with the tips of her fingers. She appeared conscience-stricken at having ventured to come in, but at the same time she looked as though she had every right to do so.

Paul Petrovich knitted his brows sternly, while Nicholas Petrovich showed traces of embarrassment.

"Good morning, Fenichka," he mumbled through his clenched teeth.

"Good morning," she replied in a voice that carried without being too loud. Glancing out of the corner of her eye at Arcady, who was smiling at her in a friendly fashion, she quietly retired. She walked with a slight waddle, but that, too, became her.

For a few seconds silence reigned on the terrace. Paul

Petrovich sipped his cocoa and then suddenly raised his head. "Here is Sir Nihilist deigning to pay us a call," he brought out in an undertone.

And sure enough, Bazarov came hurrying through the garden, taking the flower-beds in his stride. His linen jacket and trousers were spattered with mud; a clinging marsh plant had twined itself round the crown of his circular hat; in his right hand he held a small sack, and something was wriggling inside it. He strode up to the terrace and exclaimed with a nod: "Good morning, gentlemen. Apologies for being so late for tea; I shall be back at once; I must put my captives away."

"What have you got there? Leeches?" Paul Petrovich inquired.

"No, frogs."

"Do you eat them? Or do you breed them?"

"I experiment with them," Bazarov replied indifferently as he went in.

"He'll cut them up," Paul Petrovich remarked. "He has no faith in prin*cee*ples, only in frogs."

Arcady glanced reprovingly at his uncle while his father stealthily shrugged his shoulders. Paul Petrovich realized that his jest was misplaced and turned the conversation to the management of the estate. The new steward had approached him the previous day with a complaint about Foma, the labourer, who had been "debauching" and had got out of hand. "He's such an Æsop, this Foma," the steward had added. "He's made a bad name for himself in the district; but he'll live and learn, and shake off his stupid ways."

VI

On returning, Bazarov sat down at table and began hastily to drink his tea. The brothers stared at him in silence, while Arcady stole a stealthy glance now at his father and now at his uncle.

"Have you been far?" Nicholas Petrovich inquired at last.

"You have a marsh here, near the aspen copse. I started

some five snipe. Perhaps you'd like to go and shoot them, Arcady?"

"Then you're not a keen sportsman yourself?"

"No."

"Is physics your chief occupation then?" Paul Petrovich inquired in turn.

"Physics, yes; and the natural sciences in general."

"They say that the Teutons, of late, have done wonders in this domain."

"Yes, the Germans are our masters there," Bazarov replied casually.

Paul Petrovich had used the word "Teutons" instead of "Germans" with ironical intent, but this had passed unnoticed.

"You have a very high opinion of the Germans then?" Paul Petrovich asked with exquisite courtesy. Inwardly he was beginning to feel irritated. His aristocratic nature was revolted by Bazarov's utter detachment. This surgeon's son not only did not quail before him, but even gave his answers brusquely and reluctantly. His voice had a caustic and almost insolent note.

"Their scientists at least know their business."

"Quite so. Then you must hold less flattering views of Russian scientists."

"Very likely so."

"That's very laudable and self-denying of you," Paul Petrovich exclaimed, straightening his back and holding up his head. "But is it true, as Arcady was just telling us, that you admit no authorities? That you have no belief in them?"

"Why should I admit them? And what am I to believe? If they talk sense, I'll agree with them. That's all there is to it."

"But do all Germans talk sense?" Paul Petrovich asked, while his features assumed such a distant and aloof expression that he looked withdrawn into the empyrean.

"Not all," Bazarov replied with a stifled yawn; he was manifestly tired of this inquisition.

Paul Petrovich glanced at Arcady as though he wished to say to him: "Your friend is excessively polite, I must say." "As far as I am concerned," he went on again, not without an effort, "sinner that I am, I hold no brief for the Germans. I don't need to mention the Russian Germans: we all know their kind. But I can't stomach German Germans either.

The old kind of Germans just passed muster; then they had —well, there was Schiller, Goethe, let's say.... My brother is particularly taken with them.... But nowadays they merely churn out some sort of chemists and materialists ..."

"A good chemist is more useful than a score of poets," Bazarov interrupted him.

"Really?" Paul Petrovich said, raising his eyebrows slightly as though he were dozing off. "So you don't acknowledge art?"

"The art of coining or that of claiming to banish hæmorrhoids!" Bazarov exclaimed with a contemptuous smile.

"Quite so. A joke, I presume. Evidently you're bent on denying everything? Let's assume it. In that case, science is the only thing you believe in?"

"I have already informed you that I do not believe in anything. And what is science—science in general? There are only particular sciences just as there are particular trades and callings; but science in general does not exist at all."

"Very well then. Now as regards the other socially accepted conventions—do you maintain the same negative attitude towards them?"

"What is this? A cross-examination?" Bazarov asked.

Paul Petrovich turned slightly pale.... His brother thought it his duty to intervene.

"Another time we shall discuss this matter with you in greater detail, my dear Eugene Vassilich; we shall get to know your views, and we shall state our own. For my part, I am very glad that you are studying the natural sciences. I have heard that Liebig has made some wonderful discoveries for improving the soil. You may be able to help me in my agricultural work and to give some useful advice."

"I am at your service; but Liebig is far beyond us! We must first of all learn the alphabet and only then attempt to read; as it is, we haven't even so much as glanced at our A B C."

"Well, it's quite clear that you are a Nihilist and no mistake," Nicholas Kirsanov thought. "All the same, you must allow me to apply to you for assistance in case of need," he added aloud. "And now, brother, I think it's time for us to go and have a talk with the steward."

Paul Petrovich got up from his chair.

"Yes," he said, without looking at anyone, "what a calamity it is to have spent five years buried like this in the country, so far removed from intercourse with great minds! It's enough to turn one into a fool twice over. One does one's best to remember what one was taught, but behold— it all turns out to be rubbish. One is told that people in the know no longer bother with such trifles, and that one is, as it were, backward and a dunce. What's to be done? Obviously the younger generation is really more intelligent than we are."

Paul Petrovich slowly spun round on his heels and then slowly left the room. Nicholas followed him.

"Is he always like that?" Bazarov coolly inquired of Arcady as soon as the door had closed behind the brothers.

"Listen, Eugene, you were a bit curt with him," Arcady remarked. "You have offended him."

"Do you think I'm going to pander to these provincial aristocrats! Why, it's nothing but sheer personal vanity, playing the lion, ostentation. If that's the way he's made, let him carry on like that in Petersburg. . . . But why worry about him! I have just discovered a fairly rare specimen of water beetle. *Dytiscus marginatus,* do you know it? Let me show it to you."

"I promised to tell you his history," Arcady began.

"The history of the beetle?"

"No, don't be so exasperating, Eugene. My uncle's history. You will then see that he is not the sort of man you imagine. He's deserving of compassion rather than ridicule."

"I don't dispute that. But why are you so full of him?"

"One must be fair, Eugene."

"How does that follow?"

"Now listen . . ."

And Arcady proceeded to tell him his uncle's history. The reader will find it in the next chapter.

VII

LIKE his younger brother Nicholas, Paul Petrovich was, to begin with, brought up at home, and then enrolled in the Imperial Corps of Pages. From childhood his strikingly handsome appearance had been his greatest distinction;

moreover, his manner was self-assured, faintly ironical and quite amusingly caustic—he could not fail to please. As soon as he had gained his commission, he began to circulate in society. The environment spoilt him and he started to indulge himself, play the fool, and affect mannerisms; but that also became him. Women lost their heads over him, while men called him a coxcomb and secretly envied him. As we have already indicated, he shared an apartment with his brother, whom he sincerely loved though he did not resemble him in the least. Nicholas Petrovich had a limp, his features were small and pleasant, though a shade gloomy, while his eyes were on the small side and his hair soft and sparse; he was inclined to be indolent and shy of society, but was fond of books. Paul Petrovich never spent an evening at home, enjoyed a reputation for courage and agility (it was said that he had set the fashion for gymnastics among the gilded youth of the city), and had read in all some five French novels. By the age of twenty-eight he was already a captain; a brilliant career lay ahead of him. Suddenly everything was changed.

At that time a woman, a certain Princess R. who is still remembered, occasionally used to frequent Petersburg society. She had a well brought up, respectable but stupid husband, and no children. She paid sudden visits abroad and returned as suddenly to Russia; on the whole she led a strange life. She passed for a frivolous coquette, eagerly gave herself up to every sort of pleasure, danced till she could hardly stand on her feet, laughed and joked with the young men whom she used to receive before dinner in the twilight of her drawing-room. But at night she wept and prayed, unable to find peace of mind anywhere and would often pace up and down her bedroom restlessly till dawn, mournfully wringing her hands or sitting all pale and chilled over a psalter. In the daytime, she was once more transformed into a society lady, went out to pay her calls again, laughed, chattered, and behaved as though she were flinging herself at anything that might afford her the least distraction. She was wonderfully proportioned; her golden tresses —which were also as heavy as gold—fell below her knees, but no one would have called her a beauty. Her eyes were the most striking thing about her face; no, not her eyes— they were grey and less than large—but rather their expression, which was swift and penetrating, carefree to the point of rashness and thoughtful to the brink of despondency: an enigmatic expression. Even when she was engaged in lisping the most fatuous phrases her eyes had the most extraordinary glint. And she dressed with exquisite care.

Paul Petrovich met her at a ball and, after dancing a mazurka with her during which she did not utter a single sensible word, fell head over heels in love. Accustomed to conquests, he very soon gained his objective; but his easy triumph failed to cool his ardour. On the contrary, his passion for her only increased and grew ever more tormenting; for this woman, even after an absolute surrender, seemed to preserve in her depths a sanctum into which no one ever succeeded in penetrating. God alone knows what nestled in her soul! She might have been in the power of some mysterious forces unknown even to herself; they played on her as they willed; her limited intelligence could not cope with their impulses. . . . Her whole conduct was made up of inconsistencies; the only letters she ever wrote, which might have excited her husband's just suspicions, were addressed to a man who was almost a stranger to her, and her expressions of love were tinged with melancholy; she never laughed or joked with the man of her choice, but only listened to him and gazed at him in wonder. Sometimes, usually quite suddenly, her look of wonder would change into a stare of frigid terror; her face would assume an expression of deathly pallor and frenzy; she would lock herself in her bedroom, and her eavesdropping maid would catch the sound of dismal sobbing. More than once, on returning home from a tender tryst with her, Paul Petrovich felt his heart oppressed with a lacerating and bitter nostalgia, such as overwhelms a man after utter failure. "What more do I want from her?" he would ask himself while his heart ached. One day he made her a present of a ring engraved with the image of a sphinx.

"What is that?" she asked. "A sphinx?"

"Yes," he replied. "The sphinx is you."

"Me?" she asked, slowly raising her enigmatic eyes to his. "Do you realize that you are being extremely flattering?" she added with a meaningless little smile, while her eyes gleamed as strangely as ever.

Paul Petrovich suffered torments even when the Princess R. reciprocated his affection; but when, as was to happen soon enough, she chilled off towards him, he almost went out of his mind. He fell into a state of anguish, threw fits of jealousy, gave her no peace, and dogged her footsteps. Tired of his persistent importunity, she went abroad. In spite of the entreaties of his friends and the exhortations of his superiors, he resigned his commission and followed her; he spent some four years in foreign parts, now chasing after her, now intentionally losing her from sight. He felt ashamed of himself, angry at his own lack of fortitude . . . but nothing availed. Her image, that incomprehensible, almost meaningless but alluring image, had bitten too deeply into his soul. They happened to come together again in Baden and resumed their relationship; to all appearance, she had never loved him so passionately. . . . But within a month it was all over: the fire had kindled for the last time and then had died for ever. Having a presentiment of the inevitable break, he wanted at least to remain her friend, as though friendship with such a woman were possible. . . . But she left Baden in secret, and thereafter consistently avoided him. He returned to Russia and tried to resume his former life, but failed to get into the swing of it. Like a drugged man, he strayed from place to place; he still drove out to receptions and preserved all the habits of a man about town; he could boast of two or three new conquests; but he had abandoned all hope of anything either from himself or anyone else, and shunned all serious activity. He grew old and grey. To spend his evenings in the club, to be scathing or bored, to indulge in trivial arguments in the society of bachelors, that was all he required—and, as we all know, that is a bad sign. Needless to say, he entertained no thought of marriage. Ten years passed in this wise, dully, fruitlessly and quickly—terribly quickly. Nowhere does time fly so fast as it does in Russia! In prison, they say, it flies even more quickly. One day, as he was dining at his club, Paul Petrovich learned of the death of the Princess. She had died in Paris in a state verging on frenzy. He got up from the table and for a long time paced up and down the rooms of the club, halting like one rooted to the spot near some card-table, but he returned home no earlier than usual. After a time he received a package: it contained the ring he had presented to the Princess. On the image of the sphinx she had scratched some lines in the form of a cross, and the message it conveyed told him that the Cross was the final solution of the enigma.

This had occurred at the beginning of 1848, at a time when Nicholas Petrovich, just bereaved of his wife, had arrived in Petersburg. After Nicholas had settled in the country, his brother had hardly seen him at all; Nicholas's marriage had coincided with the early phase of his infatuation with the Princess. On his return from abroad, Paul Petrovich had gone to his brother's estate with the intention of spending a couple of months with him and enjoying the sight of his happiness, but he only managed to stay a week. The brothers' ways of life had become too different. By 1848 this difference had narrowed: Nicholas Petrovich had lost his wife, and Paul Petrovich his memories; after the Princess's death, he had tried to forget her. Nicholas could look back on a well-spent life and had a son growing up under his eyes; whereas Paul, the lonely bachelor, was just crossing the threshold of that troubled, twilit period, when regrets come to resemble hopes, and hopes are beginning to resemble regrets, when youth is fled and old age is fast approaching.

For Paul Petrovich this period proved more trying than for most others: in losing his past, he had lost everything.

"I am not inviting you to Maryino," Nicholas Petrovich once said to him (he had called his village by that name in memory of his wife), "because you found it so tedious even when my wife was alive, but now, I am sure, you would just die of nostalgia."

"I was silly and fussy in those days," Paul Petrovich replied. "I have since grown calmer if not wiser. Now, if you will allow me, I am ready to come and settle down with you permanently."

By way of reply, Nicholas Petrovich embraced him; but a year and a half passed from the day of that conversation before Paul Petrovich finally made up his mind to carry out his intention. On the other hand, once he had settled down in the country, he did not forsake it—not even during the three winters which Nicholas had spent with his son in Petersburg. He became an assiduous reader, mostly of English books; in general, he modelled his whole life on English taste, frequented his neighbours but seldom, and visited town only at election time, when for the most part he preserved a discreet silence, only occasionally venturing to provoke and startle the landowners of the old school by his liberal gestures. At the same time he kept the representatives of the new generation at a distance. Both the former and the latter considered him supercilious; but they respected him for his exquisite, aristocratic manners, and for the rumours that had reached them of his former conquests; they honoured him for the superb way he dressed and for always putting up in the best room at the best hotel. They also admired him because he always dined like a lord and had once even sat at table with the Duke of Wellington at the court of Louis Philippe; because, wherever he went, he took with him a dressing-case of real silver and a portable bath; because the perfume he used was out of the ordinary and amazingly 'aristocratic'; because he played a masterly game of whist and invariably lost; and finally, they respected him for his irreproachable honesty. The ladies thought him charming and melancholic, but he avoided them. . . .

"So you see, Eugene," Arcady exclaimed, "how unfair you were in judging my uncle! I shall not dwell on the fact that he has come to my father's help more than once when he has been in financial difficulties—you may not know it, but the property was never divided equally between them. But uncle is always ready to help anyone and, besides, he is always prepared to intervene on behalf of the peasants; it is true, when talking to them, he puckers his face and sniffs eau-de-Cologne . . ."

"Clearly, a nervous case," Bazarov interrupted.

"Perhaps. But he is the kindest of men and far from being stupid. What valuable advice he has given me . . . particularly . . . particularly as regards relations with women!"

"Aha! 'When you scald yourself with your own boiling milk, you start blowing on another's water.' We know that!"

"Well, in short," Arcady went on, "he is deeply unhappy, I assure you. It would be a sin to despise him."

"But who despises him?" Bazarov retorted. "All the same, I maintain that a man who has staked his whole life on the card of a woman's love, and then, when he has lost it, turns sour and lets himself drift—a creature like that is not a man but just a male animal. You inform me that he is unhappy, you know that best; but he just hasn't quite shaken off his former stuff and nonsense. I am convinced that he imagines in all seriousness that he is a capable person, just because he reads *Galignani* and, once a month, intervenes to save some peasant from the rod."

"But you must take into account his upbringing as well

as the times in which he lived the best part of his life,"
Arcady rejoined.

"His upbringing?" Bazarov exclaimed. "Every man
should educate himself—well, just as I did, for example. . . .
As to the times, why should I depend upon them? Much
better they should depend on me. No, brother, all that is
just loose thinking, there's nothing solid behind it! And
what are those mysterious relations between men and
women? We physiologists, we know what sort of relations those are. Just study the anatomy of the eye: how is
one to explain that mysterious glance, as you term it? It's
all sheer romanticism, stuff and nonsense, putrefaction,
artiness. Let us rather go and examine our beetle."

And the friends sauntered off towards Bazarov's room,
in which a sort of medical or clinical smell, mingled with
the reek of cheap tobacco, had already had time to affirm
itself.

VIII

PAUL PETROVICH did not assist long at his brother's inter-
view with the steward, a tall gaunt man with a mellifluous,
consumptive voice and roguish eyes, who, in reply to every
remark of Nicholas Petrovich's, answered, "Certainly, that
goes without saying," and tried to make out that all the
peasants were drunkards and thieves. The recently mod-
ernized system of estate management was creaking as badly
as home-made furniture knocked together out of damp,
unseasoned wood. Nicholas Petrovich did not despair, but
kept sighing and racking his brains: he felt that his enter-
prise would fail to flourish without capital, but all his
resources had already been swallowed up. Arcady had
spoken the truth: Paul Petrovich had helped his brother
more than once. On more than one occasion, when he had
seen his brother in difficulties and puzzling to find a way
out, he had walked slowly up to the window and, thrusting
his hands into his pockets, had muttered through his teeth,
"Mais je puis vous donner de l'argent," and had given him
money. On this particular day, however, he had none to

spare and so had preferred to stride away. The unsavoury details of household management depressed him; moreover, although he could not himself have put his finger on the weak spot, he was often under the impression that Nicholas, for all his eagerness and diligence, was setting about things in the wrong way. "My brother is not practical enough," he would argue with himself. "He allows himself to be cheated." Nicholas Petrovich, on the other hand, had a very high opinion of his brother's practical ability and always asked his advice. "I am too easy-going and lack firmness, I have spent too much time in the wilds," he used to say; "but it's not for nothing that you have mixed with the world and know it so well; you are as sharp-eyed as an eagle." By way of reply, Paul Petrovich merely averted his head and did not attempt to disillusion his brother.

Leaving Nicholas in the study, he walked down the corridor which separated the front part of the house from the back, and, on reaching a low doorway, stopped, reflected for an instant, tugged at his moustache, and then knocked.

"Who is there? Come in," Fenichka's voice could be heard saying.

"It's me," said Paul Petrovich, opening the door.

Fenichka leapt from the chair on which she had been sitting with her child and, handing the baby over to a young maid who carried him out of the room, hastily adjusted her kerchief.

"Pardon me for intruding," Paul Petrovich began, without looking at her, "I only wished to ask you . . . I believe someone is being sent to town to-day. . . . Will you get him to buy me some green tea?"

"Certainly," Fenichka replied. "How much would you like?"

"Oh, half a pound will do. I notice you have made some alterations here," he added, casting round him a quick glance which flitted over her face. "I mean the curtains."

"Nicholas Petrovich very kindly gave them to me; they have been hanging for some time already."

"It's quite a while since I was last in your room. You have now arranged it very cosily."

"Thanks to Nicholas Petrovich," Fenichka whispered.

"Are you more comfortable here than in the wing?" Paul Petrovich inquired politely, but without a trace of a smile.

"Of course I am."

"Who's taken your place there?"

"The laundry-maids are there now."

"Ah!"

Paul Petrovich was silent. "He'll go away now," Fenichka thought; but he made no move to depart, and Fenichka stood in front of him as though rooted to the ground, playing nervously with her fingers.

"Why did you have the baby taken away?" Paul Petrovich asked at last. "I love children; let me have a look at him."

Fenichka blushed with confusion and joy. She was frightened of Paul Petrovich, who hardly ever addressed her.

"Dunyasha," she cried, "will you bring in Mitya, if you please?" (Fenichka was very polite to everyone in the house.) "No, wait a moment: we must first put on his dress for him." And Fenichka made for the door.

"Why bother?" Paul Petrovich asked.

"I shall be back in a second," Fenichka replied, disappearing promptly.

When left alone, Paul Petrovich gazed about him with keen attention. The small low room in which he found himself was very clean and comfortable. There was a smell of paint from the freshly painted floor, of camomile and other dried flowers. Against the wall stood a set of chairs with lyre-shaped backs; the late General Kirsanov had acquired them once upon a time in Poland during one of his campaigns; in a corner next to an iron-clamped chest with a round lid was a small bed under a muslin canopy. In the opposite corner a lamp glowed in front of a large dark icon, representing St. Nicholas, the Miracle-worker; a minute porcelain egg, fastened to the halo with a red ribbon, hung down over the saint's breast. The window-sills were stocked with jars of carefully sealed jam, through which a green light filtered; the jam had been made the previous year and was tied up with meticulous care; on the paper covers Fenichka had written in her own hand, "Gooseberry." Nicholas Petrovich was particularly fond of that jam. From the ceiling on a length of string hung down a cage with a short-tailed greenfinch in it; he was twittering and hopping about ceaselessly, and as ceaselessly the cage swayed and quivered: hemp seeds kept falling and faintly tapping on the floor. On the partition-wall above a small chest of drawers hung several photographs of Nicholas

Petrovich in various poses, all rather unsuccessfully taken by some travelling photographer; here also hung a complete failure of a photograph of Fenichka herself: a sort of eyeless face was straining to smile from a dark frame—it was impossible to distinguish more. Above Fenichka's picture and beneath a satin pin-cushion slipper, General Yermolov, in a shaggy Caucasian cloak, glowered at the far-off peaks of the Caucasus.

Five minutes elapsed; a whispering and rustling was still going on next door. Paul Petrovich picked up a greasy, tattered volume of Massalsky's *The Streltsy*,[1] and turned over a few pages. . . . The door opened and Fenichka came in, holding Mitya in her arms. She had dressed him up in a little red shirt with an embroidered collar, combed his hair and wiped his face: he was breathing strenuously, straining to break away with his whole little body, and jerking his hands as all healthy infants do; but his foppish little shirt had evidently produced an effect on him; an expression of pleasure had spread over his chubby face. Fenichka had also tidied her hair, and wore her kerchief more neatly; but she could very well have stayed as she was. For is there anything in the world really more enchanting than a young and beautiful mother with a healthy-looking child in her arms?

"What a pumpkin!" Paul Petrovich said condescendingly, tickling Mitya's double chin with the tapering nail of his forefinger; the child stared up at the greenfinch in the cage and burst out laughing.

"This is your uncle," Fenichka said, putting her face close to his and shaking him a little, while Dunyasha, after first of all putting down a brass coin on the window-sill, carefully placed a lighted smoker's candle on it.

"How many months is he?" Paul Petrovich inquired.

"Six months; the seventh is not far off—on the eleventh of the month."

"You don't mean it, seven months! How is that possible?"

"Wouldn't it be eight months, Fedosya Nicolaievna?" Dunyasha interposed shyly.

"No, seven; how could it be otherwise!"

The child laughed again, staring at the chest in the corner,

[1] The Streltsy were the Musketeers of Moscow.

and then suddenly gripped his mother by the nose and lips with all the five fingers of one hand.

"You little wretch!" Fenichka exclaimed, without disengaging her face from his fingers.

"He's very like my brother," Paul Petrovich remarked.

"Whom else could he be like?" Fenichka thought.

"Yes," Paul Petrovich pursued, as though talking to himself, "the likeness is unmistakable." He glanced at Fenichka attentively, almost sadly.

"This is uncle," she repeated in a whisper this time.

"Ah! Paul! So this is where you are!" Nicholas Petrovich's voice suddenly rang out.

Paul hastily turned round, frowning; but his brother was looking at him with such joy and gratitude that he could not fail to return his smile.

"A fine little lad you've got," he said, glancing at his watch. "I dropped in here about my tea. . . ."

And assuming an air of indifference, Paul Petrovich at once quitted the room.

"Did he come of his own accord?" Nicholas Petrovich asked Fenichka.

"Yes, he did. He just knocked and came in."

"Well, and hasn't Arcady been here again?"

"He hasn't. Had I not better move back to the wing, Nicholas Petrovich?"

"Why should you?"

"I think it might be better for a time at the beginning?"

"N-no," Nicholas Petrovich replied hesitantly, rubbing his forehead. "Better it had been done earlier. . . . Hello, bubble," he said with sudden animation and, approaching his son, kissed him on the cheek; then stooping slightly, he kissed Fenichka's hand, which stood out as white as milk against Mitya's red shirt.

"Nicholas Petrovich! What are you doing?" she mumbled, lowering her eyes and then suddenly raising them. . . . Her expression was enchanting whenever she looked like that, from under her eyelids, laughing affectionately and a trifle vacantly.

Nicholas Petrovich had become acquainted with Fenichka in the following fashion. One day, some three years previously, he happened to spend a night at a hostelry in a remote district town. He was pleasantly surprised at the cleanliness of the room set aside for him and at the immaculate whiteness of the bed linen. "Is the woman of the inn a German?" was the first question he asked himself; but the woman turned out to be Russian, some fifty years of age, tidily dressed, with an agreeable, intelligent face, and a dignified way of speaking. He chatted with her over tea; he had taken a great liking to her. At that time, Nicholas Petrovich had just moved into his new house and, loath to employ any of his former serfs, was in search of hired domestic staff. For her part, the woman of the inn complained of the small number of travellers who passed through the town and of hard times. Nicholas had therefore suggested that she should take up an appointment in his house as his chief housekeeper; and she had agreed. Her husband had died long ago, leaving her with an only daughter, Fenichka. About a fortnight later, Arina Savishna (such was the new housekeeper's name) arrived at Maryino together with her daughter, and took up residence in the wing of the house. Nicholas Petrovich's choice proved a happy one. Arina put the house in order. No one ever mentioned, and few ever saw, Fenichka, who had just turned seventeen: she lived quietly and modestly, and it was only on Sundays that Nicholas Petrovich would notice the delicate profile of her milk-white face in some corner of the parish church. Thus a whole year passed.

One morning Arina Savishna came into his study and, bowing low as was her custom, asked if he could help her daughter whose eye had been struck by a spark. Like all domesticated people, Nicholas Petrovich dabbled in medicine and had even ordered a homœopathic medicine chest for himself. He at once commanded Arina Savishna to bring in the patient. On learning that the master had summoned her, Fenichka was very startled but nevertheless accompanied her mother. Nicholas Petrovich led her up to a window and took her head in his hands. Having thoroughly examined her red and swollen eye, he prescribed an eye-wash, which he then made up on the spot and, tearing up his handkerchief, showed her how to apply the solution. Fenichka heard him to the end and then prepared to leave the room. "Kiss the master's hand, silly," Arina Savishna said to her. But Nicholas Petrovich withheld his hand and, in some confusion, kissed her bowed head on parting. Fenichka's eye was quickly healed, but the impression she had made on Nicholas Petrovich was not to be dissipated so rapidly. He kept picturing that pure, tender, apprehensively uplifted face; the sensation of her soft hair still tingled in his hands; he kept seeing those innocent, slightly parted lips which in the sunlight revealed a moist glitter of diamond-like teeth. At church he began to peer at her more attentively and tried to engage her in conversation. At first she was very shy and once, in the late afternoon, when she happened to run into him on a narrow footpath leading through a field of rye, she had turned aside into the tall, thick rye, all overgrown with cornflowers and wormwood, so as to avoid meeting him face to face. He caught sight of her little head through the golden network of the ears of rye, whence she peeped like a wild animal. He shouted in a friendly tone:

"Good evening, Fenichka, I don't bite."

"Good evening," she had whispered back, without emerging from her retreat.

Though still shy in his presence, she was gradually beginning to get used to him, when her mother, Arina Savishna, unexpectedly died of the cholera. Where was Fenichka to go? From her mother she had inherited a love of order, intelligence and decency; but she was young and lonely; Nicholas Petrovich was himself such a kind and modest person. . . . There is no need to describe the rest. . . .

"So my brother dropped in to see you after all?" Nicholas asked Fenichka. "He just knocked and came in?"

"Yes."

"Well, that's excellent. Just let me rock Mitya."

And Nicholas Petrovich began to throw him up almost as high as the ceiling, to the huge delight of the infant and the great perturbation of the mother who, at each throw, stretched her arms towards his twinkling little feet.

In the meantime, Paul Petrovich had returned to his elegant study. Its walls were covered with wall-paper of a greyish tint and hung with an assortment of weapons on a Persian wall-carpet. The room was stocked with walnut furniture, a Renaissance book-case of ancient oak, several bronze statuettes displayed on a sumptuous writing-desk, a fireplace. . . . He threw himself down on a sofa, put his hands to his head and remained quite motionless, staring almost in despair at the ceiling. Whether he wished to conceal the expression on his face from the very walls or for some other reason, he got up, unfastened the heavy window-curtains, and then again slumped back on the sofa.

IX

THE same day Bazarov made Fenichka's acquaintance. He was strolling with Arcady in the garden and explaining to him why some of the newly planted trees, the oaks in particular, had not taken to the soil.

"What you should do is to plant more silver poplars here and fir trees, and limes maybe, but you must first put down some black earth. Now this arbour here is flourishing," he added, "because acacia and lilac are sturdy fellows and require the minimum of nursing. Ah, there's someone in it."

Fenichka was sitting in the arbour with Dunyasha and Mitya. Bazarov halted while Arcady nodded to Fenichka like an old friend.

"Who's that?" Bazarov inquired as soon as they had gone past. "What a charming girl!"

"Whom are you referring to?"

"It's clear enough: only one of them is pretty."

Arcady, not without embarrassment, told him briefly about Fenichka.

"Aha!" Bazarov exclaimed. "Your father obviously has taste. I quite like your father! He's a fine chap. But I must make her acquaintance," and he retraced his steps towards the arbour.

"Eugene!" Arcady shouted after him in alarm. "Be careful, for God's sake."

"Don't be perturbed," Bazarov replied. "I've knocked about and lived in cities."

Approaching Fenichka, he doffed his cap.

"May I introduce myself?" he began with a polite bow. "A friend of Arcady Nicolaievich and an inoffensive person."

Fenichka rose from the bench and stared at him in silence.

"What a wonderful baby!" Bazarov pursued. "Don't

worry, I haven't cast a spell on anyone yet. Why are his cheeks so red? Is he teething by any chance?"

"Yes," Fenichka replied. "He has already cut four teeth, but his gums are swollen again."

"Let me see them . . . don't be afraid. I'm a doctor."

Bazarov picked up the child in his arms and to both Fenichka's and Dunyasha's surprise, the infant offered no resistance and showed no alarm.

"I see, I see. . . . It's nothing . . . everything is in order; he'll have a strong set of teeth. If there's any trouble, just let me know. And are you in good health yourself?"

"I am, thank God."

"Thank God indeed—that's the best of all things. And you?" he added, turning to Dunyasha.

Dunyasha, who was very strait-laced in the house and an inveterate giggler out of doors, only snorted by way of an answer.

"Well, that's excellent. Here's your little champion."

Fenichka took the child back in her arms.

"How quiet he was in your arms," she said in an undertone.

"Children are always quiet in my arms," Bazarov replied. "I know a trick or two."

"Children instinctively recognize those who love them," Dunyasha remarked.

"That's right," Fenichka confirmed. "Now, as a rule, Mitya will not let anyone handle him at any price."

"May I try?" ventured Arcady who, after keeping his distance for a while, had approached the arbour. He tried to lure Mitya into his arms, but much to Fenichka's perturbation the infant only threw back his head and squalled.

"I'll try again when he's got used to me," Arcady said condescendingly, and the friends walked away.

"And, pray, what is her name?" Bazarov inquired.

"Fenichka . . . Fedosya," Arcady replied.

"And her patronymic? I must know that too."

"Nicolaievna."

"*Bene*. What I like about her is that she doesn't show too much embarrassment. Another might blame her for that. But it's sheer nonsense. Why be embarrassed? She is a mother, and quite right too."

"She's in the right," Arcady remarked, "but my father . . ."

"He's also in the right," Bazarov interrupted him.

"No, I don't agree."

"I suppose you can't stomach a second heir!"

"You should be ashamed to impute such ideas to me!" Arcady retorted hotly. "That is not why I criticize my father; I think he should marry her."

"Aha!" Bazarov said quietly. "What magnanimity! You attach then some importance to the marriage tie; I did not expect that from you."

The friends walked on a few steps in silence.

"I have seen all your father's installations," Bazarov began again. "The cattle are of poor quality, the horses mere hacks. The buildings are tumbledown, and the labourers look arrant loafers; as for the steward, he is either a fool or a rogue, I'm not yet sure which."

"You are very censorious to-day, Eugene."

"Nor will the good peasants fail to cheat your father. You know the proverb, 'A Russian peasant will get the better of God Himself.'"

"I'm beginning to think my uncle was not far off the mark," Arcady remarked. "You have decidedly a poor opinion of Russians."

"As if that mattered! The best thing about a Russian is the poor opinion he has of himself. What's important is that two and two make four, the rest is just trivial."

"And is nature trivial?" Arcady inquired, staring thoughtfully at the far-spread, variegated fields, suffused with the beautiful and mellow light of the declining sun.

"Nature *is* trivial in the sense you mean. Nature is no temple but merely a workshop, and man is the craftsman."

At that instant the lingering notes of a 'cello were wafted towards them from the house. Someone was playing Schubert's "Expectation" with sensibility, but without the professional touch, and, like honey, the melody flowed through the air.

"What's that?" Bazarov inquired in amazement.

"It's my father."

"Your father plays the 'cello?"

"Yes."

"And how old is your father?"

"Forty-four."

Bazarov burst out laughing.

"What are you laughing at?"

"Good Lord! At forty-four, a *pater familias,* in the province of X, playing the 'cello!"

Bazarov continued to laugh: but, on this occasion, Arcady, though he venerated his mentor, did not even smile.

X

ABOUT a fortnight had elapsed. Life at Maryino was pursuing its normal course: Arcady played the Sybarite, and Barazov kept his nose to the grindstone. Everyone in the house had got used to him, to his casual ways, as well as to his curt and brusque manner of speech. Fenichka, in particular, had come to take him so much for granted that one night she even had him wakened: Mitya was suffering from cramp; and Bazarov had come along, as was his wont, partly jesting and partly yawning, spent a couple of hours in her room, and eased the child's pains. On the other hand, Paul Petrovich had developed a violent dislike for Bazarov: he deemed him an arrogant, impudent fellow, a cynic and a plebeian: he suspected that Bazarov held him in little esteem, that he almost despised him—him, Paul Petrovich Kirsanov! Nicholas Petrovich was a shade frightened of the young Nihilist and doubted the value of his influence on Arcady: but he listened willingly enough to him, and assisted just as willingly at his experiments in physics and chemistry. Bazarov had brought a microscope and pored over it for whole hours on end. The servants had become attached to him; even though he poked fun at them, they felt that he was one of them and no "master." In his presence Dunyasha was very ready to burst out giggling and to trip past him like a fluttering quail, casting significant glances at him from the corner of her eyes; Peter, who was an extremely conceited and stupid person with an intent expression and a perpetually wrinkled forehead, a person whose entire dignity depended on his respectful mien, his ability to spell out a text syllable by syllable, and his habit of frequently brushing his jacket—even he grinned and cheered up as soon as Bazarov paid the least attention to him. As for the servant lads, they followed the "doctor" about like puppies. Prokofyich was the only person to dislike him; he served him at table with a sullen expression on his face, called him a "skin-alive" and a "rapscallion," and maintained that he was, with his side-whiskers and all, a regular pig in the poke. In his own way, Prokofyich was no less of an aristocrat than Paul Petrovich.

The year was at its best in early June. The weather was beautiful; in the remote background, it is true, there was a renewed threat of cholera, but the inhabitants of the province had already grown accustomed to its visitations. Bazarov used to rise early and set off for a walk of a mile or two, not just for the sake of exercising his limbs—he could not bear purposeless jaunts—but in order to gather herbs and insects. Sometimes he took Arcady with him. On their way back they usually became engrossed in argument and, though more eloquent than his friend, Arcady usually came out the loser.

One morning they were out longer than usual; Nicholas Petrovich had strolled into the garden to meet them and, as he drew level with the arbour, he suddenly heard the sound of quick steps and young men's voices. They were walking along on the other side of the arbour and could not see him.

"You don't know my father well enough," Arcady said.

Nicholas Petrovich kept in the background.

"Your father is a good-natured old boy," Bazarov replied, "but he's a back number. He's sung his swan-song."

Nicholas Petrovich pricked up his ears. . . . Arcady made no reply.

For a couple of minutes the "back number" stood motionless and then slowly trudged back home.

"A couple of days ago I caught him reading Pushkin," Bazarov went on meanwhile. "Will you please explain to him that this won't do? He's no youth, it's time he gave up such nonsense. Where's the sense in being a romantic nowadays! Give him something practical to read."

"What can I give him?" Arcady inquired.

"I should think Büchner's *Stoff und Kraft* would do for a start."

"I'm inclined to agree," Arcady replied approvingly. "*Stoff und Kraft* is written with an eye on the general reader. . . ."

"So it seems both you and I are 'back numbers,' and our

swan-song is sung," Nicholas Petrovich said to his brother
after dinner that day. "Well? Maybe Bazarov is right; but I
confess to being hurt by one thing: I had hoped that the
time was ripe for me to establish a really close friendship
with Arcady, but it turns out that I have been left standing
while he has forged ahead, and we cannot understand each
other."

"And why should he have forged ahead? In what way is
he so different from us?" Paul Petrovich inquired impa-
tiently. "All that's been stuffed into his head by that *signor,*
that Nihilist. I can't stand that petty surgeon; in my opinion,
he's a mere charlatan; I am convinced that, for all his frogs,
he hasn't got very far with his physics."

"No, brother, you mustn't say that: Bazarov is intelligent
and knowledgeable."

"But he's so horridly arrogant!" Paul Petrovich exclaimed.

"Yes," Nicholas agreed, "he is arrogant. But evidently he
can't do without it. I can't make head or tail of just one
thing. I seem to be doing everything possible not to lag
behind the age: I have split up the land among my former
serfs, I have inaugurated a model farm and acquired
throughout the province the reputation of being a Radical;
I read, study, do my best, on the whole, to keep level with
contemporary demands—and yet here they are talking
about my swan-song. And once it has reached that stage,
brother, I really begin to think that I have sung it."

"Why is that?"

"This is why. To-day I was sitting and reading Pushkin.
. . . Arcady came up and without a word, though with a
look of affectionate pity on his face, gently took away my
book as he might have taken it from a child, and put another
one in front of me, a German one. . . . He smiled and then
went out, carrying off my Pushkin."

"Really! What book did he give you?"

"This one."

From the back pocket of his frock-coat Nicholas Petrovich pulled out a volume of the ninth edition of Büchner's
celebrated treatise.

Paul Petrovich turned it over in his hands. "H'm!" he
growled. "Arcady is trying to educate you. Well? Have you
attempted to read it?"

"I have."

"And what do you make of it?"

"Either I'm stupid or it's sheer rubbish. I must be stupid."

"You haven't forgotten your German?" Paul Petrovich inquired.

"I can understand German quite well."

Paul Petrovich turned the book over again in his hands and glanced sideways at his brother. They were both silent for a while.

"By the way," Nicholas Petrovich began, obviously anxious to change the subject. "I have just received a letter from Kolyazin."

"From Matvey Ilyich?"

"From the very man. He's just arrived in town to inspect the province. He's risen in the world and writes to say that, as a relative of ours, he would like to see us, and so he invites you and me, and Arcady, to go and stay in town with him."

"Are you going?" Paul Petrovich asked.

"No. Are you?"

"I won't go either. It's not worth while traipsing thirty miles for that! *Mathieu* wishes to display himself in all his glory. The devil take him! He will have the whole province at his feet, so he can dispense with us. As though a Privy Councillor were such big fish! If I had continued in the service, carrying that stupid knapsack on my back, I'd have been an Adjutant-General by now. Anyway, we are both in retirement."

"Yes, brother. Evidently the time has come for us to order our coffins and to fold our arms," Nicholas Petrovich replied with a sigh.

"As for me, I shan't capitulate so quickly," his brother muttered. "I intend to do battle royal with that surgeon yet, I can feel it in my bones."

The battle royal took place that very day, at tea-time. Paul Petrovich came down to the drawing-room in an irritable mood, all itching for battle. He was only waiting for a pretext to rush upon the enemy, but the pretext was long in presenting itself. As a rule, Bazarov talked little in the presence of the "old Kirsanovs" (so he called the brothers), and that evening he felt out of sorts as he sipped one cup of tea after another in silence. Paul Petrovich was consumed with impatience; but at last his wish was granted.

The conversation turned on one of the neighbouring

landowners. "A rotter, a petty aristocrat," Bazarov, who had met him in Petersburg, remarked indifferently.

"May I ask you," Paul Petrovich began, his lips trembling, "whether, as you understand it, the words rotter and aristocrat are synonymous?"

"I said a petty aristocrat," Bazarov replied, lazily taking a sip of tea.

"Exactly so. But I assume that you are of the same opinion about aristocrats as you are about petty aristocrats. I consider it my duty to declare that I do not share this opinion. I venture to say that I am known as a liberal and progressive person; and that is why I respect aristocrats—real aristocrats. You must remember, my dear sir" (at these words Bazarov raised his eyes to Paul Petrovich), "you must remember, my dear sir," he repeated with exasperation, "the English aristocrats. They never yield a jot of their own rights and, for that reason, they respect the rights of others; they insist on the fulfilment of obligations due to them and, because they do that, they fulfil *their own* obligations. The aristocracy gave England her freedom and have maintained it ever since."

"We have heard that refrain often enough," Bazarov retorted. "But what do you wish to prove by this?"

"By 'phthis' I wish to prove, my dear sir," (when angry, Paul Petrovich used to say deliberately "phthis" and "phthat," though he knew very well that no such words existed in the dictionary. This caprice was a tradition he had inherited from Alexander I's reign. The blades of those days, on the rare occasions when they did speak their native language, used to employ the terms "phthis" and "phthat." "We are, as it were, *real* Russians," they meant it to be understood, "and at the same time nobles who can dispense with grammatical rules")—"by 'phthis' I wish to prove that without a sense of personal dignity, without any respect for one's self—and these feelings are highly developed among the aristocracy—there can be no solid foundation for the social . . . *bien public* . . . for the social order. The personality, my dear sir—that is the chief thing; the human personality must be as strong as a rock, for on it everything else is founded. I know very well, for instance, that you deign to ridicule my habits, my way of dressing and, above all, my neatness, but all that comes from a feeling of self-respect, a sense of duty—yes-s, yes-s, a sense of duty. I live in the country, in the wilds, but I do not demean myself, I respect the man in myself."

"But if you will allow me, Paul Petrovich," Bazarov said, "you may respect yourself and yet you sit doing nothing; of what use is that for the *bien public*? If you had no respect for yourself, you would do the same thing."

Paul Petrovich turned pale.

"That is quite a different question. I am under no obligation to explain to you now why I sit doing nothing, as you are pleased to put it. I only wish to say that aristocracy is a principle, and only immoral or empty-headed people can dispense with principles in our times. I said this to Arcady the day after he arrived, and I repeat it to you now. Isn't that so, Nicholas?"

Nicholas Petrovich nodded assent.

"Aristocracy, liberalism, progress, principles," Bazarov said in the meantime, "just think, what a lot of foreign— and useless—words! Russians have not the least need of them."

"What do you think they need then? To hear you talk, we might all be living outside human society, beyond the pale of its laws. I ask you—the logic of history demands . . ."

"What need have we of that logic? We can get on quite well without it."

"What do you mean?"

"Just that. I hope you have no need of logic to find a bite of bread when hungry. What have we to do with such abstractions!"

Paul Petrovich threw up his hands.

"After that, I fail to understand you. You insult the Russian people. I don't understand how one can fail to admit principles and rules. What is the motive of your conduct?"

"I have already told you, uncle, that we admit no authorities," Arcady intervened.

"Our actions are governed by utility," Bazarov said. "In these days, negation is the most useful thing of all—and so we deny."

"Everything?"

"Everything."

"What? Not only art, poetry . . . but also . . . I am afraid to say it . . ."

"Everything," Bazarov repeated with inexpressible calm.

Paul Petrovich stared at him. He had not expected this, and Arcady blushed with pleasure.

"However, if I may say so," Nicholas Petrovich interjected, "you deny everything or, to put it more precisely, you are destroying everything. . . . But it's essential to construct as well."

"That is not our affair. . . . First, we must make a clean sweep."

"The present state of the people makes it necessary," Arcady solemnly added. "We must fulfil these demands. We have no right merely to indulge in the satisfaction of our personal egotism."

This last phrase evidently displeased Bazarov; it smelt of philosophy, that is, of romanticism, for Bazarov identified the two; but he did not think it necessary to contradict his youthful disciple.

"No, no!" Paul Petrovich exclaimed with unexpected heat. "I will not believe that you gentlemen have any exact notion of the Russian people, that you represent its strivings! No, the Russian people is not what you imagine it to be. It has a holy respect for traditions, it is—a patriarchal people. It cannot live without faith . . ."

"I shall not attempt to dispute that," Bazarov interrupted. "I am even prepared to agree that you are right in this."

"But if I am right . . ."

"That still proves nothing."

"Exactly. It proves nothing," Arcady repeated with the assurance of an expert chess player who had foreseen an obviously clever move on the part of his opponent, and as a result was in no way nonplussed.

"What do you mean—it proves nothing?" Paul Petrovich muttered in amazement. "You are going against your own people then?"

"And even if I were?" Bazarov exclaimed. "When it thunders, the people assume that the Prophet Ilya is riding through the heavens in his chariot. Well? Am I to agree with them? And besides—the people may be Russian, but am I not Russian too?"

"No, you are no Russian after what you have just said! I cannot accept you as a Russian."

"My grandfather tilled the soil," Bazarov replied haughtily. "Ask any of your peasants in which of us—in you or me—he would sooner recognize a compatriot. You don't even know how to talk to them."

"And you talk to them and despise them at the same time."

"Well, and what if they deserve contempt? You deprecate my attitude, but who told you that it was an accidental thing in me rather than something called forth by the spirit of the people themselves, in whose name you are protesting?"

"I don't think so! Nihilists are not so very essential!"

"Whether they are essential or not—it's not for us to decide. You don't regard yourself as quite useless either!"

"Gentlemen, gentlemen, you mustn't be personal!" Nicholas Petrovich exclaimed, standing up.

Paul Petrovich smiled and, laying his hand on his brother's shoulder, made him sit down again. "Don't worry," he said. "I shall not forget myself, just because of the sense of personal dignity which is being so savagely assailed by Mister—Doctor Bazarov. If you will allow me," he continued, turning anew to Bazarov, "perhaps you think your doctrine is a novelty? A pity you imagine that. The materialism you preach has gained currency more than once and has invariably proved bankrupt . . ."

"Again a foreign word!" Bazarov interrupted him. He was beginning to get angry and his face had assumed a coarse coppery tint. "In the first place, we preach nothing; that is no habit of ours. . . ."

"What are you doing then?"

"This is what we are doing. Formerly, not so very long ago, we used to say that our officials took bribes, that we had no roads, no trade, no justice. . . ."

"Well, yes, yes, you are castigators of social maladies—that's what you're called, I believe. I agree with a great many of your criticisms, but . . ."

"And then we concluded that to chatter and only chatter about our maladies was not worth a candle, that it only led to a petty and doctrinaire attitude. We realized that our 'bright men,' the so-called 'advanced men' who castigated social maladies, were good-for-nothings, that we were merely preoccupied with trivialities, debates about types of art, unconscious creation, parliamentarianism, justice, and the devil knows what, when the gist of the matter was our daily bread, when the most vulgar superstitions were stifling us, when our industrial enterprises were failing for lack of honest men at their head, when even the emancipation of the serfs—the emancipation the government is making such a fuss about now—will hardly be to our advantage, because the peasants are only too delighted to filch from each other in order to drink themselves silly in the gin-shops."

"So," Paul Petrovich interrupted him, "so, you are convinced of all this and are resolved to avoid any serious undertaking."

"And are resolved to avoid any undertaking," Bazarov repeated grimly. He suddenly felt depressed at having been so expansive in front of this lordling.

"But only indulge in abuse?"

"To indulge in abuse."

"And that is what you call Nihilism?"

"And that is what you call Nihilism," Bazarov repeated again, this time with emphatic insolence.

Paul Petrovich screwed up his eyes slightly.

"So that's it!" he exclaimed in a strangely calm voice. "Nihilism is a remedy for all our maladies, and you—you are the saviours and heroes. But why do you pick on the others—the castigators of social maladies? Don't you chatter quite as much as the rest of them?"

"Anything you like, but don't lay that particular sin at our door," Bazarov muttered through his teeth.

"Well then? Are you *already* in active conspiracy? Or are you preparing for action?"

Bazarov did not answer. Paul Petrovich quivered, but mastered himself at once.

"H'm! . . . To act, to break up . . ." he continued. "But how can you break things up without knowing even why?"

"We break things up because we are a force," Arcady remarked.

Paul Petrovich looked at his nephew and laughed.

"Yes, a force need give no account of itself," Arcady said, drawing himself up.

"Wretched lad!" Paul Petrovich wailed; he was decidedly in no state to control himself any longer. "If only you gave a thought to *what* you were supporting in Russia by your silly judgments! No, it's enough to make an angel lose patience! A force! The wild Kalmuk and the Mongolian

have force—but what do we need it for? We value civilization—yes, yes, my dear sir; its fruits are dear to us. And
don't you tell me those fruits are insignificant: the pettiest
dauber, *un barbouilleur,* a cheap musician who makes five-
pence an evening—even they are of more use than you,
because they represent civilization rather than crude Mongolian force! You imagine that you are advanced, but your
real home is a Kalmuk tent! A force! And finally, my
forceful gentlemen, you must remember this, there are
only four and a half of you, whereas the others number
millions, and they will not allow you to trample on their
most sacred beliefs. They will crush you underfoot!"

"If they do crush us, such is our destiny," Bazarov replied. "Only you can't have your cake and eat it. We are not
as few as you suppose."

"What? You seriously think you can deal—deal with the
whole people?"

"A penny candle, you know, set Moscow on fire,"
Bazarov retorted.

"I see. First of all, a pride that is almost satanical, and
then a gibing tone. Indeed, that is what attracts young men,
that is what conquers inexperienced boyish hearts! Just
look, Bazarov, there's one sitting beside you, almost
adoring you, just look and admire." (Arcady turned away
and frowned.) "That disease has already made great in-
roads. I am told that our painters in Rome refuse to set
foot in the Vatican. They consider Raphael almost a fool
—on the grounds that he is, as it were, an 'established
authority'; and as for themselves, they show themselves
impotent and barren to the point of disgusting one, and,
however much they try, their fantasy goes no further than
a picture like 'Girls at the Fountain'! And the painting of
the girl is rotten into the bargain. In your opinion, they are
fine fellows, isn't that so?"

"In my opinion," Bazarov retorted, "Raphael isn't worth
a brass farthing; and they are no better."

"Bravo! Bravo! Listen, Arcady . . . that's the way modern
young men should express themselves! When one reflects,
it's no wonder they follow you! Formerly, young men had
to study; they had no wish to be known as ignoramuses,
and so willy-nilly they had to apply themselves. Now all
they can say is, 'Everything is rubbish!' And they have
made their point. The young men are simply delighted.

To be sure, before they were only blockheads, now they have suddenly become Nihilists."

"So, your boasted sense of dignity has failed you," Bazarov remarked phlegmatically, while Arcady went all hot and his eyes flashed. "Our argument has gone too far . . . we'd better stop it. I shall be prepared to agree with you," he added, getting up, "when you confront me with at least one form of our contemporary life, in the family or the social order, which does not call for absolute and ruthless negation."

"I can confront you with a million such," Paul Petrovich exclaimed. "A million! Now take the Peasant Commune, for example."

A cold sneer twisted Bazarov's lips.

"Well, as to the Peasant Commune," he said, "you had better discuss it with your brother. He seems to have had some practical experience of the Commune—of its mutual guarantees, sobriety and other devices of the sort."

"There's the family, finally, the family, as it exists among our peasantry!" Paul Petrovich shouted.

"I suggest you had better not examine that question in detail either. You have, I suppose, heard of the way the head of the family can select his daughter-in-law? Listen to me, Paul Petrovich, take a couple of days to consider it, you won't tumble on it at once. Sift over all our social classes, and ponder well on each of them, while Arcady and I will . . ."

"Will sneer at everything," Paul Petrovich picked him up.

"No, we shall dissect frogs. Let's go, Arcady; good-bye, gentlemen!"

The friends went out. The brothers remained alone and, for a time, only stared at each other.

"There," Paul Petrovich began at last, "there you have the young men of to-day! Such are our heirs!"

"Our heirs," Nicholas Petrovich repeated with a despondent sigh. While the disputation was going on, he had sat as on red-hot coals, stealing now and then a stealthy and pained glance at Arcady. "Do you know what it reminds me of, brother? Once I had a quarrel with our late mamma; unwilling to hear me, she was shouting her head off. . . . I finally told her that she was incapable of understanding me: 'We belong to different generations,' I had said. She was terribly offended, while I thought to myself,

'What's to be done?' It is a bitter pill—but I shall have to swallow it. Now our turn has come, and our heirs can say to us: 'You don't belong to our generation, you can swallow the pill.' "

"You're far too good-natured and modest," Paul Petrovich expostulated. "I am convinced that you and I are much more in the right than these little gentlemen, even though we may express ourselves in somewhat out-of-date, *vieilli* language, and may lack their impudence and self-assurance. . . . They are so swollen-headed, these young men of to-day! If you ask one of them, 'Which wine do you prefer, red or white?' 'I am in the habit of preferring red!' he will answer in a bass voice and with such a solemn expression on his face as though the whole of the universe were looking at him at that instant. . . ."

"Would you like some more tea?" Fenichka asked, thrusting her head through the door: she had hesitated to enter the drawing-room while voices had been raised in dispute.

"No, you may tell them to remove the samovar," Nicholas Petrovich replied, getting up to meet her. With a brusque, *"Bon soir!"* Paul Petrovich retired to his study.

XI

HALF an hour later, Nicholas Petrovich was in the garden, sauntering in the direction of his favourite arbour. He was oppressed with sad thoughts. For the first time he had clearly realized the gulf that separated him from his son, and he had a foreboding that with each day the gap would widen. Therefore, he felt that he had merely wasted his time when, as he had sometimes done during his winter stay in Petersburg, he had spent whole days poring over the latest books; he had merely wasted his time in listening to the young men talk and in feeling elated at his own success in inserting a word or two into their heated discussions. "My brother maintains that we are right," he thought, "and discarding all personal vanity it seems to me also that these young men are further removed from the truth, and yet I cannot help feeling that they have something we lack, an advantage over us. . . . Is it their youth? No, it can't be only a question of youth. Perhaps their advantage lies in their having fewer traces of the serf-master in their character?"

Nicholas Petrovich lowered his head and passed a hand over his face.

"But to reject poetry?" he asked himself again. "To lack all feeling for art, for nature . . ."

And he gazed about him as though he wished to grasp how it was possible not to share the feeling for nature. The evening was already creeping on: the sun had hidden behind a small aspen grove, some half a mile away from the garden, and its shadow spread endlessly over the motionless fields. A peasant was riding a white horse at a trot along the dark, narrow path that skirted the grove: though he was riding in the shadow, his horse's hooves could be perceived flashing up and down with pleasing precision. The rays of the sun, for their part, filtered into the grove and, forcing their way through the thicket, drenched the trunks of the aspen trees in such a suffusion of light that they began to assume the appearance of pine trunks, and their foliage showed blue beneath an azure sky, slightly tinged by the beams of the setting sun. The larks were soaring on high; the breeze had quite died away; belated bees were buzzing lazily and drowsily among the lilac; a column of swarming gnats was crowding over an isolated projecting branch. "How beautiful it all is, O Lord!" Nicholas Petrovich thought, and some favourite lines of verse rose to his lips. Suddenly he remembered Arcady—his *Stoff und Kraft*— and restrained himself; but he kept his seat, surrendering himself to the bitter and consoling play of solitary reflections.

He was fond of meditation; his life in the country had developed this capacity in him. Only recently he had meditated in this manner when waiting for his son to arrive at the posting-station, but since then things had changed, and how they had changed! their relations, nebulous until then, had now become defined. . . . He conjured up the image of his late wife, not as he had known her through the many years of their married life, not as an efficient and painstaking housewife, but as a slender young maiden with innocent, searching eyes, and a plait of hair knotted tightly over her girlish neck. He remembered his first glimpse of her. He had met her on the staircase leading to his apartment: and having accidentally pushed her, he had turned round intending to apologize, but could only mumble, *"Pardon, monsieur."* At that she had nodded, laughed and run away as though frightened; but at the turning of the stair, she had glanced quickly round at him, looking grave, and had blushed. Then had followed their first shy meeting, the half-uttered phrases, the half-smiles, the perplexity, the depressions and the surges of emotion, which were finally crowned by breathless happiness. . . . Where had all that gone? She had become his wife, he had been happier than most mortals. . . . "But," he thought, "why should not those first sweet moments remain eternal and immortal?"

He made no attempt to clarify this thought, but longed to arrest that blissful time by some means stronger than memory; he yearned to have his Maria near him once more, to feel her warmth and her breath, and he fancied that yonder, above him . . .

"Nicholas Petrovich," Fenichka's voice rang out nearby. "Where are you?"

He started. He felt no pain or shame. . . . He did not even admit the possibility of comparison between his late wife and Fenichka, but he regretted that she had taken it into her head to seek him out. Her words reminded him at once of his grey hairs, his age, his present . . .

The magic world, which he was just entering and which was just looming out from the misty waves of the past, wavered—and vanished.

"Here I am," he replied. "I'll be along soon, don't wait for me."

As he said this, he instantly thought, "That's the serf-master in me talking!" Fenichka peeped silently into the arbour and was gone; and he noticed with surprise that darkness had already descended while he had been musing. In the vicinity everything was dark and quiet; and the glimpse he had caught of Fenichka's face threw into relief its pallor and frailness. He rose and was about to make for the house; but his agitated heart gave him no peace. He began to pace up and down the garden, now staring thoughtfully at his feet, now raising his eyes to the sky where the stars were already swarming and winking at each other. He went on walking till he felt almost exhausted, but his anxiety, an undefined probing and sorrowful anxiety, did not diminish. Oh, how Bazarov would have laughed at him, if he had known what was going on in his mind! Arcady himself would have reproved him. Here he was at forty-four, a gentleman farmer and landowner, shedding tears, inexplicable tears; that was a hundred times worse than playing the 'cello.

Nicholas Petrovich pursued his pacing, unable to make up his mind to return home—to that peaceful and cosy nest whose lighted windows peeped at him so invitingly; he had not the strength to tear himself away from the gloom, from the garden, from the fresh air that played on his face, from the nostalgia, from the anxiety....

At the turning of the path, he ran into Paul Petrovich.

"What's the matter with you?" Paul Petrovich asked. "You look as pale as a ghost. Aren't you feeling well? Why don't you go to bed?"

Nicholas Petrovich explained his state of mind and then walked away. Paul Petrovich strolled as far as the end of the garden, grew pensive too, and likewise lifted his gaze to the sky. But his fine dark eyes reflected only the glimmer of the stars. He was not born a romantic, and his soul, so dry and elegant, passionate and misanthropic in the French way, was incapable of reverie....

"Do you know what?" Bazarov said that night to Arcady. "I've just had a marvellous idea. Your father was telling us to-day of the invitation he had received from that highfalutin relative of yours. Your father does not wish to go; let us make a dash for town—the gentleman in question has invited you too. We could stay there five or six days, and that would be a change!"

"But will you come back here afterwards?"

"No, I'll have to travel on and see my father. As you know, he lives only some twenty miles from town. I haven't seen him for ages, nor my mother; I must cheer up the old folk. They are splendid people, both of them, especially my father: he's a most amusing person. I'm the only son."

"And will you stay long with them?"

"Not very long. I'd find it a bit boring."

"And will you call on us on the way back?"

"I don't know. . . . We'll have to see. Well, are you game? Shall we go?"

"Maybe," Arcady replied lazily.

In his heart he rejoiced at his friend's suggestion, but he thought it his duty to disguise his feelings. He was not a Nihilist for nothing!

The following day Arcady and Bazarov set off for town. The younger folk at Maryino regretted their departure; Dunyasha even shed a tear . . . but the older men breathed a sigh of relief.

XII

THE town which was the object of our friends' visitation was in the charge of a Governor of the younger generation —a man who, as is often the case in Russia, was at once progressive and despotic. Within a year of assuming office he had quarrelled not only with the Marshal of the Nobility, a retired cavalry captain of the Guards, who ran a stud farm and kept open house, but also with his own subordinates. The conflicts engendered as a result assumed such proportions that the Ministry in Petersburg had been finally obliged to dispatch an official entrusted with the task of investigating the pros and cons on the spot.

The choice of the authorities fell on Matvey Ilyich Kolyazin, the son of that particular Kolvazin who had once upon a time acted as guardian to the brothers Kirsanov. He was also one of the "younger men," that is to say, he had just turned forty, but already he aimed at the higher posts of state and displayed a star on each side of his chest. As a matter of fact, one of these stars was of foreign provenance and of a none too illustrious order. Like the Governor, whom he was about to judge, he had the reputation of being a progressive but, as he was already a big shot, did not conduct himself as most of them are wont to do. He had the highest opinion of himself; his vanity knew no bounds, but his manner was simple, his glance encouraging, his attention indulgent and his laughter so good-natured that, for a short while, he might have passed for a "splendid fellow." However, on important occasions he was quite capable, as they say, of "beating the carpet." "Energy is essential," was his favourite maxim at the time. *"L'énergie est la première qualité d'un homme d'état"*; but despite it all, he was extremely gullible, and any experienced official could ride over him rough-shod. Matvey Ilyich used to speak with the greatest respect of Guizot, and tried to instil in all and sundry the notion that he himself did not belong to the category of routine officials and backward bureaucrats; that he never missed any important "manifestations" of social life. . . . All such words and phrases were only too familiar to him. He even followed the development of contemporary literature, though he did so with casual condescension, like an adult who, on occasion, might join in a procession of boys he happened to meet in the street. Actually, Matvey Ilyich was but little ahead of those statesmen of Alexander I's reign who, before attending a *soirée* at Madame Svyechin's, then resident in Petersburg, would peruse a page of Condillac in the morning; but his approach was different by virtue of its modernity. He was a subtle courtier, a man of great wile, and that was all; he had no sense for handling public affairs, no intelligence—only a knack for making ends meet; no one could outsmart him in this domain, and that is what really matters.

Matvey Ilyich greeted Arcady with all the affability— and even playfulness—that becomes an enlightened hierarch. He was amazed, however, to learn that the relations whom he had invited had preferred to stay at home in the country. "Your father was always an eccentric," he remarked, fingering the tassels of his sumptuous velvet dressing-gown. Then turning brusquely to a young official, who wore an undress uniform carefully buttoned up for the occasion, he exclaimed with a worried look: "What is it?" The young man, whose lips were glued together from prolonged silence, leapt up and stared at his chief in perplexity. But having set his subordinate a problem, Matvey Ilyich paid no more attention to him. As a rule, our higher officials like to startle their subordinates; and they employ a great variety of methods to achieve this end. Among others, the following method is in vogue, "is quite a favourite," as the English say: a high official will suddenly fail to understand the simplest words and simulate deafness. For instance, he will inquire, "What day of the week is it?"

He will be respectfully informed, "To-day is Friday, your Ex . . . len . . . cy."

"Eh? What? What did you say?" the high official will repeat with great intensity.

"To-day is Friday, your Ex . . . len . . . cy."

"What? How's that? What is Friday?"

"Friday, your Ex . . . len . . . cy, is a day of the week."

"Well, I . . . Are you trying to teach me something?"

Although he was reputed to be a liberal, Matvey Ilyich was first and foremost a high official.

"I advise you, my friend, to pay a call on the Governor," he told Arcady. "You will understand that I counsel you to do this out of no predilection for the old convention, according to which the authorities must be placated, but simply because the Governor is quite a decent fellow; besides, you would probably like to mix in local society. . . . You're no bumpkin, I trust? The day after to-morrow the Governor is giving a large ball."

"Are you going?" Arcady inquired.

"He is giving it for me." Matvey Ilyich replied almost in a tone of regret. "Do you dance?"

"I do, but not very well."

"That's a pity. There are some charming girls here and, besides, a young man should be ashamed of not being able to dance! I'm not saying this out of prejudice; I don't in the least assume that one's brain should go into one's feet, but the Byronic attitude is ridiculous now, *il a fait son temps.*"

"But, uncle, the Byronic attitude has nothing to do with my . . ."

"I shall introduce you to the young ladies, I'll take you under my wing," Matvey Ilyich interrupted him, laughing in a self-satisfied sort of way. "You'll find it quite warm, eh?"

A manservant appeared and reported the arrival of the President of the Finance Department, a doting-eyed old man with wrinkled lips; he was inordinately partial to nature, particularly in summer when, according to him, "Each bee takes its wee bribe from each wee flower. . . ." Arcady took his leave.

He found Bazarov at the inn where they had put up and

spent quite a time trying to persuade his friend to call on the Governor.

"There's no way out!" Bazarov exclaimed at last. "We must go through with it. Since we have come to spy upon the landed gentry, we might as well inspect them at close quarters."

The Governor received the young men cordially, but did not ask them to sit down and himself remained standing. He was very fussy and always in a hurry; in the morning he donned his tight-fitting undress uniform and an exceedingly stiff cravat; he never found time to finish his meals or drinks, and was constantly issuing orders. In the province he had been nicknamed "Bourdaloue"; this implied no affinity with the well-known French preacher of that name but rather with a muddy beverage called "bourda." He invited both Kirsanov and Bazarov to the ball, and within two minutes repeated the invitation under the impression that the friends were brothers and that their name was Kaysarov.

As they were walking back from the Governor's, a passing droshky pulled up and a squat man in a jacket of Hungarian cut much favoured by the Slavophils jumped out and, with a shout of "Eugene Vassilich!" rushed to meet him.

"Ah! So it's you, Herr Sitnikov!" Bazarov exclaimed without halting in his stride. "What fates bring you here?"

"Just imagine, a pure accident," the other replied. Turning towards the driver of the droshky and waving his hand at him four or five times, he bawled: "Follow us, will you? My father has a concern here," he went on, leaping over the gutter, "well, and so he asked me. . . . This morning I learnt of your arrival and have already called on you. . . ." (As a matter of fact, when our friends returned to their rooms, they found a visiting-card with the corners turned down and the name of Sitnikov printed on one side in French and on the other in a Slavonic scrawl.) "I hope you are not coming from the Governor's?"

"Don't hope. We have come straight from him."

"In that case, I shall call on him too. . . . Eugene Vassilich . . . Will you introduce me to your . . . to him? . . ."

"Sitnikov, Kirsanov," Bazarov growled without halting.

"I am highly flattered," Sitnikov began, sidling up to Arcady, smirking and hurriedly pulling off his over-elegant gloves. "I have heard a great deal . . . I am an old friend of Eugene Vassilich's and, if I may say so, his disciple. I am obliged to him for my regeneration. . . ."

Arcady stared at Bazarov's disciple. The small but agreeable features of his smoothly shining face wore a dull and anxious expression; his smallish eyes, which looked as if they had been crushed into his face, stared restlessly ahead of him, and he had an anxious laugh, a sort of jerky wooden laugh.

"Would you believe it," he went on, "when I heard Eugene Vassilich say for the first time that we must respect no authorities, I was simply bowled over with enthusiasm. . . . It was like having a new vision of the world! Here, I thought, I have at last found a man! By the way, Eugene Vassilich, you must not fail to call on a certain lady here. She is quite capable of understanding you, and your visit would be a real joy to her. I am sure you must have heard of her?"

"Who is she?" Bazarov reluctantly inquired.

"Kukshin, *Eudoxie,* Eudoxia Kukshin. She is a woman of remarkable disposition; she is *emancipée* in the real sense of the word—an advanced woman. Do you know what? Let's go and visit her now. She lives only a couple of steps away. We can have lunch with her. You haven't lunched yet, have you?"

"Not yet."

"Well, that's grand. She's separated from her husband, you know, and is quite independent."

"Is she attractive?" Bazarov interrupted.

"No-o-o, I wouldn't say that."

"Then why the devil are you asking us to call on her?"

"You like your little joke. . . . She's sure to stand us a bottle of champagne."

"That's better! One can see at once that you're a practical man. By the way, is your father still in the liquor business?"

"He is," Sitnikov hurriedly replied, emitting a shrill laugh. "Well? Are you game?"

"I really don't know."

"Since you wanted to see how other people live, you might as well go," Arcady interjected in an undertone.

"And what about you, Monsieur Kirsanov?" Sitnikov asked. "You must come too, we couldn't go without you."

"But wouldn't we be intruding if we all went?"

"That's quite all right. Kukshin is a marvellous woman."

"And are you certain she will provide a bottle of champagne?" Bazarov queried.

"Three!" Sitnikov exclaimed. "I guarantee that."

"With what?"

"With my own head."

"Your father's money-bags would be better. However, let us go."

XIII

THE small aristocratic house in the Moscow style, where Avdotya Nikitishna or Eudoxia Kukshin resided, was situated in one of the recently burnt-out streets of the town; as everyone knows, our provincial towns are ravaged by fire every five years. In the doorway, above a crookedly fixed visiting-card, a bell handle could be perceived, and in the entrance hall the visitors were met by a woman who must have been either a maid or a lady's companion. She was wearing a mob-cap—a manifest sign of the progressive strivings of the lady of the house. Sitnikov inquired whether Madame Kukshin was at home.

"Is that you, Victor?" a shrill voice asked from an adjoining room. "Come in."

The woman in the mob-cap immediately disappeared.

"I'm not alone," Sitnikov replied, as he dashingly threw off his Hungarian jacket, revealing beneath it a sort of sleeveless undercoat or jerkin, and glanced eagerly at both Arcady and Bazarov.

"Never mind," the voice replied. *"Entrez!"*

The young men entered. The room in which they found themselves resembled a working cabinet more than a drawing-room. Papers, letters, thick volumes of Russian periodicals for the most part uncut, were strewn over the dusty tables; white cigarette-ends lay scattered all over the place. On a leather sofa a lady reclined, still young, fair-haired, a trifle dishevelled, wearing a none too tidy dress, heavy bracelets on her short arms and a lace kerchief on her head. She got up from the sofa, absent-mindedly pulling over her shoulders a short velvet coat lined with ermine and, as she shook hands with him, drawled lazily, "Good morning, Victor."

"Bazarov, Kirsanov," Sitnikov said curtly after the manner of Bazarov.

"You are very welcome," Madame Kukshin replied and, fixing Bazarov with her round eyes between which a tiny snub nose was just visible, added, shaking hands with him also, "I know you."

Bazarov knitted his brows. There was nothing ugly about the small, matt face of the emancipated lady; but its expression left a disagreeable impression on the beholder. Instinctively one longed to ask her, "Why are you so hungry? Are you bored? Do you lack confidence? Why are you so fidgety?" Something was continually gnawing at her soul just as it was at Sitnikov's. Her conversation and her movements were disconnected and awkward, she evidently looked upon herself as an affable and simple creature, but her actions invariably gave the impression that she intended the opposite; everything she attempted looked "intentional," as children say—in short, neither simple nor natural.

"Yes, yes, I know you, Bazarov," she repeated. (Like many provincial and Moscow ladies, she was in the habit of calling men by their family names on first acquaintance.) "Would you like a cigar?"

"A cigar's a cigar," interjected Sitnikov who, with one of his legs in the air, was already sprawling in an arm-chair, "but do let's have some lunch. We are quite famished; and tell them also to send up a bottle or two of champagne."

"Sybarite!" Eudoxia exclaimed, laughing. (Whenever she laughed, the gums of her top teeth showed.) "He's a Sybarite, isn't he, Bazarov?"

"I appreciate the comforts of life," Sitnikov solemnly declared. "That doesn't prevent my being a liberal."

"Yes, it does, it does!" Eudoxia exclaimed. Nevertheless she ordered her attendant to see to both the lunch and the champagne. "Now what do you think?" she added, turning to Bazarov. "I'm positive you share my opinion."

"Not quite," Bazarov retorted. "Even from the chemical point of view, a chunk of meat is better than a morsel of bread."

"So you are a student of chemistry? It's my great passion; I have even invented a new compound."

"A new compound? You?"

"Yes, I. And do you know for what purpose? For making dolls—to prevent their heads from breaking off. I'm quite a practical person. But I haven't got quite into shape yet. I have still to read Liebig. *Apropos,* have you seen Kislyakov's article on female labour in the *Moscow Gazette?* Do read it. I'm sure you are interested in the question of women's emancipation, aren't you? And also in the problem of the schools? But what does your friend do? What is his name?"

Madame Kukshin let drop her questions one after the other with feminine insouciance, without expecting any answers; it was the way in which spoilt children talk to their nannies.

"My name is Arcady Nicolaievich Kirsanov," Arcady informed her, "and I don't do anything."

Eudoxia guffawed.

"That's charming! Don't you smoke? Victor, you know I am angry with you."

"Why?"

"They say you've been praising Georges Sand again. She's already out of date and that's the end of it! How can one compare her with Emerson! She has no ideas about education or physiology or anything. I am sure she has never heard of embryology, and in these days what can we do without it?" (Eudoxia even threw up her hands.) "Ah, what a wonderful article Yeliseyivich has just written on that topic! He's quite a genius of a gentleman!" (Eudoxia constantly used the word "gentleman" instead of "man.") "Bazarov, come and sit down beside me on the sofa. You may not be aware of it, but I am terribly afraid of you."

"Why's that? May I inquire the reason?"

"You're a dangerous gentleman; you are so very critical. Oh Lord, oh Lord! How funny! I'm talking like any staid lady-landowner. However, I actually am a landowner. I manage my own estate and, just fancy it, my steward Yerofey is an amazing character, just like Fenimore Cooper's Pathfinder: he has something in common with him! I have now definitely taken up my quarters here; it's quite unbearable, this town, isn't it? But what's to be done?"

"It's much the same as any other town," Bazarov remarked coolly.

"All these niggling interests, that's what is so terrible! Formerly I used to spend the winter in Moscow. . . . But now my worthy husband, Monsieur Kukshin, lives there. Besides Moscow is now . . . I don't know what's the matter, but it's not the same. I am thinking of going abroad; I was already on the point of departing last year."

"To Paris presumably?" Bazarov inquired.

"To Paris and Heidelberg."

"Why Heidelberg?"

"Why? Because Bunsen is there."

Bazarov was at a loss how to cap this.

"*Pierre* Sapozhnikov . . . do you know him?"

"No, I don't."

"But goodness me, *Pierre* Sapozhnikov . . . he still comes regularly to Lydia Khostatova's."

"I don't know her either."

"Well, he's taken it upon himself to accompany me abroad. Thank God, I'm free, I have no children. . . . Did I say 'Thank God'? Not that it matters anyway."

With her nicotine-stained fingers Eudoxia rolled herself a cigarette, licked it, sucked it and then lit it. The attendant entered with a tray.

"Ah, here's the lunch! Will you have a bite? Victor, uncork a bottle; that's your specialty."

"It is, it is," Sitnikov mumbled, laughing shrilly again.

"Are there any attractive women in this town?" Bazarov inquired as he emptied his third glass of champagne.

"There are," Eudoxia replied, "but they are all lightheaded. But *mon amie* Odintzov, for example, is not so bad. What a pity she has such a reputation. . . . However, that would not matter so much, but she has no freedom of outlook, no breadth, nothing . . . of *that*. Our whole system of education needs changing. I have already been pondering on it; our women are all very badly brought up."

"Better give it up as a bad job!" Sitnikov exclaimed. "Women should be despised, and I do despise them, completely and absolutely!" (The chance to be scathing and to express his contempt for anyone was for Sitnikov a most agreeable sensation; he made a particular point of attacking women, little suspecting that within a few months he would have to crawl before his own wife for no other reason than that she was born a Princess Durdoleosov.) "None of them would be capable of understanding our conversation; none of them deserves to be discussed by us serious-minded men!"

"But they have no need to understand our conversation," Bazarov retorted.

"Whom are you talking about?" Eudoxia intervened.

"Attractive women."

"What? You must share the views of Proudhon!"

Bazarov drew himself up haughtily.

"I share no one's views: I have my own."

"Down with all authorities!" Sitnikov shouted, rejoicing at an opportunity to express himself critically in the presence of the man whom he slavishly imitated.

"But even Macaulay—" Madame Kukshin tried to say.

"Down with Macaulay!" Sitnikov thundered. "Are you attempting to defend those females?"

"Not those females, but the rights of women which I swore to champion to the last drop of my blood."

"Down with them all!" Sitnikov cried and then pulled himself up. "I am not against their rights," he added.

"Yes, you are. I can see you are a Slavophil!"

"No, I'm not a Slavophil, though of course . . ."

"No, no, no! You are a Slavophil. You're an upholder of the *Domostroy,* of patriarchal tyranny. You want to rule with the rod!"

"The rod's sound enough," Bazarov remarked. "But we have just reached the last drop . . ."

"Of what?" Eudoxia interrupted him.

"Of the champagne, my most respected Avdotya Nikitishna," Bazarov replied. "Of the champagne—not of your blood."

"I cannot remain indifferent when women are being attacked," Eudoxia went on. "It's terrible, simply terrible. Instead of blackguarding them, you would do better to read Michelet's book, *De l'Amour.* It's a miracle! Gentlemen, let us talk of love," Eudoxia added, letting her hand fall languorously on the crumpled cushion of the sofa.

A sudden silence followed.

"No, why should we?" Bazarov said. "But you referred to Madame Odintzov. . . . That is what you called her, I believe? Who is this lady?"

"She's simply charming!" Sitnikov squeaked. "I'll introduce you to her. She's intelligent, affluent, and a widow. A pity she's not more developed: what she needs is to get to know Eudoxia more intimately. I drink your health, Eudoxia! Let's clink! *Et toc, et toc, et tin-tin-tin. Et toc, et toc, et tin-tin-tin! . . .*"

"Victor, you're a scamp."

The luncheon lasted a long time. The first bottle of champagne was succeeded by a second, then a third, and finally a fourth. Eudoxia chattered away without respite; Sitnikov echoed her. They had much to say about the nature of marriage—whether it was prejudice or crime. They debated whether men were born equal or not. And they discussed the essence of individuality. The proceedings ultimately reached a stage when Eudoxia, all flushed with the wine she had drunk, began to thump with her close-cut fingernails on the keys of an out-of-tune piano and to sing in a hoarse voice, first, some gipsy songs and then Seymour Schiff's romance, "Granada Lies Slumbering," while Sitnikov, a scarf tied around his head, mimed the swooning lover at the passage:

> And when your lips and mine
> In burning kiss shall twine . . .

Arcady could bear it no longer. "Gentlemen," he exclaimed loudly, "this is very like bedlam."

Bazarov, who had contented himself with dropping a sarcastic word every now and then into the conversation—he was more engrossed in the champagne—yawned noisily, got up and, without so much as bidding good-bye to the hostess, strode out from the house followed by Arcady. Sitnikov leapt up and tried to catch up with them.

"Well, well!" he exclaimed, running now to the right, now to the left of them. "Didn't I tell you she was a remarkable personality! There should be more women like her! In her own way, she is a supra-ethical phenomenon."

"And is *that* establishment of your father's also an ethical phenomenon?" Bazarov inquired, pointing to a gin-shop which they were passing at that instant.

Sitnikov laughed shrilly again. He was very ashamed of his origin, and was at a loss whether to feel flattered or hurt by Bazarov's unexpected familiarity of speech.

XIV

A FEW days later the Governor gave his ball. Matvey
Kolyazin was indeed the guest of honour. The Marshal of
the Nobility made it clear to all and sundry that he had
only attended out of respect for him; and the Governor
persisted in ordering everyone about even while the ball
was in full swing and he himself was standing still. Matvey
Kolyazin's suppleness of approach was equalled only by
his stately manner. He had soft words for everyone, with a
shade of fastidiousness for some and of deference for others;
in front of the ladies he sparkled with compliments *en vrai
chevalier français* and laughed continuously with a hearty,
resounding and solitary laugh, as befits a dignitary. He
patted Arcady on the back and in a loud voice dubbed him
"nephew." On Bazarov, who was arrayed in an oldish dress-
coat, he bestowed an absent-minded but condescending
sideways glance, which slipped over his cheek, and a vague
but friendly grunt, which sounded something like, "I . . .
greatly." To Sitnikov he held out one of his fingers, smiling
at him as he turned his head away. Even to Madame
Kukshin, who had arrived at the ball without a crinoline,
wearing a pair of soiled gloves and with a bird of paradise
in her hair, he vouchsafed an *"enchanté."* There were lots
of people and no lack of cavaliers; the civilians tended to
bunch along the walls, while the officers danced with gusto,
especially a certain officer who had spent about six weeks in
Paris, where he had picked up a variety of dashing expressions, such as *"zut," "Ah fichtrrre," "pst, pst, mon bibi,"*
and others of the sort. His pronunciation was perfect, full of
real Parisian *chic,* and yet at the same time he used to say,
"si j'aurais" instead of *"si j'avais,"* and *"absolument"* when
he meant *"certainly"*—in short, he delivered himself in that
Franco-Great-Russian jargon at which the French poke fun
when they have no need to assure us that we speak their
language like angels, *"comme des anges."*

As we already know, Arcady danced badly, while
Bazarov did not dance at all: they both retired to a corner

and there Sitnikov joined them. With a mocking expression on his face and letting fall a few venomous remarks, he stared round him provokingly; to all appearance he was thoroughly enjoying himself. Then of a sudden his expression changed and, turning to Arcady, he said in an embarrassed sort of way, "Madame Odintzov has just arrived."

Arcady looked round and perceived a tall woman in a black dress pausing in the doorway of the ballroom. The dignity of her carriage astonished him. Her bare arms hung gracefully beside her stately figure; from her glossy hair light sprays of fuchsia fell gracefully upon her rounded shoulders; from under a slightly prominent, white forehead, her bright eyes looked calm and intelligent, calm above all and not pensive, and a barely perceptible smile played on her lips. A sort of affectionate and tender strength beamed in her face.

"Are you acquainted?" Arcady inquired from Sitnikov.

"Intimately. Would you like me to introduce you?"

"If you like . . . after the quadrille."

Bazarov had also directed his attention to Madame Odintzov.

"Who is that figure?" he asked. "She's unlike the other women."

Having waited for the quadrille to end, Sitnikov led Arcady up to Madame Odintzov; but he proved to be anything but intimately acquainted with her: he grew embarrassed as he addressed her and she, for her part, stared at him with a certain amount of surprise. However, her face assumed an affable expression when she heard Arcady's family name. She inquired whether he was not the son of Nicholas Petrovich.

"That is so," Arcady replied.

"I have met your father twice and have heard a great deal about him," she went on. "I am very glad to make your acquaintance."

At that moment some adjutant flew up to her and invited her to dance the next quadrille with him. She consented.

"So you dance?" Arcady asked her respectfully.

"I do. But why should you think I didn't? Or do I seem too old for it?"

"I beg your pardon, I didn't intend . . . But in that case may I invite you for the mazurka?"

Madame Odintzov smiled indulgently. "Certainly," she

replied, glancing at Arcady not so much with condescension as in the way a married sister might look at a younger brother. Madame Odintzov was a little older than Arcady; she had turned twenty-nine, but in her presence he felt himself a schoolboy, a young student, as though the difference of years between them were much greater. Then Matvey Kolyazin came walking towards her with stately mien and flattering speeches. Arcady stepped aside, but continued to keep her under observation: he did not take his eyes off her while she danced the quadrille. She was as unconstrained in her conversation with her partner as she had been with the high official; she made a few gentle motions with her head and eyes, and laughed softly once or twice. Her nose, like that of most Russians, was a trifle thick, and her complexion matt; for all that, Arcady decided that he had never met such an entrancing woman. The sound of her voice haunted his ears; the very folds of her dress, it seemed to him, hung down in a way no other woman could imitate, in a fashion more stately and flowing, and all her movements seemed particularly smooth as well as natural.

Arcady felt inwardly a little shy when, at the first strains of the mazurka, he sat out with his partner and, as he was on the point of engaging her in conversation, he could only stroke his hair without uttering a single word. But his shyness and agitation did not last long; Madame Odintzov's self-possession communicated itself to him also: within a quarter of an hour he was already talking quite freely about his father, his uncle and his life both in Petersburg and in the country. Madame Odintzov listened to him with obliging readiness, opening and shutting her fan a little as she did so; his chatter was interrupted whenever a new partner claimed her for a dance; Sitnikov, incidentally, invited her twice. She would return, sit down again and pick up her fan, without appearing to breathe any faster; Arcady would resume his chatter, feeling full of happiness at finding himself so close to her, talking to her, gazing into her eyes, at her lovely forehead, at the whole of her charming, grave and intelligent face. She herself spoke little, but her words showed a wide knowledge of life; from some of her remarks Arcady concluded that this young woman had already experienced and pondered on many things.

"With whom were you standing," she asked him, "just before Monsieur Sitnikov brought you over to me?"

"You noticed him then?" Arcady inquired in his turn. "What a fine face he has, don't you think? That's Bazarov, a friend of mine."

Arcady launched into a description of "his friend."

He spoke about him in such detail and with such enthusiasm that Madame Odintzov directed her gaze on Bazarov and attentively scrutinized him. Meanwhile the mazurka was drawing to an end. Arcady felt sorry at having to give up his partner: for almost an hour he had been very happy with her! It is true, during that time he had a persistent feeling that she was being indulgent to him, that he should have been grateful to her . . . but such feelings do not weigh heavily on youthful hearts.

The music came to a stop.

"Merci," Madame Odintzov murmured, getting up. "You have promised to visit me; do also bring your friend with you. I am very curious to meet a man who dares have no belief in anything."

The Governor came up to Madame Odintzov, announced that supper was served and, with a worried look on his face, offered her his arm. As she departed, she glanced back with a smile of farewell and a nod to Arcady. He made her a low bow and, following her with his eyes (how well proportioned her figure seemed, sheathed in the greyish glitter of black silk!) he thought to himself, "By now she's already forgotten my existence." As he did so, a feeling of exquisite resignation welled up in his heart. . . .

"Well? How goes it?" Bazarov inquired of Arcady, as soon as the latter had rejoined him in a corner. "Did you get any pleasure out of it? A certain gentleman was just telling me that the lady in question was—'quite hot'; but he looks a fool. Well? What is your opinion? Is she really—'quite hot'?"

"I completely fail to grasp the allusion," Arcady replied.

"Come, come! What innocence!"

"In that case, I fail to understand your gentleman. Madame Odintzov is very charming—there is no doubt on that score, but her manner is so cold and reserved that . . ."

"Still waters . . . you know the rest!" Bazarov exclaimed. "You say she is cold. That merely improves the flavour. You're fond of ices, aren't you?"

"Maybe," Arcady mumbled. "I'm no judge of such things. She would like to make your acquaintance. She has asked me to bring you along when I pay her a visit."

"I can imagine the portrait you daubed of me! However, you have acted sensibly. Take me along. Whatever she may be—a mere provincial lioness or just an *emancipée,* like Kukshin—she has a pair of shoulders I have not seen this many a day."

Bazarov's cynicism jarred on Arcady, but—as happens often enough—the reproach he levelled against his friend did not correspond exactly with what he really held against him. . . .

"Why are you unwilling to admit that women are capable of freedom of thought?" he asked in an undertone.

"Because, my dear brother, my observations lead me to suppose that free-thinking women are monstrosities."

On that the conversation ended. Both the young men departed immediately after supper. Madame Kukshin gave vent to a nervously spiteful but rather faltering laugh in their wake: her vanity had been deeply hurt because neither of them had paid the least attention to her. She was among the last to leave the ball, and towards four o'clock in the morning she and Sitnikov danced a polka-mazurka in the Parisian style. With this edifying entertainment the Governor's festival culminated.

XV

"WE shall soon find out to what category of mammals this personage belongs," Bazarov said to Arcady next day as they mounted the staircase of the hotel where Madame Odintzov was staying. "I can smell something not quite right here."

"You amaze me!" Arcady exclaimed. "What? To have you, Bazarov, of all people, uphold the narrow morality which . . ."

"What a queer chap you are!" Bazarov interrupted carelessly. "Don't you realize that, in our jargon and for people like us, 'not quite right' signifies 'quite all right'? It implies that some advantage can be gained. Did you not say yourself earlier on that she had made an odd marriage? Though, as I see it, to marry a rich old man is not in the least odd; on the contrary it is a sensible decision. I distrust the gossip of the town; but I should like to think, as our cultured Governor puts it, there is some foundation in it."

Without replying, Arcady knocked at the door. A young manservant in livery conducted our friends into a large room, which was furnished in as bad taste as the majority of rooms in Russian hotels but was embellished with a profusion of flowers. Very soon Madame Odintzov in person appeared on the scene in a simple morning dress. The spring sunshine made her look younger than ever. Arcady introduced Bazarov and noted with concealed surprise that his friend exhibited signs of embarrassment, whereas Madame Odintzov remained as self-possessed as she had been on the previous day. Bazarov became aware of his confusion and felt ashamed. "Well I never!" he thought. "Here's a woman who has put the wind up me!" Thereupon, sprawling in an arm-chair in the Sitnikov manner, he began to hold forth in an exaggeratedly free and easy tone, while Madame Odintzov kept her glowing eyes fixed on him.

Anna Sergeyevna Odintzov was born the daughter of Sergey Nicolaievich Loktyev, a speculator and gambler, who had been renowned for his good looks. Having succeeded in staying the course and gaining some notoriety in Petersburg and Moscow, Loktyev had ended by losing all he had at cards and by being obliged to retire into the country; there he soon died, leaving a tiny income to his two daughters—Anna, aged twenty, and Katerina, aged twelve. Their mother, a descendant of the impoverished line of the Princess K, had died in Petersburg while her husband was still at the height of his prosperity. After her father's death, Anna found herself in a very difficult situation. Her brilliant Petersburg education had not fitted her for the worries connected with the management of an estate and a manor house, or for the dull life of the provinces. She had absolutely no friends in the neighbourhood, and there was no one whose advice she could ask. Her father had done his best to avoid contacts with his neighbours; he despised them and they returned the compliment, each in his own way. However, she did not lose her head and at

once wrote to a maternal aunt of hers, the Princess Avdotya
Stepanovna K, a spiteful and conceited old lady, inviting
her to come and stay in the house. This the Princess did,
appropriating to herself all the best rooms, growling and
grumbling from morning till night, and even going to the
lengths of having herself accompanied whenever she went
out for a stroll in the garden by her one and only serf-
retainer, a sulky footman in a threadbare, pea-green livery
trimmed with pale-blue braid and in a three-cornered hat.

Anna bore patiently with her aunt's oddities, supervised
her young sister's education in her spare time, and seemed
resigned to the idea of withering away in this wilderness.
. . . But fate had other things in store for her. She happened
to meet a certain Odintzov, a very wealthy man of about
forty-six, eccentric, hypochondriac, bloated, ponderous and
sour, but neither stupid nor ill-tempered; he fell in love
with her and proposed marriage. She consented to become
his wife; after living with her for some six years he died,
bequeathing to her his whole fortune. For about a year after
his death Anna Sergeyevna did not leave the country; then
she went abroad with her sister, but stayed only in Ger-
many; becoming homesick, they returned to their favourite
estate at Nicolskoye, some thirty miles from town. There
she kept up a sumptuous, excellently furnished house with
a lovely garden and conservatories: the late Odintzov had
denied himself nothing. Anna Sergeyevna visited town but
rarely and then for the most part on business which did
not take up much time. But she was not liked in the
province. Her marriage with Odintzov had caused quite a
stir, and the most incredible rumours about her were in
circulation. It was affirmed that she had helped her father
in his nefarious deals, that she had an ulterior motive for
travelling abroad—that of concealing the unfortunate con-
sequences . . . . "You know what," the indignant interlocu-
tor would exclaim. "She's been through fire and water,"
others said of her; and a notorious provincial wit usually
threw in: "And through a brass band." All this gossip
reached her ears, but she paid no attention to it: she had a
firm and independent character.

Leaning back in an arm-chair with hands clasped,
Madame Odintzov listened to Bazarov. He was talking
more than his wont, garrulously and, to Arcady's great
surprise, obviously trying to intrigue her. He could not

make up his mind whether Bazarov was succeeding in his purpose. From Anna Sergeyevna's face it was hard to guess her thoughts: its expression remained unchanged, cordial and sympathetic; her beautiful eyes were bright with attention, yet her glance seemed imperturbable. At first, Bazarov's attitudinizing produced a disagreeable impression on her, like a bad smell or a too strident note; but she quickly realized that he was ill at ease, and this even flattered her. Paltriness was the only thing that revolted her, and Bazarov could not be accused of paltriness. That day Arcady was destined to be in a state of recurring amazement. He had expected Bazarov to converse with Madame Odintzov as with an intelligent woman about his convictions and opinions: she herself had expressed the wish to listen to a man "who dared have no belief in anything," but instead Bazarov discoursed on medicine, homœopathy and botany. It turned out that Madame Odintzov had not wasted her time in solitude: she had read through several good books and spoke faultless Russian. She brought the conversation round to music, but perceiving that Bazarov did not relish art, quickly veered the conversation back to botany despite the fact that Arcady had already begun to discuss the significance of folk melodies. Madame Odintzov continued to treat him like a younger brother: she seemed to appreciate his good qualities and youthful simplicity—and no more. Their leisurely, varied and animated conversation lasted for over three hours.

At length the friends rose to go and began to take their leave. Anna Sergeyevna eyed them amiably, held out her beautiful white hand to each of them in turn and, after a moment of reflection, said with a hesitant but impressive smile, "If you are not afraid of boredom, gentlemen, come and visit me at Nicolskoye."

"How can you say that, madame!" Arcady exclaimed. "I shall be delighted. . . ."

"And you, Monsieur Bazarov?"

Bazarov merely bowed—and Arcady was again amazed: he noticed that his friend had blushed.

"Well?" he asked when they were out in the street. "Are you still of the opinion that she is—'quite hot?' "

"One can never tell! Just look at the way she has put herself on ice!" Bazarov retorted, and after a pause added: "A regular duchess, a commanding personality. She only needs to have a train trailing behind her and a coronet on her head."

"Our duchesses don't speak such faultless Russian," Arcady remarked.

"She's been through the mill, my lad. She's tasted of our common bread."

"And yet she's beautiful," Arcady rejoined.

"A really opulent body!" Bazarov pursued. "Just ripe for the dissecting table."

"For Heaven's sake, Eugene, shut up! This won't do."

"Well, you mustn't be angry, you ninny. First class—that's what I really meant. We must go and pay her a visit."

"When?"

"The day after to-morrow, if you like. What is there to do here! Drink champagne with Kukshin? Or listen to your relative, the liberal big-noise? . . . We'll make a dash for it the day after to-morrow. By the way—my father's property is not very far from here. Isn't Nicolskoye on the X road?"

"Yes."

"*Optime.* Why dawdle then? Only fools delay—and the wise. Didn't I tell you, she's got an opulent body!"

Three days later, the friends were on the road to Nicolskoye. It was sunny without being too hot, and the well-nourished post-horses raced along in good fettle, gently swishing their knotted and plaited tails. Arcady stared at the road and, for some unknown reason, smiled to himself.

"You must congratulate me," Bazarov suddenly exclaimed. "This is the twenty-second of June, my name-day. We'll see how well my Patron Saint will watch over me. They are expecting me at home to-day," he added, lowering his voice. . . . "Well, they can wait a little longer—it's not so important!"

XVI

ANNA SERGEYEVNA's country house stood on the slope of a bare hill, within easy reach of a yellow stone church with a green roof, white columns and a fresco of the Resurrection painted in the Italian style over the main entrance. The figure of a swarthy warrior in a helmet, lying prostrate in the foreground, was particularly remarkable for its well-rounded contours. Behind the church a village spread for some distance in a double row of houses, whose chimneys projected here and there over the thatched roofs. The manor house was built in the same style as the church, the style so well known in Russia as the "Alexandrine"; this house was also painted yellow and had a green roof, as well as a row of white columns and a pediment with an escutcheon. The chief architect of the province had erected both buildings with the approval of Anna's late husband, who could not bear any "pointless and arbitrary innovations," as he called them. The house was flanked on each side with the sombre trees of an ancient park, while an alley of clipped fir trees stretched towards the main porch.

Our friends were met in the hall by two stalwart footmen in livery; one of them at once ran off to fetch the butler. The butler, a stout man in black tails, appeared promptly on the scene and directed the guests up a carpeted staircase to the room reserved for them, which already contained two beds as well as all the essential toilet requisites. Order evidently reigned in the house: everything was spick and span, and everywhere there was an odour of respectability such as is to be found in ministerial reception rooms.

"Madame would like you to call on her in half an hour," the butler reported. "Have you any instructions for me in the meantime?"

"No instructions at all, my worthy fellow," Bazarov replied, "unless you will deign to serve us with a glass of vodka."

"Certainly, sir," the somewhat puzzled butler replied as he went off with boots creaking.

"What *grand genre!*" Bazarov remarked. "I believe that's what it's called in your parlance? A regular duchess, that's what she is."

"A fine duchess," Arcady retorted, "to have invited at first sight two such obvious aristocrats as you and me."

"Me in particular, a country doctor in the making, and the son of one, and the grandson of a deacon. . . . You knew, didn't you, that I was the grandson of a deacon? . . ."

"Like Speransky,"[1] Bazarov added, after a brief pause,

---

[1] Speransky (1772-1839)—A Russian statesman of "westernizing" and reformist tendencies.

with a wry smile. "Anyhow, she's pampered. Oh, how she has pampered herself, this lady! Hadn't we better don our dress clothes?"

Arcady merely shrugged his shoulders . . . but he also felt slightly embarrassed.

Half an hour later Bazarov and Arcady descended into the drawing-room. It was a spacious, lofty room, furnished fairly luxuriously but without any distinctive taste. The ponderous, expensive furniture was set out in the usual, rather frigid order along the walls, which were covered in a buff wall-paper with golden arabesques; the late Odintzov had ordered the furnishings from Moscow through an agent friend of his, a wine merchant. Over the centre sofa hung a portrait of a somewhat flabby, fair-haired man—he seemed to stare rather disapprovingly at the guests. "It must be *him*," Bazarov whispered to Arcady and, wrinkling up his nose, added, "Shall we beat it?" But at that instant the lady of the house came in. She was wearing a summery muslin dress; her hair was smoothly brushed back behind her ears, imparting a girlish expression to her pure, fresh face.

"I am grateful to you for keeping your word," she began. "You must stay with me for a while: it is really not at all unpleasant here. I shall introduce you to my sister, she plays quite well. That is of no interest to you, Monsieur Bazarov; but I believe that Monsieur Kirsanov is fond of music; besides my sister, I have living here an old aunt, and one of our neighbours drives in occasionally for a game of cards: that is the whole of our society. And now let us sit down."

Madame Odintzov uttered the whole of her little speech very precisely, as though she had learnt it by rote: then she turned to Arcady. It transpired that her mother had known Arcady's mother, and had even acted as her confidante when the latter had fallen in love with Nicholas Kirsanov. Arcady began to speak with great warmth of his late mother, while Bazarov proceeded to inspect some of the albums. "I've grown quite tame," he was thinking.

A handsome borzoi with pale-blue collar ran into the drawing-room, tapping on the floor with its paws; it was followed by a girl of eighteen, with black hair, an olive-complexioned, slightly oval but winsome face, and dark eyes. In her hands she held a basket full of flowers. "This is

Katya," Madame Odintzov said, with a nod in her direction.

Katya made a slight curtsy, sat down beside her sister and began to sort out the flowers. The borzoi, whose name was Fifi, approached each of the guests in turn, wagging its tail and thrusting its cool muzzle into their hands.

"Did you pick them yourself?" Madame Odintzov inquired.

"Yes, I did," Katya replied.

"And is auntie coming down for tea?"

"She's coming."

Katya, when she spoke, had a charming smile, at once bashful and candid, and she had an amusingly severe way of looking up at one: everything about her was still innocently fresh; the downy bloom on her face, her rose-pink hands with white palms, and her rather compact shoulders. . . . She was constantly blushing and apt to catch her breath.

Madame Odintzov turned to Bazarov. "You are looking at those pictures merely out of politeness, Monsieur Bazarov," she began. "They don't really amuse you. You had better come closer, and then we can start an argument about something."

Bazarov moved closer. "What shall we argue about?" he inquired.

"Anything you like. I warn you, I'm a fierce wrangler."

"You?"

"Yes, I am. You seem surprised. Why?"

"Because, as far as I can judge, you have a calm, cold temperament. Argument implies an excitable nature."

"How can you sum me up so quickly? In the first place, I am very impatient and obstinate—you'd better ask Katya; and in the second, I am easily carried away."

Barazov looked at Anna Sergeyevna.

"Perhaps, you know best. So you would like us to have an argument—all right then. I was examining some views of German Switzerland in your album, and you remarked that they could not possibly interest me. You said that because you assumed that I had no artistic sense—yes, I really have none. But those views might have interested me from a geological standpoint, for instance that of the way mountains are formed."

"If I may say so, as a geologist you had better consult a manual, some special work on the subject, rather than those drawings."

"A drawing may provide a visual image of what it takes ten pages of text to describe."

Anna Sergeyevna was silent for a moment.

"And so you have no drop of artistic sense in you?" she brought out, leaning on the table, and, as a result of that movement, bringing her face nearer to Bazarov's. "How can you do without it?"

"And may I inquire why I need it?"

"It might help you to read people's characters."

Bazarov smiled.

"First, one's experience suffices for that; and secondly, may I state that it's not worth the trouble to make a separate study of individuals? All men are similar in body and soul; each one of us has a brain, a spleen, a heart, and identically formed lungs; and the so-called moral qualities attributed to us are the same in all: slight variations only prove the rule. One human specimen affords an adequate basis for judging all the rest. People are like trees in a forest; no botanist would dream of studying each birch tree in detail."

Katya, who was leisurely matching the flowers one by one, raised her eyes in perplexity and, encountering Bazarov's quick, casual glance, flushed to the tip of her ears. Madame Odintzov shook her head.

"The trees in a forest," she repeated. "According to you, then, there is no difference between a stupid and an intelligent man, between a good and a bad man."

"Oh yes, there is: it's like the difference between a sick and a healthy man. A consumptive's lungs, although identically formed, are differently conditioned from ours. We know approximately the cause of physical ailments; but moral ailments are induced by the wrong sort of education, by all sorts of rubbish with which it has been the custom to stuff people's heads, by the monstrous state of society—in short, if society is put right, then the ailments will vanish."

As Bazarov delivered himself of this, he had the air of thinking, "Believe me or not, it's all the same to me!" As he slowly stroked his side-whiskers with his long fingers, his eyes flitted round the corners of the room.

"You assume then," Anna Sergeyevna said, "that when society is put right, no more stupid or bad people will be left?"

"In a properly functioning society, it wouldn't matter a

jot whether a man were stupid or intelligent, good or bad."

"Yes, I understand. They will have identical spleens."

"Exactly so, madame."

Anna Odintzov turned to Arcady. "And what is your opinion, Monsieur Kirsanov?"

"I agree with Eugene," he replied.

Katya looked at him from under her eyelids.

"You amaze me, gentlemen," Madame Odintzov said, "but we shall discuss this further. And now I can hear auntie coming down for tea; we must be merciful to her."

Princess K, Anna Odintzov's aunt, a thin, little woman with a clenched fist of a face and glaring spiteful eyes under a grey wig, came in and, with barely a bow to the guests, sank into a roomy velvet arm-chair which no one but herself was privileged to use. Katya placed a hassock under her feet; the old lady did not bother to thank her, she did not even so much as glance at her, but kept twitching her hands under a yellow shawl, which covered almost the whole of her infirm body. The princess was fond of yellow, and her cap was also hung with bright yellow ribbons.

"Did you sleep well, auntie?" Madame Odintzov inquired, lowering her voice.

"That dog is here again," the old lady growled in reply. Then observing that Fifi had taken a couple of hesitant steps in her direction, she exclaimed, "Go away, go away!"

Katya called Fifi and opened the door.

Fifi rushed out joyously, expecting to be taken for a walk, but on being left alone outside the door, began to scratch with her paws and to whine. The princess frowned. Katya was on the point of going out. . . .

"I think tea is served," Madame Odintzov said. "Gentlemen, let us go. Auntie, please come and have some tea."

The princess silently vacated her arm-chair and was the first to leave the drawing-room. Everyone followed her into the dining-room. The little Cossack boy in livery noisily pushed back from the table another sacred arm-chair, laden with cushions, into which the princess sank; Katya, who was pouring out the tea, served her first with a cup emblazoned with a coat of arms. The old lady put some honey in her tea (although she never spent a penny of her own on anything, she considered it sinful and expensive to drink tea with sugar), and suddenly inquired in a husky voice:

"And what does *Preence* Ivan write?"

She received no reply. Bazarov and Arcady soon divined
that, although she was treated with respect, no one paid
any attention to her. "They keep her for the sake of appear-
ances, because she comes of a princely house," Bazarov
concluded. . . . After tea Anna Sergeyevna suggested a
stroll, but a drizzle had set in, and the company, with the
exception of the princess, returned to the drawing-room.
Then the neighbour arrived. A squat, grizzled old man, with
short spindly legs, very courteous and humorous, he was
Porfiry Platonich by name, and a great lover of cards. Anna
Sergeyevna, who talked with Bazarov more than anyone
else, asked him whether he would not care to pit himself
against them in a game of old-fashioned preference. Bazarov consented, remarking that it behoved him to train in
advance for his impending duties as a country doctor.

"Take care," Anna Sergeyevna said, "Porfiry Platonich
and I, between us, will rout you. As for you, Katya," she
added, "play something for Monsieur Arcady: he likes
music, and we shall listen too."

Reluctantly Katya approached the piano; and, though
fond of music, Arcady followed her as reluctantly; it had
occurred to him that Madame Odintzov was sending him
away—and his heart, like that of every young man at his
age, was beginning to seethe with a sort of vague and nostalgic sensation akin to a foreboding of love. Katya raised
the lid of the piano and, without a glance at Arcady, asked
him in an undertone:

"What shall I play for you?"

"Whatever you like," Arcady replied indifferently.

"What music do you prefer?" Katya inquired again,
without changing her position.

"Classical," Arcady replied in the same sort of tone.

"Do you like Mozart?"

"Very much."

Katya brought out Mozart's Sonata Fantasia in C minor.
She played very well, although a trifle too mechanically
and dryly. She sat motionless and stiffly, without taking her
eyes off the music, her lips tightly pressed, and it was only
as the Sonata neared its end that her face began to glow,
and a small tress of hair fell uncoiling over her dark brow.

The last part of the Sonata in particular impressed
Arcady—the part where transports of the most woeful and

almost tragic grief come suddenly bursting through in the middle of the enchanting joyousness of the heedless refrain. . . . But the reflections which were stimulated in him by the music of Mozart bore no reference to Katya. As he looked at her, he merely concluded, "This young lady doesn't play at all badly, and she is not bad-looking either."

When she had come to the end of the Sonata, Katya asked him, without taking her hands off the keys, "Will that do?" Arcady declared that he did not dare to impose on her any further, and began to talk to her about Mozart; he asked her whether she had selected the Sonata herself or whether anyone had recommended it to her. But Katya's replies were monosyllabic: she was hiding herself, she had withdrawn into herself. Whenever this happened to her, it took her a long time to come to the surface again; her very face as a result assumed an expression of obstinancy and almost of blankness. She was not so much shy as distrustful, and somewhat intimidated by the sister who had brought her up—a fact which the latter did not even suspect. For the sake of appearing at ease, Arcady finally fell back upon Fifi, now back in the room once more; calling her over to him and smiling benevolently, he stroked her head. Katya busied herself again with the flowers.

Meanwhile Bazarov was losing one game after another. Anna Sergeyevna was an expert player, Porfiry Platonich could also hold his own. Bazarov came out the loser of a sum which, though it was by no means considerable, he nevertheless found regrettable. Over supper Anna Sergeyevna once more broached the subject of botany.

"Let us go for a stroll to-morrow morning," she said to him. "I should like to learn from you the Latin names of various wild herbs and the properties."

"What do you want with Latin names?" Bazarov inquired.

"There must be order in everything," she replied.

"What a wonderful woman!" Arcady exclaimed as soon as they were alone in their room.

"Yes," Bazarov replied, "a woman with brains. I'm sure she's seen quite a lot."

"In what sense do you mean, Eugene?"

"In the good sense, in the good sense, my dear friend Arcady! I am also persuaded that she is an excellent estate manager. But it's her sister, not herself, who is the miracle."

"What? That little dark thing?"

"Yes, that little dark thing. She's fresh, untouched, apprehensive, anything but talkative, and whatever else you like. But she would be worth a lot of trouble. You could shape her to your fancy; but the other is too spry." Arcady made no reply. They went to bed, each pondering his own thoughts.

That night Anna Sergeyevna was also thinking about her guests. She had taken a liking to Bazarov—his lack of airs and the downright severity of his judgments appealed to her. She detected something new in him, something she had never encountered before, and her curiosity was roused.

Anna Sergeyevna was an odd enough person. Free from all prejudice, she yet lacked strong convictions; and though she was not put off by obstacles, she had no goal in life. She had clear ideas about many things and a variety of interests, but nothing ever fully satisfied her; nor did she seek complete satisfaction. Her mind was at once probing and apathetic: any doubts she may have entertained were never banished to the point of oblivion; nor were they ever allowed to provoke a state of inner alarm. If she had not been rich and independent, she might have thrown herself into the battle of life, experienced passion. . . . But she had an easy life, boring as it may sometimes have been, and continued to pursue her daily round without haste or undue agitation. From time to time a rainbow would loom in her sky, but when the mirage had faded she rediscovered peace and did not pine. Her imagination ranged beyond the bounds of what was considered permissible by the laws of conventional morality, but even then the rhythm of her blood pulsed no quicker as it circulated through her magnificently proportioned and tranquil body. Sometimes, emerging all warm and languorous from a fragrant bath, she would begin to muse on the insignificance of life, its sorrows, labours and evils. . . . Her soul would be filled with sudden resolve and would seethe with noble ardour; but a draught from a slightly open window was enough to make her shrink, complain, and almost be angry; in a moment like that her most urgent desire was to prevent the horrid draught from blowing on her.

Like all women who had failed to fall in love, she expeperienced a yearning for something she could not define. In reality, she yearned for nothing, although she seemed to long for everything. She could hardly bear her late husband (she had married him for practical reasons, although she probably would not have consented to become his wife unless he had been, as she imagined, of a kindly disposition), and had developed a secret revulsion for men, whom she represented as being all untidy, clumsy, limp and impotently wearisome creatures. On one occasion, somewhere abroad, she had met a handsome young Swede with a chivalrous face and a pair of honest pale-blue eyes beneath an open forehead; he made a powerful impression on her, but that did not prevent her from returning to Russia.

"What an odd man that doctor is!" she thought as she lay in her sumptuous bed, on lace pillows, beneath a silk quilt. . . . From her father Anna Odintzov had inherited a propensity for luxury. She had been very fond of her sinful but indulgent father; and, in his turn, he had adored her, joked with her as a friend and equal, confided in her and sought her counsel. She hardly remembered her mother.

"What an odd doctor!" she repeated. Stretching herself, she smiled, clasped her hands behind her head, and then, after letting her eyes stray over a couple of pages of a silly French novel, dropped the book and fell asleep, all pure and frigid in her spotless and fragrant linen.

Next morning, immediately after breakfast, Anna Odintzov set out on a botanizing expedition with Bazarov and came back just before dinner: Arcady did not venture to go out and spent about an hour with Katya. He did not feel bored in her company. She had suggested of her own accord that she might play yesterday's Sonata for him again; but when Madame Odintzov returned at last, when he saw her—his heart instantly contracted. . . . She was walking through the garden with a somewhat tired gait; her cheeks had flushed crimson and her eyes beneath the round straw hat shone more brightly than usual. In her fingers she was twirling a slender stalk of some wild flower, a light mantilla hung down to her elbows, and the broad grey ribbons of her hat clung to her bosom. Bazarov strode behind her, looking as self-confident and casual as ever, but the expression of his face, though cheerful and even affectionate, displeased Arcady. With a muttered "Good morning!"

Bazarov stalked off to his room. Madame Odintzov absent-mindedly pressed Arcady's hand and also went past him.

"Good morning," Arcady thought to himself. . . . "As if we had not seen each other earlier!"

XVII

TIME, as we all know, is sometimes a bird on the wing, and sometimes a crawling worm; but men are happiest when oblivious of time's quick or slow pace. In this mood Arcady and Bazarov spent about a fortnight at Madame Odintzov's. Her regular life and the order she had instituted in her household were partly responsible for this. She adhered strictly to her time-table and obliged others to observe it. There was a fixed time for everything throughout the day. In the morning, at eight o'clock punctually, the company assembled for morning tea; from tea-time till lunch everyone followed his own bent; the lady of the house attended to the steward (her estate had been put on a rent basis), the servants and the head housekeeper. Before dinner the company gathered again for conversation or reading; the evening was given up to walks, card-games and music; at half-past ten Anna Sergeyevna would retire to her room, give her final instructions for the following day and go to bed.

The measured, rather dignified precision of this daily round was not to Bazarov's taste: "It's like rolling on rails," he used to declare: the footmen in livery, the decorous butlers and servants, offended his democratic sentiments. According to him, the next logical step would have been to dine in English fashion, in evening dress and white ties. One day he broached the subject to Anna Sergeyevna. Her manner disposed everyone to express his opinions frankly, and without reserve. When Bazarov had had his say, she rejoined, "You are right from your point of view, and maybe in this particular case I am too much of a 'lady'; but one cannot live in the country without routine, otherwise it would only lead to boredom." And she pursued her course. Bazarov grumbled, but the reason why Arcady and he

found life so smooth at Madame Odintzov's was that everything in her house did "roll on rails." Nevertheless, since
the day of their arrival at Nicolskoye's, both the young
men had undergone a change. An unfamiliar anxiety had
overtaken Bazarov, whom Anna Sergeyevna treated with
obvious favour, even though she hardly ever saw eye to eye
with him: he was easily irritated, reluctant to talk, bad-
tempered in his looks and, as though impelled by an inward
anguish, could hardly sit still for a moment. Arcady, who
finally made up his mind that he was in love with Anna,
began to suffer from subdued fits of depression. However,
his depression did not prevent him from becoming more intimate with Katya; it even helped him to establish affectionate and comradely relations with her. "Anna doesn't think
much of me! So be it! . . . But this good-hearted creature
does not spurn me," he thought to himself, and his heart
once more indulged in the sweetness of magnanimous
sensations.

Katya vaguely grasped that he was seeking some consolation in her company, and she did not deny either herself
or him the innocent pleasure of a half-shy, half-trusting
friendship. In Anna Sergeyevna's presence they refrained
from talking to one another. Katya invariably shrank into
herself under her sister's probing glance, and Arcady, as
befits a young man in love, had no eyes for anything but
the object of his passion; but he felt happiest of all when
alone with Katya. He knew that it was not in his power to
hold Anna Sergeyevna's interest; when left alone with her,
he grew shy and lost his poise; nor did she know what to
say to him—he was too young for her. On the other hand,
Arcady felt himself quite at home with Katya; he treated
her indulgently, allowed her to air the impressions excited
in her by the music, the reading of novels, verse and other
such "trifles," without observing or, rather, failing to realize
that these trifles also amused him. Katya for her part did
not inhibit his feelings of melancholy. Arcady felt happy
with Katya, Anna—with Bazarov; and this usually resulted
in the two couples, especially when they went for a stroll,
going their different ways so as to enjoy their intimacy for
a while. Katya *adored* nature, and Arcady loved it too,
though he did not dare to admit it; like Bazarov, Anna
Sergeyevna was fairly indifferent to it. The fact that they
were almost continuously separated from each other was

not without its consequence for our friends: their relationship underwent a change. Bazarov stopped referring to Anna Sergeyevna when talking to Arcady; he even stopped railing at her "aristocratic ways"; he continued, it is true, to praise Katya as before, counselling his friend to tone down her sentimental inclinations, but his praise was hurried, his counsels dry, and, on the whole, he chatted with Arcady far less than was his wont . . . it looked as though he were avoiding him or felt ashamed in his presence. . . .

Arcady noted all this, but kept his observations to himself.

.   .   .   .   .

The real cause of all these "innovations" was the feeling inspired in Bazarov by Anna Sergeyevna—a feeling which tormented and enraged him, and which he would have at once repudiated with scoffing laughter and cynical vituperation if anyone had even distantly hinted at the possibility of what was going on in his mind. Bazarov was a great lover of women and feminine beauty, but love in the ideal sense or, as he would have put it, in the romantic sense, he called tomfoolery and unpardonable idiocy; he regarded chivalrous feelings as something in the nature of malformation or disease. On more than one occasion he had voiced his amazement at the fact that Toggenburg, with all his Minnesingers and Troubadours, had not been locked up in bedlam. "If you are attracted by a woman," he used to say, "try and gain her; but if that proves impossible—well, don't bother, drop her. A forest is not made up of one tree."

He liked Anna: the rumours about her, the freedom and independence of her mind, her undoubted penchant for him—all these seemed to argue in his favour; but he was quick to grasp that he could not "gain her." Moreover, to his amazement, he discovered that he lacked the resolution to "drop her." His blood took fire as soon as her image impinged on his mind; he could have controlled his blood easily, but something else had got into him, something he would not admit at any price, something which he had always scoffed at and which revolted his pride. In his conversations with Anna he used to indulge to an even greater extent than usual in his scathing indifference to everything savouring of romanticism; but when left to himself, he became indignantly aware of the romantic strain in his own composition. On these occasions he would set off into the forest and walk about there with large strides, breaking off any branch that barred his way and cursing both her and himself in a low voice, or he would clamber into a hayloft, into a barn, and, obstinately shutting his eyes, force himself to fall asleep, though he did not always succeed in achieving that result. Suddenly he would imagine those chaste hands one day twining themselves round his neck, those proud lips responding to his kisses, those intelligent eyes gazing lovingly—yes, lovingly—into his own; his head would go round and he would find an instant of oblivion before his indignation flared up again. As though tempted by the devil, he caught himself thinking all sorts of immodest thoughts. Sometimes, it seemed to him that a change was coming over Anna too, that there was something particular about the expression of her face, that perhaps . . . But at this point he would usually stamp his feet, grind his teeth and shake his clenched fist menacingly under his own nose.

And yet Bazarov was not entirely mistaken. He had excited Anna Sergeyevna's imagination; he had intrigued her, and she devoted much thought to him. In his absence she did not long for him, she did not yearn for him, but his presence always stimulated her; she was glad to be alone with him and glad to converse with him, even when he irritated her or shocked her taste and her refined habits of mind. She behaved as though she wished both to test him and to explore her own depths.

One day, as they were strolling in the garden, he suddenly informed her in a grim voice of his intention to depart in the near future and to visit his father. . . . Anna turned pale as though something had pricked her heart, and pricked it so painfully that she was surprised; she worried for a long time afterwards about the significance of this. Bazarov had told her of his intended departure without any idea of testing her or checking her reaction; he was not in the habit of "fabricating effects." That very morning he had seen his father's steward, Timofeyich, who was by way of being the "uncle" of his childhood. This Timofeyich, an experienced and astute old man, with faded yellow hair, red weather-beaten face and tiny teardrops in his shrunken eyes, had unexpectedly confronted Bazarov, wearing a short coat of greyish-blue cloth, belted with a leather thong, and tarred boots.

"So it's you, old Timofeyich! How goes it?" Bazarov had exclaimed.

"Greetings to you, young master," the old man had begun, smiling joyously, so that his face had suddenly dissolved into wrinkles.

"What have you come for? Were you sent to fetch me or what?"

"If it please your honour, how can that be!" Timofeyich had started to mumble (he remembered his master's strict injunctions when setting off). "I was on the way to town on the master's business when I happened to hear of your honour's being here, so I turned aside from the main road, that is—to have a peep at your honour ... it wouldn't do to disturb you otherwise."

"Now don't tell fibs," Bazarov interrupted him: "Is this the way to town?" Timofeyich looked sheepish and made no reply. "Is my father well?"

"Yes, thank God."

"And my mother?"

"Arina Vlassyevna is very well too, the Lord be thanked."

"No doubt they are expecting me!"

Old Timofeyich hung his small head to one side.

"Ah, your honour, how could they not be expecting you! As God's my witness, my heart's grown sick with watching your parents worry."

"Well, that'll do, that'll do, don't exaggerate. Tell them I'll be coming soon."

"As you will," Timofeyich had replied with a sigh.

As he quitted the house, he had pulled his cap over his eyes with both hands. On getting into the rickety droshky, which had been left standing at the gateway, he had started off at a trot—but not in the direction of the town.

The same evening Anna Sergeyevna was sitting in her study with Bazarov, while Arcady was pacing up and down the music-room, listening to Katya as she played. The princess had retired upstairs; as a rule, she could not bear guests, especially these "new loony ones," as she had dubbed them. In the drawing-room, she merely sulked, but in her own quarters, in the presence of her maid, she sometimes gave vent to such a stream of abuse as made her cap jerk up and down on her head together with her wig. Anna Sergeyevna was well aware of this.

"Why are you thinking of going away?" she began. "What about your promise?"

Bazarov stirred.

"Which promise?"

"You've forgotten then? You were going to give me a few lessons in chemistry."

"What's to be done! My father is expecting me; I can't dawdle here any longer. However, you can read Pelouse and Frémy, *Notions générales de la Chimie*; it's a good book and clearly written. You will find in it everything you need."

"But don't you remember, you tried to persuade me that a book was no substitute for . . . I forget how you put it, but you know what I want to say . . . do you remember?"

"What's to be done!" Bazarov repeated.

"Why must you go?" Anna Sergeyevna asked, lowering her voice.

He glanced at her. She had thrown her head back against the arm-chair and folded her arms, which were bare to the elbow. She looked paler in the light of a solitary lamp, hung over with a gauze-like paper shade. She was swathed in the soft folds of a voluminous white dress; the tips of her feet, which were also crossed, were just visible.

"And why should I stay?" Bazarov replied.

Anna Sergeyevna turned her head slightly.

"What do you mean by that? Aren't you enjoying yourself here? Or do you imagine that no one here will regret your going?"

"Of that I am positive."

Anna Sergeyevna had nothing to say for a moment.

"A pity you think so. However, I don't believe you. You could not have meant it seriously." Bazarov made no move. "Why don't you speak?"

"And what am I to say to you? There's no point in having regrets about people, and even less so about me."

"Why do you say that?"

"I am a serious and uninteresting person. I'm no conversationalist."

"You're angling for a compliment, Eugene Vassilich."

"That is no habit of mine. Don't you know yourself that the refinements of life are beyond my reach—the refinements on which you set so much store?"

Anna Sergeyevna nibbled a corner of her handkerchief.

"You can think what you like, but I shall miss you when you go."

"Arcady is staying behind," Bazarov replied.

Anna Sergeyevna gave a slight shrug of her shoulders.

"I shall miss you," she said.

"Really? In any case you won't miss me for long."

"Why do you assume that?"

"Because you told me yourself that you feel bored only when your routine is upset. You have arranged your life with such blameless rectitude that there could be no place in it for boredom or grief . . . or any disturbing emotions."

"You find that I am blamelessly . . . that is, that I have arranged my life with such rectitude?"

"Exactly so! Now take this, for example: in a few minutes it will strike ten, and I already know in advance that you will send me packing."

"No, I won't. You may stay. Will you open the window? . . . It feels stuffy."

Bazarov got up and pushed at the window. It flew open at once with a rattle. . . . He had not expected it to open so easily; moreover, his hands were shaking. The dark, mild evening peeped into the room with its almost black sky, faintly rustling trees and the fresh fragrance of the pure untrammelled air.

"Draw the blind and sit down," Anna Sergeyevna said. "I'd like to have a talk with you before you depart. Tell me something about yourself; you never talk of yourself."

"I try and chat with you about useful subjects."

"How very modest of you. . . . But I should like to learn something about you, your family, your father, for whom you are forsaking us."

"Why is she talking like this?" Bazarov thought.

"It's not at all interesting," he said aloud, "especially for you; we're obscure sort of folk. . . ."

"And according to you, I am an aristocrat?"

Bazarov raised his eyes and looked at Madame Odintzov.

"Yes," he said with over-emphatic bluntness.

She smiled.

"I can see that you hardly know me, although you assure me that all people are alike and that they are not worth individual study. One day I shall tell you about my life . . . but you must tell me about yours first."

"I hardly know you," Bazarov repeated. "Maybe you

are right; it may be true that every person is an enigma. Now let's take you, for instance: you shun people, you find them a nuisance, and yet here you have invited two students to come and stay with you. Why does a woman of your intelligence and your beauty live in the country?"

"What? How did you put it?" Madame Odintzov cried with animation. "With my . . . beauty?"

Bazarov frowned.

"It doesn't matter," he muttered. "I wished to say that I don't quite understand why you have settled in the country."

"You don't understand. . . . However, you must explain it in some way?"

"Yes. . . . I assume that you remain fixed in one and the same spot because you have been spoilt, you have grown too fond of comfort and all that goes with it, and are quite impervious to anything else."

Madame Odintzov smiled again.

"You are determined to disbelieve in my capacity for enthusiasm?"

Bazarov glanced at her from under his eyebrows.

"Out of curiosity, maybe; not otherwise."

"Indeed? Well, now I understand what brought us together; you are exactly like me."

"Brought us together . . ." Bazarov repeated in a hollow voice.

"Yes! . . . but I forgot that you were intending to go away."

Bazarov rose. The lamp was burning dimly in the middle of the dusky, fragrant and secluded room; the irritating freshness of the nocturnal air came pouring through the blind as it stirred occasionally, and its mysterious whispering seeped through. Anna sat perfectly still, but a secret agitation was gradually invading her. . . . It communicated itself to Bazarov. He suddenly realized that he was alone with a young and beautiful woman. . . .

"Where are you going?" she slowly asked.

Without replying he sank back into his chair.

"So you regard me as a placid, spoilt and self-indulgent creature," she went on in the same tone, without taking her eyes off the window. "But the one thing I know about myself is that I am unhappy."

"Unhappy! Why? You don't mean to say that you attach any importance to slanderous tittle-tattle?"

Madame Odintzov frowned. She felt annoyed at his interpreting her so well.

"These slanders don't even amuse me, and I am too proud to let them upset me. I am unhappy because . . . I have no desire, no longing for life. You look distrustfully at me, you think: there's an 'aristocrat,' covered in lace and seated in a velvet arm-chair. I shall not disguise the fact that I am fond of what you call comfort, but at the same time I have very little desire to live. Interpret this contradiction as you will. However, all this is romanticism in your eyes."

Bazarov shook his head.

"You are in good health, independent, rich. What more do you need? What is it you want?"

"What do I want?" Madame Odintzov repeated, sighing. "I have grown weary and old; I seem to have lived a great age. Yes, I've grown old," she added, gently drawing the ends of her mantilla over her bare arms. Her eyes met Bazarov's, and she flushed slightly. "I have behind me so many memories: my life in Petersburg, prosperity, then poverty, my father's death, my marriage, my trip abroad, it had to be . . . There are plenty of memories, but nothing to remember, and ahead, in front of me, stretches a long, long road, but I have no goal. . . . So I have no desire even to tread the path."

"You are so disillusioned?" Bazarov asked.

"No," Madame Odintzov replied with deliberation. "But I am incomplete. It seems to me that, if I were capable of becoming strongly attached to something . . ."

"You are longing to fall in love," Bazarov interrupted her, "but you are incapable of it: that is your unhappiness."

Madame Odintzov began to inspect the mantilla which covered her arms.

"Am I incapable of love?" she asked.

"Hardly! Only I was wrong to call it unhappiness. The contrary is true, people deserve pity who do fall for that."

"Fall for what?"

"Love."

"And how do you know that?"

"By hearsay," Bazarov retorted angrily.

"You're playing the coquette," he thought to himself. "You are merely bored and want to provoke me out of idleness, but I . . ." And, indeed, his heart was being torn.

"Moreover, you may be too exacting," he said, bending his whole body forward and playing with the fringe of the arm-chair.

"Perhaps. All or nothing is the way I see it. A life for a life. If you take mine, give me yours. And, if you do so, you must have no regrets or afterthoughts. Otherwise I don't want it."

"Indeed?" Bazarov remarked. "There's justice in that, and I am surprised that until now . . . you have not found what you wanted."

"And do you think it's so easy to surrender one's self completely to whatever it might be?"

"Not so easy once you start thinking, biding your time, putting a price on yourself, growing in your own estimation. That is so; but if you stop reflecting, then it's quite easy to surrender."

"But how can one fail to set a value on one's self? If I had no price, who would want my devotion?"

"That's not my affair; it's for the other person to decide on my value. What matters is to be able to surrender yourself."

Anna detached herself from the back of the arm-chair.

"You are talking as if you had experienced it all."

"It arose out of the conversation, Anna Sergeyevna. As you know, all this is not in my line."

"But would you be capable of surrendering yourself?"

"I don't know. I don't wish to boast."

Madame Odintzov did not say anything, and Bazarov fell silent. From the drawing-room came the sound of a piano being played.

"Katya is playing very late to-night," Madame Odintzov remarked.

Bazarov got up.

"Yes, it is quite late," he said. "It's time you were in bed."

"Wait. Why are you in such a hurry? . . . I want to say a word to you."

"What is it?"

"Wait," Madame Odintzov whispered. Her eyes rested on Bazarov; she seemed to be scrutinizing him with great attention.

He took a turn about the room and then, suddenly approaching her, bade her a hurried "Good night." He squeezed her hand so hard that she almost cried out and

left the room. She raised her numbed fingers to her lips,
blew on them and, rising brusquely and impetuously from
her arm-chair, strode rapidly towards the door as though
intending to call Bazarov back. . . . A maid entered with a
decanter on a silver tray. Madame Odintzov stopped short,
ordered her to go away and sat down again, immersed in
thought. Uncoiling itself like some dark snake, her hair
spread over her shoulders. For a long while yet the lamp
burnt on in Anna Sergeyevna's room, and for a long while
she remained sitting motionless, only occasionally with her
fingers stroking her hands which were now beginning to
feel the chill of the nocturnal air.

As for Bazarov, he returned some two hours later to his
bedroom, his boots all wet with dew, his hair dishevelled
and his expression grim. He found Arcady sitting at the
writing-desk, a book in his hands and his jacket all buttoned up.

"You're not in bed yet?" Bazarov asked in a tone almost
of regret.

"You were a long time with Anna Sergeyevna to-night,"
Arcady retorted, without replying to the question.

"Yes, I was with her all the time you and Katya were
playing the piano."

"I was not playing . . ." Arcady started to say and then
stopped. He felt the tears welling to his eyes, but he did
not want to weep in front of his scoffing friend.

XVIII

WHEN Madame Odintzov appeared at tea next day,
Bazarov sat for a while hunched over his cup of tea and
then suddenly glanced up at her. . . . She turned to face
him as if he had given him a jolt, and it struck him that her
face had gone slightly pale overnight. She soon retired to
her room and did not re-emerge until lunch-time. It had
drizzled from early morning and to go walking was out of
the question. The whole of the company had gathered in
the drawing-room. Arcady had got hold of the *Gazette* and
had begun to read aloud from it. The princess, as usual,

had reacted by looking amazed at first, as though Arcady were guilty of some indecency, and then she had fixed him with a baleful stare; but he paid no attention to her.

"Eugene Vassilich," Anna Sergeyevna said at last, "come along to my room. . . . I should like to ask you . . . You mentioned a manual yesterday."

She stood up and made for the door. The princess glanced round her with an expression that seemed to say, "Well, well, just look at that!" and then she had glared at Arcady again, but he merely raised his voice and, after exchanging a few glances with Katya, who was sitting beside him, continued to read aloud to her.

With quick steps Madame Odintzov reached her study. Bazarov had followed her promptly without raising his eyes and, as she glided ahead of him, he only caught the gentle swish and rustle of her silk dress. Madame Odintzov sank down into the same arm-chair as she had occupied the previous evening, and Bazarov also sat down on his former chair.

"What was the name of that book?" she began after a short pause.

"Pelouse and Frémy, *Notions générales . . .*" Bazarov replied. "However, I can also recommend Ganot, *Traité élémentaire de la physique experimentale*. The illustrations to that treatise are much clearer and, on the whole, that manual is . . ."

Madame Odintzov held out her hand.

"Eugene Vassilich," she said, "you must pardon me, but I did not ask you to come here to discuss manuals. I wanted to pursue our conversation of yesterday. You left so abruptly. . . . You won't find this boring?"

"I am at your service, Anna Sergeyevna. But, may I ask, what was it we were discussing last night?"

Madame Odintzov glanced at Bazarov out of the corner of her eyes.

"I believe we were discussing happiness. I was telling you something about myself. Incidentally, I have just mentioned the word 'happiness.' Now will you tell me why, even when we are enjoying music, for instance, or a pleasant evening party, or a conversation in agreeable company —why it all seems no more than just a hint of some boundless happiness existing elsewhere rather than actual happi-

ness, or any such happiness as may really be granted to us?
Why is it so? Or, maybe, you never feel like that?"

"You know the proverb, 'Happiness is somewhere
else,' " Bazarov retorted. "Besides, you yourself told me
yesterday that you felt incomplete. As for myself, you are
quite right, such thoughts never occur to me."

"Perhaps you think them ridiculous?"

"I don't, but they simply never enter my head."

"You don't mean that? Do you know, I am very anxious
to learn what you *do* think about."

"How so? I don't quite understand you."

"Now just listen to me. For a long time I've been wishing
to clear up a few matters with you. There is no point in
telling you—you know it yourself—that you are not just an
average person. You are still young—you have a whole life
in front of you. For what are you preparing yourself? What
is your future going to be? I mean to say, what goal have
you set yourself? Where are you going? What is the purpose
animating you? In short, who are you? What are you?"

"You amaze me, Anna Sergeyevna. As you know very
well, I am merely a student of the natural sciences, and as
for what I am . . ."

"Yes, what *are* you?"

"I have already told you—a country doctor in the
making."

Anna Sergeyevna made an impatient gesture.

"Why tell me that? You don't believe it yourself. Arcady
might answer me so, but not you."

"And in what way is Arcady . . ."

"Do stop it! Can you possibly be satisfied with such a
modest life? And haven't you always maintained that there
is no such thing as medicine? You—with your pride—a
country doctor! You are merely trying to put me off with
such answers because you have no confidence in me. But
do you know, Eugene, I could understand you; once I was
poor and full of pride myself; I may have been through
quite as many trials as you."

"All that is very well, Anna Sergeyevna, but you must
excuse me . . . I'm not accustomed as a rule to talking about
myself; and between you and me there is such a gulf. . . ."

"What gulf? Are you going to tell me again that I am an
aristocrat? That's beside the point, Eugene Vassilich; I
think I have proved to you . . ."

"And besides," Bazarov interrupted her, "why all this eagerness to talk and think about the future, which for the most part does not depend on us? If one gets an opportunity of doing something positive, that's excellent—but if one doesn't, one should at least be content with not chattering about it in advance."

"You call our friendly talk 'chatter.' . . . Or perhaps you don't regard me as a woman worthy of your trust? You must really despise the lot of us."

"I don't despise you, Anna Sergeyevna, you should know that."

"No, I don't know anything . . . but let us suppose that I do understand your reluctance to talk about your future plans; quite apart from that, we could discuss what is happening to you now. . . ."

"Happening!" Bazarov repeated. "As though I were some sort of state or society! In any case, it is all quite uninteresting and, besides, is a man always capable of describing aloud everything that is 'happening' to him?"

"But I don't see why it should be impossible to express everything one has on one's mind."

"Can you do it?" Bazarov inquired.

"I can," Anna Sergeyevna replied after a moment of hesitation.

Bazarov inclined his head.

"You are more fortunate than I," he said.

Anna Sergeyevna looked at him questioningly.

"As you like," she went on. "But something tells me, nevertheless, that we did not meet for nothing and that we shall become the best of friends. I am convinced that this —how shall I call it?—this tension of yours, this reserve, will disappear one day."

"So you have noticed in me this reserve . . . as you put it . . . this tension?"

"Yes."

Bazarov stood up and went over to the window.

"And you would like to learn the cause of this reserve? You would like to learn what is 'happening' inside me?"

"Yes," Madame Odintzov repeated with a sort of as yet unexplained fear.

"And you will not be angry?"

"No."

"No?" Bazarov was standing with his back to her. "Then

I must tell you that I love you stupidly, madly. . . . You have forced me. Now you know."

Madame Odintzov held out both her hands to him, while Bazarov remained standing with his forehead pressed against the window-pane. He was gasping: his whole body was visibly quivering. But it was no quiver of youthful timidity, nor yet the sweet terror of a first avowal that had got possession of him: it was a wave of passion surging through him, a violent and urgent passion, not unlike the symptoms of rage and, perhaps, not unrelated to it. . . . Madame Odintzov was filled with fear as well as a feeling of compassion for him.

"Eugene Vassilich," she murmured at last, and there was a note of involuntary tenderness in her voice.

He spun round, threw a devouring glance at her, and, seizing hold of both her hands, suddenly drew her to his breast.

But she at once disengaged herself from his embrace; an instant later she was already standing distantly in a corner and gazing at him. He rushed towards her. . . .

"You misunderstood me," she whispered hastily in alarm. She looked as though she might scream if he took another step. . . . Bazarov bit his lips and strode out of the room.

Half an hour later, the maid brought Anna Sergeyevna a note from Bazarov; it consisted of a single line: "Must I leave this evening or may I stay until to-morrow?" "Why leave? I did not understand you—you misunderstood me," was Anna Sergeyevna's reply. To herself she thought, "Nor do I understand myself."

She did not show herself till dinner-time. In the meantime she paced up and down her room, with hands clasped behind her back, stopping every now and then either in front of the window or in front of the mirror, slowly mopping her neck with a handkerchief on the spot where she fancied her skin to be burning. She kept asking herself what had impelled her to "force him," as Bazarov had put it, into being frank with her. Had she not really had an inkling of something? . . . "I am to blame," she said aloud, "but I could not foresee it." She kept thinking about it, and blushed each time she remembered Bazarov's almost bestial expression as he had rushed towards her. . . .

"Or . . . ?" she exclaimed suddenly and stopped, giving her curls a shake. . . . She had caught a glimpse of herself in the mirror; the image of her head, as it was flung back, and of the mysterious smile playing on her half-closed, half-opened eyes and lips seemed instantly to tell her something which immediately threw her into confusion. . . .

"No," she resolved at last. "God knows where that might have led, it's no joking matter. A quiet life is better than anything else in the world."

Her inward calm was not shattered; but she felt sad, and once she even burst into tears—she did not know why, but the insult she had suffered was certainly not the cause. She did not feel insulted: on the contrary, she had a feeling of guilt. The pressure of various conflicting emotions—an awareness that her life was on the decline, a longing for novelty—had brought her to the brink of an abyss; and as she peered over it, she saw no abyss but only a void . . . a shapeless chaos.

XIX

FOR all her self-possession and freedom from prejudice, Madame Odintzov felt distinctly ill at ease when she entered the dining-room. However, the dinner passed off fairly happily. Porfiry Platonich arrived and recounted various anecdotes; he had just got back from town. Among other things, he related that the Governor, "Bourdaloue," had issued instructions that officials engaged on special missions should wear spurs in case they might have to be dispatched on urgent business on horseback. Arcady was chatting with Katya in a low voice and, at the same time, he was being diplomatically attentive to the princess. Bazarov preserved an obstinate and gloomy silence. Twice Madame Odintzov glanced at him—straight in the face rather than out of the corner of her eyes, but at the sight of his rigid and glowering features, his lowered eyes, and the imprint of a contemptuous resolve on each line of his face, she thought to herself, "No . . . no . . . no. . . ." After dinner she strolled out with the whole company into the garden where, noticing that Bazarov wished to speak to her, she took a few steps to one side and stopped. Without raising his eyes, he went up to her and said in a hollow voice:

"I must apologize to you, Anna Sergeyevna. You must be angry with me."

"No, I'm not angry with you, Eugene Vassilich," Madame Odintzov replied. "But I am disappointed."

"So much the worse. In any case, I am sufficiently punished. As you will probably agree, I'm in an extremely silly position. You wrote asking me why I must leave. But I cannot stay, nor do I wish to. By to-morrow I shall be gone."

"But Eugene Vassilich, why are you . . ."

"Why am I going away?"

"No, that was not what I wished to say."

"The past cannot be resurrected, Anna Sergeyevna . . . and sooner or later this was bound to happen. Therefore I must go away. As I see it, there's only one condition on which I might have remained; but that can never be fulfilled. If you will pardon my presumption, am I not correct in saying that you do not love me and never will?"

For an instant Bazarov's eyes gleamed from under his dark eyebrows.

Anna Sergeyevna made no reply. "I'm afraid of this man," was the thought that flashed through her mind.

"Farewell then," Bazarov said, as though divining her thought, and he turned back towards the house.

Anna Sergeyevna followed him slowly and, calling Katya, took her by the arm. She remained inseparable from her until evening. She kept away from the card-table and frequently laughed to herself, which contrasted strangely with her pallor and the distraught look on her face. Arcady was puzzled and kept an eye on her, as young men will do, constantly asking himself what it all meant. Bazarov had locked himself in his room; but he put in an appearance for tea. Anna Sergeyevna was longing to say a kind word to him, but was at a loss how to approach him. . . .

An unexpected incident resolved her embarrassment: the butler announced Sitnikov's arrival.

Words fail to describe the fluttering quail-like figure cut by this young "Progressive" as he flew into the room. Having decided with an importunity so characteristic of him to drive into the country to pay a visit to a lady whom he barely knew and who had never invited him, but at whose house, as he had been informed, some intelligent and close friends of his were staying, he was nevertheless stricken to the marrow of his bones with embarrassment on setting foot in the house. Instead of repeating the excuses and greetings he had learnt by heart, he merely stammered some nonsense to the effect that Eudoxia Kukshin had sent him to inquire after Madame Odintzov's health and that Arcady had always spoken of him in terms of highest praise. . . . At this point, he got stuck, and was so flustered that he sat down on his own hat. As no one ventured to show him the door, however, and as Anna Sergeyevna even went so far as to introduce him to her aunt and sister, he soon recovered his equanimity and warbled away in all his glory. The spectacle of paltriness can often prove a useful lesson in life: it may loosen strings that have been pitched too high and sober both self-assured and disinterested feelings by serving to remind one of a possible affinity between them. Sitnikov's arrival had the effect of making everything seem cruder and simpler; the company even supped more solidly and dispersed to their bedrooms half an hour earlier than usual.

"I can now repeat to you," Bazarov said, as he lay in bed, to Arcady, who had also undressed, "what you once said to me: 'Why do you look so sad? Have you just fulfilled a sacred duty?' " Of late a sort of pseudo-easy banter —the sign invariably of secret discontent or suppressed suspicions—had become a habit between our young friends.

"I'm off home to-morrow, to my father's," Bazarov went on to inform him.

Arcady sat up, leaning on his elbow. He felt both surprised and, for some reason, pleased. "Ah," he exclaimed, "doesn't it depress you?"

Bazarov yawned. "Too much knowledge makes one's hair go grey," he exclaimed.

"And what about Anna Sergeyevna?" Arcady pursued.

"What about Anna Sergeyevna?"

"What I mean is: will she let you go?"

"She is not my employer."

While Arcady ruminated, Bazarov stretched himself out, and then turned his face to the wall. For several minutes there was silence.

"Eugene!" Arcady suddenly exclaimed.

"Well?"

"I'm also coming with you."

Bazarov made no reply.

"But I mean to drive on home," Arcady continued. "We'll go together as far as the Khokhlovsky settlement, you'll be able to get a relay of horses at Fedot's. It would give me very great pleasure to make the acquaintance of your people, but I'm afraid to inconvenience them as well as yourself. But you'll visit us again, won't you?"

"I have left my apparatus at your house," Bazarov replied, without turning round.

"Why doesn't he ask me why I'm going away? And quite as unexpectedly as himself," Arcady thought. "Why indeed am I going and why is he?" he pursued his reflections. He could find no satisfactory answer to this question and a feeling of bitterness filled his heart. He found it difficult to break with this life at Nicolskoye, to which he had grown so accustomed; but to have stayed on there alone, would have created a strange impression. "What has happened between them?" he asked himself. "What excuse could I offer for sticking round here in her company after his departure? And anyhow it would only end in my boring her and thus losing my last chance." He began mentally to picture Anna Sergeyevna; then gradually other traits began to emerge in the background of the young widow's lovely features.

"I shall regret leaving Katya too!" Arcady whispered into his pillow, on which he let drop a tear. . . . Then suddenly tossing back his hair, he exclaimed aloud: "Why the devil did that idiot Sitnikov barge in?"

Bazarov stirred in his bed, and gave vent to the following:

"I can see, brother, that you are still stupid. Sitnikov is essential to us. I would have you understand that I need such louts. It is not for the gods to glaze pottery! . . ."

"Oho! . . ." Arcady thought. Only now, at this very instant, was the whole bottomless pit of Bazarov's arrogance and pride revealed to him. "So you and I are gods? Or rather, you are a god and I'm a mere lout, isn't that so?"

"Yes," Bazarov repeated firmly. "You're still stupid."

Next day, when Arcady informed her that he was leaving with Bazarov, Madame Odintzov expressed no particular surprise; she looked distraught and fatigued. Katya gazed at him gravely and silently, and he could not help noticing that the princess went so far as to make a sign of the cross under her shawl, but Sitnikov, on the other hand, was quite taken aback. He had just come down for breakfast, wearing for the occasion a modish costume instead of a Slavophil one; the previous night he had astounded the valet placed at his disposal by the quantity of linen he had brought with him, and now his friends were leaving him in the lurch! He took a few mincing steps, scurried about like a hare driven to the edge of a wood—and suddenly, almost in terror, almost with a shrill cry, declared that he also intended to depart. Madame Odintzov made no attempt to detain him.

"I have a very smooth-running barouche," the unfortunate young man added, turning to Arcady. "I can take you in it, while Bazarov can use your tarantass. That would be even better."

"But I'm going out of your way. It's quite a distance to my place."

"That doesn't matter at all; I have plenty of time and, besides, I have some business to transact in that region."

"Liquor deals?" Arcady inquired a little too contemptuously.

But Sitnikov was in such a state of despair that, contrary to his habit, he did not even simper.

"I can assure you," he muttered, "that my barouche runs very smoothly and there's plenty of room for everyone."

"You must not disappoint Monsieur Sitnikov," Anna Sergeyevna interjected. . . .

Arcady glanced at her and bowed significantly.

The guests took their leave after breakfast. When saying farewell, Madame Odintzov held out her hand to Bazarov and said: "We shall see each other again, shan't we?"

"At your orders," Bazarov replied.

"In that case, we shall see each other."

Arcady was the first to go down the steps and to clamber into Sitnikov's barouche. While a servant was respectfully helping him to get in, Arcady could have thrashed him with the greatest of pleasure or have burst out crying. Then Bazarov took his seat in the tarantass. On reaching the Khokhlovsky settlement, Arcady waited while Fedot, the keeper of the posting-station, harnessed a fresh team of horses; walking up to the tarantass, he smiled as of old and said to Bazarov, "Eugene, do take me with you; I should like to visit your home."

"Get in," Bazarov growled through his teeth.

Sitnikov, who was pacing up and down and whistling cheerfully in the vicinity of the wheels of his barouche, could only gape when he heard these words and saw Arcady coolly retrieve his belongings, get in beside Bazarov and, with a polite bow to his former travelling-companion, shout, "Drive on!" The tarantass rolled away and soon vanished from sight. . . . Sitnikov stared hopelessly at his coachman, but the latter merely flicked his whip over the tail of the offside horse. Then jumping into his barouche and shouting at a couple of peasants who happened to be passing by, "On with your caps, you idiots!" Sitnikov dragged himself off to town, where he arrived very late that night. The following day, at Madame Kukshin's house, he severely took to task a couple of "nasty and oafish pups."

On joining Bazarov in the tarantass, Arcady pressed his hand warmly and then a long silence ensued. Bazarov seemed to understand and value both the handshake and the silence. He had not slept a wink the whole of the previous night, and for some days past he had neither smoked nor eaten much.

His gaunt profile was sharply and grimly outlined beneath his cap, which was pressed well down over his forehead.

"Well, brother," he said at last, "give me a cigar. And by the way, is my tongue all coated?"

"Quite thickly," Arcady replied.

"I thought so . . . this cigar hasn't any taste. My mechanism has gone to pieces."

"You certainly have altered of late," Arcady remarked.

"Never mind! We'll get over it. I have only one thing on my mind—my mother is so fond of me that she worries to death if I don't grow a pot-belly and eat a dozen times a day. As for my father, he's got his feet on the ground, he's knocked about the world, through thick and thin. No," he added, throwing his cigar into the dusty road, "I must stop smoking."

"It's about sixteen miles to your estate, isn't it?" Arcady inquired.

"Yes, sixteen. But you'd better ask that sage," he said, pointing to the peasant in the driver's seat, one of Fedot's employees.

But the sage in question replied in this wise: "And who would be after knowing it?—the miles hereabouts are not measured." And having said that, he went on swearing in an undertone at the shaft horse for "kicking out with its headpiece"—in other words, for jerking its neck.

"Yes, yes," Bazarov began, "let this be a lesson to you,

my young friend, an instructive example of sorts. The devil take it, how absolutely absurd everything is! The life of each of us hangs by a thread, an abyss may gape beneath us any minute, and yet we go out of our way to cook up all sorts of trouble for ourselves and to mess up our lives."

"What are you driving at?" Arcady inquired.

"I'm not driving at anything, but let me tell you straight from the shoulder that we have been acting very stupidly. What's the point of talking about it! But my clinical observations have already led me to conclude that resistance is the only way of conquering pain."

"I don't quite get you," Arcady said. "It seems to me that you have nothing to complain about."

"If you don't quite get me, then let me tell you this: in my opinion, it's better to break paving-stones than to allow any woman to dominate as much as the tip of your little finger. That's all . . ." Bazarov was on the point of uttering his favourite word—"Romanticism," but he refrained and said instead: "Rubbish. You may not believe me, but it's quite clear that we were drawn into feminine society and found it agreeable; but to give up that society is as refreshing as a cold shower on a hot day. A man should have no time for such trifling: as the Spanish proverb says, 'A man must be ferocious.' Now what about you?" he added, turning to the peasant on the box. "You're a smart fellow; tell me, have you a wife?"

The peasant turned his flat and bleary-eyed face towards the friends.

"A wife, you say? I have one. How could it be otherwise?"

"Do you beat her?"

"The wife, you say? Anything can happen. But we don't beat her without cause."

"That's fine. We . . . and does she beat you?"

The peasant tugged at the reins. "Them's your words, master. You like your joke. . . ." He was evidently quite offended.

"You heard that, Arcady! But you and I have received a thrashing. . . . That's what comes of being so cultured."

Arcady uttered a forced laugh; Bazarov turned away and kept his mouth shut for the rest of the journey.

To Arcady the sixteen miles were more like thirty. But at last, at the foot of a slope, a small village came into view.

It was there that Bazarov's parents lived. Nearby, in the middle of a young birch-tree copse, a gentleman's small house could be perceived under a thatched roof. As they drove past the first of the cottages, they saw a couple of peasants with caps on standing outside and swearing at each other. "For an out-size swine," one of them said, "you're worse than any sucking-pig." "And your wife's a witch," retorted the other.

"By their free and easy ways," Bazarov remarked, "and by their playful turns of speech, you can guess that my father's peasants are not too ground down. And there he is himself coming out on the steps of the house. He must have heard the bells tinkling. It's he, it's he—I can tell him by his shape. Ay, ay! And yet how grey he's grown, poor old chap!"

XX

BAZAROV stuck his head out of the tarantass while Arcady, peering over his friend's head, caught sight of a tall, gaunt-looking individual with tousled hair and sharp aquiline nose standing on the steps of a small house, attired in an old unbuttoned military jacket. He stood there with legs wide apart, smoking a long pipe and squinting at the sun.

The horses came to a stop.

"Here you are at last," Bazarov's father exclaimed, still continuing to puff at his pipe although his trembling fingers could hardly hold the stem. "Now, out you get, out you get, let me embrace you."

He hugged his son again and again. . . .

"Enyusha, Enyusha," a woman's quavering voice rang out. The front door opened and a shortish, stoutish old lady came running down the steps, in a white cap and a brightly coloured blouse. She gave a cry, staggered, and would have fallen if Bazarov had not steadied her. Her plump little hands immediately clasped him round his neck, her head sank against his chest, and the ensuing silence was interrupted only by convulsive sobs.

Old Bazarov breathed heavily and squinted more than ever at the sun.

"Well, that's enough, that's enough, Arina! Stop it now," he exclaimed after exchanging glances with Arcady, who had remained standing motionless near the tarantass; even the peasant driver on his box-seat had turned away his head. "It's quite unnecessary! Do stop it, please!"

"Ah! Vassily Ivanich," the old woman quavered, "it's ages and ages since I've seen my little lord, my darling, my Enyushenka. . . ." And without unclasping her hands she drew away her face, which was all tear-stained, crumpled and melting with emotion; gazing at him again with eyes at once blissful and comic, she clasped her arms once more round his neck.

"Well, yes, of course, it's all very natural," said Vassily Ivanich, "but it would be better if we went in. Eugene has brought a guest. Excuse me," he added, turning to Arcady with a slight scrape of his foot, "but I'm sure you understand, a woman's frailty; yes, and a mother's heart too. . . ."

But his own lips and eyebrows were also twitching, and his chin trembled . . . he was evidently trying to master his emotions and to appear indifferent. Arcady bowed.

"Let's go in, mother, indeed let us," Bazarov said, conducting the old lady, who was overcome by the scene, into the house. Making her sit down in a comfortable arm-chair, he hastily embraced his father once more and then introduced Arcady to him.

"Heartily glad to make your acquaintance," Vassily Ivanich said, "but you mustn't expect too much: we lead a simple, soldierly life here. My dear Arina, do calm yourself, oblige me please: why show yourself so faint-hearted? Our gentleman visitor will form a poor opinion of you."

"My good sir," the old lady managed to stutter through her tears, "I have not the honour of knowing your name . . ."

"Arcady Nicolaievich," her husband prompted in a low but solemn voice.

"You must excuse me, I am a stupid old thing." The old lady blew her nose and bending her head now to the right, now to the left, wiped each eye thoroughly in turn. "You must excuse me. Why, I thought I'd die and never see my da . . . dar . . . ling again."

"Well, your patience has been rewarded, my dear lady,"

Vassily Ivanich took her up. "Tanyushka," he cried, turning to a barefooted girl of about thirteen in a bright red cotton dress, who was peeping from behind the door, "bring a glass of water for the lady—on a tray, do you hear? As for you, gentlemen," he added with a sort of old-fashioned play of civility, "allow me to invite you to pass into the study of a retired veteran."

"Let me embrace you just once more, Enyushenka," Arina Vlassyevna moaned. Bazarov stooped down. "What a handsome lad you've grown!"

"Handsome or not," Vassily Ivanich remarked, "but he looks a man all right—'om fay, as they say. And now, Arina Vlassyevna, I hope that, having satiated your maternal heart, you will take the trouble to satisfy our dear guests, because, as you must know very well, a nightingale cannot live only on fables."

The old lady got up from her arm-chair.

"The table will be laid in a minute, Vassily Ivanich. I shall run along to the kitchen myself and order the samovar to be got ready. We shall have everything, everything. Why, it's three years since I have seen him, since I have given him to eat and drink. It's not easy, is it?"

"Well, attend to it, my little housewife, get it all ready, and don't disgrace us; and as for you, gentlemen, I beg you to follow me. Ah, Eugene, here's Timofeyich coming to greet you. He's delighted too, I expect, the old poodle. What? You're glad, aren't you, you old poodle. Now, pray, follow me."

And Vassily Ivanich fussily led the way, shuffling and flapping along in his well-worn slippers.

His whole house consisted of six minute rooms. One of them—the room into which he conducted our friends—was called the study. The space between the two windows was entirely filled by a table on sturdy legs, heaped with papers that had turned black with ancient dust and looked as if they had been smoked. The walls were hung with Turkish flint-locks, whips, sabres, a couple of maps, a series of anatomical drawings, a portrait of Hufeland, a monogram woven from hair set in a black frame and a diploma under glass. A leather sofa, holed and torn in places, stood between two enormous cupboards of Karelian birch; the shelves were packed with a welter of books, little boxes, stuffed birds, jars, phials; a broken electric battery lay in one of the corners.

"I warned you, my dear guest," the father began, "we are living here, as it were, in a camp. . . ."

"Do stop apologizing all the time," Bazarov interrupted him. "Kirsanov knows very well that we are no Crœsuses and that you don't own a palace. Where shall we lodge him, that's the question?"

"That's no problem, Eugene; we have an excellent room in the wing: our guest will find it quite comfortable."

"So you've had a new wing put in?"

"Indeed we have—on the site of the bath-house," Timofeyich intervened.

"That's to say, next door to the bath-house," the father hastened to interject. "It's summer now. . . . I shall run along and see that everything is put in order; and you, Timofeyich, had better take charge of their baggage. As for you, Eugene, I shall of course let you have my study. *Suum cuique*."

"Well, that's that! An amusing old man, a heart of gold," Bazarov said as soon as his father had gone out. "He is as eccentric as your father, but in a different way. He's a chatterbox."

"Your mother seems a wonderful woman," Arcady remarked.

"Yes, she has no wiles. Just wait and see what a spread she will give us."

"We were not expecting you to-day, master. We didn't get any beef," said Timofeyich, who had just brought in Bazarov's trunk.

"We can do without beef; 'one can't blame the innocent.' They say poverty is no crime."

"How many serfs does your father own?" Arcady suddenly inquired.

"The property is not his, but my mother's; as far as I remember, there are fifteen."

"Twenty-two in all," Timofeyich remarked with evident displeasure.

There was a sound of shuffling slippers and Vassily Ivanich reappeared on the scene.

"Your room will be ready to receive you in a few minutes," he exclaimed triumphantly. "Arcady . . . Nicolaievich, isn't that how you're pleased to be called? And here is your valet," he added, pointing to a lad who had just entered, dressed in a blue kaftan with ragged elbows and wearing someone else's boots.

"His name is Fedka. Although my son forbids it, I must ask you again not to expect too much. However, the lad can fill a pipe. You smoke, don't you?"

"I usually prefer cigars," Arcady replied.

"How very sensible of you. My preference also goes to cigars, but it's extremely difficult to procure them in these remote parts."

"Stop playing Lazarus," Bazarov again interrupted him. "You'd better sit down here on the sofa and let me have a look at you."

Vassily Ivanich laughed and sat down. His face closely resembled his son's, only the forehead was lower and narrower, the mouth a trifle broader, and he seemed always in motion, perpetually shrugging his shoulders as though his suit were too tight for him under the armpits, blinking his eyes, coughing and twitching his fingers, whereas a certain air of detached immobility was his son's distinguishing trait.

"Play Lazarus!" Vassily Ivanich repeated. "Don't imagine, Eugene, that I wish, as it were, to excite our guest's compassion by complaining of our life here in the wilds. On the contrary, I am of the opinion that no wilds can exist for any thinking person. At least, I do my best, as far as I can, not to grow stale, as they say, and to keep up with the times."

From his pocket Vassily Ivanich pulled out a new yellow silk handkerchief, which he had managed to pick up while running to attend to Arcady's room. Fanning himself with it, he went on: "I am not referring now to the fact that, at some sacrifice to myself, I have established my peasants on a rent-paying system and have transferred my land to them on a profit-sharing basis. I consider that I have done no more than my duty as dictated by common sense, although plenty of other landowners don't even dream of attempting it. But I am speaking now of the sciences, of education."

"Yes, I notice you have a copy of the *Friend of Health* for 1855," Bazarov remarked.

"An old comrade of mine sends them to me for old times' sake," Vassily Ivanich hastily replied. "But to give you an

example, we are not without some knowledge of phren-
ology," he added, speaking more for the benefit of Arcady
and pointing to a small plaster head divided up into
squares, which was standing on the top of the cupboard.
"Even Shönlein has not remained unknown to us—and
Rademacher."

"Is Rademacher still regarded as an authority in this
province?" Bazarov asked.

Vassily Ivanich coughed. "In the provinces . . . Of
course, you know better, gentlemen; how is one to keep
up with you? You are here to succeed us. In my day some
humoralist like Hoffman, some Brown with his *vitalism*—
they all seemed quite ridiculous, and yet they too had made
a lot of noise in their time. Now someone has taken
Rademacher's place in your estimation, and you worship
him, but in twenty years' time he will very likely also be a
laughing-stock."

"Let me tell you by way of consolation," Bazarov
retorted, "that we now laugh at medicine as a whole, and
worship no one."

"How can that be? But you intend to become a doctor,
don't you?"

"I do, but there is no contradiction involved."

With his middle finger Vassily Ivanich poked about in
his pipe, which still contained a little hot ash. "Well, that
may be, that may be—I will not dispute it. For who am I?
A retired army doctor, *voyla-too,* now turned agronomist.
Yes, I served in your father's brigade," he added, turning
again to Arcady. "Yes, yes—I have seen many sights in my
day. And what circles have I not moved in! What people
have I not met! I—the person you are pleased to see
before you—I felt Prince Wittgenstein's pulse and Zhukov-
sky's too! All those people who were with the southern
army in the 1814, you know" (hereupon the old doctor
pursed his lips significantly), "I knew them all without
exception. Yes, but my job was very lop-sided: to be
proficient with the lancet, that's all there was to it! Now
your grandfather was a very honourable man, a real
soldier."

"Come, come, confess he was a first-class blockhead,"
Bazarov said lazily.

"Ah, Eugene, how can you say such things! Do be con-

siderate. . . . Of course, General Kirsanov was not one
of . . ."

"Well, drop him then," Bazarov interrupted him. "As I
was driving here, I was very pleased to see your birch-
plantation. It has sprouted beautifully."

Vassily Ivanich grew animated. "You must see the
garden now! I planted each tree myself. We have fruit-
trees, raspberry canes and all sorts of medicinal herbs.
However clever you young gentlemen may think yourselves, old Paracelsus put his finger on the truth: *in herbis,
verbis et lapidibus.* . . . As you know, I gave up my practice,
but a couple of times a week I am obliged to revert to my
old pastime. Folk will come for consultation—I can't drive
them away. Sometimes a poor man will ask for help. There
are no other doctors in the locality. One of our neighbours
—just imagine it—a retired major, goes about healing too.
I made some inquiries about him: had he studied medicine?
They told me, 'No, he hasn't studied, but he does it for
the sake of philanthropy.' . . . Ha, ha, ha—for the sake of
philanthropy! Ah? Now what do you think of that? Ha,
ha, ha!"

"Fedka, fill my pipe for me!" Bazarov said sternly.

"We have another doctor here who once came to visit
a patient," Vassily Ivanich went on in a sort of despairing
way, "and the patient was already *ad patres*; the servant
would not let the doctor in since there was no longer any
need for him. The doctor did not expect this and, in his
confusion, inquired: 'Tell me, did your master hiccup
before he died?' 'Yes, he did.' 'And did he hiccup a lot?'
'Quite a lot.' 'Well, that's fine!' he exclaimed and went
off. Ha, ha, ha!"

The old man was alone to laugh; Arcady just managed a
smile. Bazarov only puffed at his pipe. The conversation
continued in this wise for about an hour; Arcady had time
to pay a visit to his room, which turned out to be the anteroom of the bath-house, but it was very cosy and clean.
At last Tanyusha came in to announce that the dinner was
served.

Vassily Ivanich was the first to get up. "Come along,
gentlemen! You must be indulgent to me if I have bored
you. Perhaps my good wife will give you better satisfaction."

The dinner, though hastily prepared, turned out to be

excellent and even abundant; only the wine was a trifle dubious, as they say: the almost black sherry, which Timofeyich had bought in town from a merchant of his acquaintance, tasted slightly of copper or resin; and the flies also were a pest. Usually the servant boy chased them away with a leafy branch; but on this occasion the host had sent him away for fear of being misjudged by the younger generation. The mistress of the house had had time to change; she had donned a high cap ornamented with silk ribbons and a pale-blue flowered shawl. On catching sight of her Enyusha, she burst into tears again; but there was no need for her husband to chide her, for she wiped away her tears promptly to avoid staining her shawl. The young men were alone to eat, for the old folk had already dined. Fedka waited at table, obviously encumbered by his unfamiliar boots, and was assisted by a woman of masculine looks, who went by the name of Anfisushka and fulfilled the duties of housekeeper, pantry-maid and washerwoman. Throughout the dinner Vassily Ivanich marched up and down the room and, with a happy and even blissful expression on his face, talked about the grave anxieties roused in him by Napoleon III's policy and the complications of the Italian question. Bazarov's mother paid no attention to Arcady and did not even press him to eat more; with her tiny fist propping her rounded face, to which her puffy little cherry-tinted lips and the moles on her cheeks imparted a very benign expression, she glued her eyes on her son and sighed continuously; she was desperately anxious to learn how long he intended to stay, but was afraid to ask him. "And what if he should say, 'I've come for two days only,'" she thought to herself, and her heart would stop beating. After the roast Vassily Ivanich disappeared for an instant and then returned with an uncorked bottle of champagne.

"Here!" he exclaimed, "even though we do live in the wilds, yet we always have something special in reserve for festive occasions!" He filled three large glasses and a smaller one, proposed a toast to "our invaluable guests," and emptied his glass at one draught in the military fashion. He forced his wife to drink her little glass to the very last drop. When the turn of the jam came, Arcady, who as a rule could not bear anything sweet, nevertheless deemed it his duty to taste four different kinds of freshly made jam. He did this also because Bazarov had bluntly refused to try them and had at once lit a cigar. Then the tea was brought, with cream, butter and cracknels: afterwards the old man led them out into the garden so that they might admire the beauty of the evening. As they passed a certain bench, he whispered to Arcady: "On this spot I love to philosophize, gazing at the sunset: it becomes a recluse. And over there I have planted several trees so greatly favoured by Horace."

"What are the trees?" inquired Bazarov, who had overheard.

"Why . . . acacias."

Bazarov began to yawn.

"I suppose it is time for the weary travellers to fall into the embraces of Morpheus," Vassily Ivanich remarked.

"You mean it's time for us to sleep," Bazarov retorted. "A very just remark that. It is time, indeed it is."

Bidding his mother good night, he kissed her on the forehead, while she hugged him and blessed him thrice stealthily behind his back. Vassily Ivanich conducted Arcady to his room and wished him "such sweet repose as I also have enjoyed in the flower of my youth." And, indeed, Arcady slept excellently in his bath-house anteroom: the place smelt of mint, and two crickets behind the stove competed with each other in drowsy chirping. On leaving Arcady, Vassily Ivanich went into the study where, curling himself up on the sofa at his son's feet, he prepared to have a chat with him: but Bazarov sent him away at once, saying that he felt sleepy, though actually he did not fall asleep until the early morning. With eyes wide open he glared banefully into the gloom; childhood memories had no hold over him and, besides, he had not yet succeeded in shaking off his last bitter impressions. As for his mother, she first of all prayed her fill; afterwards, she spent a long while chatting with Anfisushka who stood in front of her mistress, like a person rooted to the ground, with her one and only eye fixed on her, imparting in a whisper all her impressions and notions regarding the young master. The old mother's head was spinning with joy, wine and cigar smoke; her husband made an attempt to converse with her, but soon, with a hopeless gesture, gave it up as a bad job.

Arina Vlassyevna was a genuine Russian gentlewoman of the old school; she might have lived some two centuries back, in the old days of Muscovy. Very devout and impres-

sionable, she believed in all sorts of omens, fortune-telling,
charms and dreams; she believed in the visions of mad
prophets, in spirits, in wood-sprites, in the evil eye, in
spells, in folk remedies, on "Thursday salt," and in the
imminent end of the world; she believed that, if the candles
failed to go out at vespers on Easter Sunday, a good crop
of buckwheat would result, and that mushrooms stopped
growing when seen by the human eye; she believed that
water was the devil's haunt, and that every Jew had a
bloody mark on his breast. She was afraid of mice, adders,
frogs, sparrows, leeches, thunder, cold water, draughts,
horses, goats, ginger-haired people and black cats, and
deemed crickets and dogs unclean creatures; she ate no veal
or pigeon, crayfish or cheese, asparagus or Jerusalem arti-
chokes, hare or, finally, water melon, because a sliced
water melon reminded her of John the Baptist's head. The
mere mention of oysters made her shudder; she loved food
but also kept strict fasts; she slept ten hours out of twenty-
four—and did not go to bed at all when her husband happened to have a headache. She read no book except *Alexisa,
or the Hut in the Forest*; she wrote one, never more than
two, letters a year, but she knew all about housekeeping,
preserving fruit and jam-making, although she did not
touch anything with her own hands and disliked moving
about. Arina Bazarov was very kind of heart and, in her
own way, not at all stupid. She was convinced that the
gentry were there to give orders and the common people
to obey them—and so she felt no repugnance at the sight
of servility and obsequience; but she was always mild and
gentle with those who served her, no beggar was allowed
to pass by without receiving alms and, although at times
she was inclined to gossip, she never criticized anyone. In
her youth she had been very comely, had played the clavi-
chord and prattled a little in French; but in the course of
many years of peregrination with her husband, whom she
had married against her will, she had grown stout and forgotten both her music and her French. Her son she both
loved and feared to an incredible degree; and as for her
estate, she let her husband manage it and never interfered
with him: she merely moaned and waved her handkerchief, while her brows shot up higher and higher in alarm,
whenever the old man broached the subject of the imminent
land reforms and his projects. She was very apprehensive,

lived in constant expectation of some great misfortune
about to befall them, and burst out sobbing whenever she
happened to recall any sorrow. . . . In our time, women like
her have grown rare. God alone knows whether that is a
matter for rejoicing.

XXI

GETTING out of bed, Arcady flung the window wide
open, and Vassily Ivanich was the first object to catch his
eye. Wearing a dressing-gown of Bokhara silk, fastened
round the waist with a handkerchief, the old man was
busily digging in the orchard. Perceiving the young guest
and leaning on his spade, he exclaimed: "The best of health!
Did you have a good night's rest?"

"Indeed, I had," Arcady replied.

"As you can see, here I am like some Cincinnatus,
knocking up a bed for the late turnips. Such are the times
we live in—and thank God for that!—each one of us has
to provide for his nourishment with his own hands; it's
no use relying on others—one must labour oneself. It
turns out that Jean-Jacques Rousseau was right. Half an
hour ago, my dear sir, you would have seen me in quite a
different posture. I had a peasant woman here who complained of 'gripes'—that's what they call it, dysentery is
the term we would use, and there was I . . . how shall I put
it best? . . . there was I pumping opium into her; I also
pulled out a tooth for another woman. I offered to give
her an anæsthetic . . . but she wouldn't have it. All that I
did gratis—*in amature*. However, I am quite used to that;
for I am a plebeian, *homo novus*—not out of Debrett, like
my dear spouse. . . . Wouldn't you like to join me here, in
the shade, and breathe the morning freshness before
breakfast?"

Arcady joined him.

"Welcome once more!" Vassily Ivanich exclaimed,
raising his hand to his greasy skull-cap in a military salute.
"I know you are accustomed to luxury and pleasure, but

the great ones of this world would not disdain to spend a short time under a humble roof."

"Good Heavens," Arcady protested. "What sort of a great personage of the world do you take me for? Nor am I accustomed to luxury."

"I beg to differ," Vassily Ivanich retorted with an amiable grimace. "Although I am already filed away in the archives, I have had some experience of the world—I can spot a bird by the way it flies. In my own way, I am also a psychologist and a physiognomist too. If I had not possessed that gift—if so I may call it—I would have been a failure long ago; they would have just trodden on an insignificant man like me. Let me tell you, compliments apart, that I am sincerely glad of the friendship which I have noted between you and my son. I have just seen him; according to his habit, one you very likely know, he was up very early and off into the country. If you don't mind my curiosity, may I ask if you have known my Eugene long?"

"Since the winter."

"I see. May I also inquire . . . but won't you sit down? May I also inquire, as a father, quite frankly, what is your opinion of my Eugene?"

"Your son is one of the most remarkable men I have ever met," Arcady replied with feeling.

Vassily Ivanich's eyes suddenly opened wide and a faint blush spread over his cheeks. The spade dropped out of his hands.

"So, you suppose . . ." he began.

"I am convinced," Arcady took him up, "that a great future awaits your son, that he will make your name famous. I was sure of that as soon as I met him."

"And how . . . how did you meet him?" Vassily Ivanich inquired, hardly able to speak. A smile of delight had parted his lips and stayed there.

"You would like me to tell you how we met?"

"Yes . . . and moreover . . ."

Arcady launched on an account of their meeting and talked of Bazarov with even greater warmth and enthusiasm than on the evening when he had danced a mazurka with Madame Odintzov.

Vassily Ivanich was all ears, he listened, blew his nose, with both hands rolled his handkerchief into a ball, coughed, ruffled his hair—and, finally, unable to restrain himself any longer stooped and kissed Arcady on the shoulder.

"You have made me perfectly happy," he said, smiling all the while. "I must tell you that I . . . I worship my son; as for my old woman, there is no need even to mention it: she is the mother, of course!—but I dare not show my feelings in his presence, because he dislikes it. He is an enemy to all expressions of emotion; many people even criticize him for this firmness of character and interpret it as a sign of arrogance or insensibility; but men like him should not be measured with a common yardstick, should they now? Here is an example: in his place another would have drawn and drawn on his parents; but would you believe it, he never took a penny too much from us from the day he was born, and that's God's truth!"

"He is quite unselfish and honest," Arcady remarked.

"Yes, exactly, unselfish. But I not only worship him, I am also proud of him, and the whole of my vanity comes to this, that in due course I should like to see the following written in his biography: 'The son of an army doctor who, however, was able to understand him early in life and who spared nothing for his education. . . .'" The old man's voice quavered.

Arcady pressed his hand.

"Now what do you think?" Vassily Ivanich asked him after a pause. "It will not be in the field of medicine that he will attain the fame you prophesy for him?"

"Of course not, although his will be one of the great minds in that field."

"What will be his particular field then, Arcady?"

"It is hard to tell yet, but he is bound to be famous."

"Bound to be famous?" the old man repeated, falling into a reverie.

"Arina Vlassyevna sends me to tell you breakfast is served," Anfisushka called out as she passed them, carrying a great big dish of ripe raspberries.

Vassily Ivanich came to life.

"Will there be any cold cream with the raspberries?"

"Yes, plenty of cream."

"Make sure it's put on ice! Don't stand on ceremony, do help yourself to the raspberries. I wonder why Eugene isn't back yet."

"I am here," Bazarov's voice rang out, coming from Arcady's room.

His father spun quickly round.

"Aha! You called on your friend, but you were too late, *amice*. I have already been having a long chat with him. Now we must go in and have breakfast: mother is calling us. Incidentally, I must have a word with you."

"What about?"

"We have a peasant here who suffers from *icterus*. . . ."

"You mean jaundice?"

"Yes, a chronic and very persistent *icterus*. I have prescribed centaury and St. John's wort, I have made him eat carrots and given him soda; but these are merely palliative measures: something more drastic is required. I know you laugh at medicine, but I'm pretty sure you will be able to give me some sound advice. But we must talk of that later. And now let's go in and have tea."

Leaping nimbly from the bench, Vassily Ivanich started to hum an air from *Robert le Diable*:

A law, a law, a law let's make
To live . . . to live for joy and pleasure!

"What remarkable vitality!" Bazarov said to himself, moving away from the window.

Midday came. From behind a diaphanous curtain of spreading whitish clouds, the sun was scorching. Everything was still: only the cocks crowed lustily in the village, exciting a strange sensation of drowsiness and boredom in all who heard them; and somewhere high up above, in the tree-tops, throbbed the querulous and persistent squeaking of a young hawk. Arcady and Bazarov lay stretched out in the shade of a small hayrick; beneath them they had strewn two or three armfuls of grass that was still green and fragrant though it rustled drily.

"That poplar," Bazarov remarked, "reminds me of my childhood; it grows on the edge of a pit, which is all that remains of the brick shed, and at the time I was convinced that both the pit and the poplar had the powers of a talisman; in their vicinity I was never bored. I failed to understand then that I was not bored just because I was a child. Well, now that I'm grown up, the talisman has lost its charm."

"How long were you here in all?" Arcady inquired.

"Two years running. Then we had our fill of travelling. We led a vagabond sort of life; we mostly traipsed from town to town."

"And has this house been long built?"

"Yes, quite a time. My maternal grandfather had it put up."

"And what was your grandfather?"

"The devil only knows. An army major of sorts. He served under Suvorov, and was always telling us how he had crossed the Alps. No doubt he was making it up."

"That explains the portrait of Suvorov in the drawing-room. I like small houses, such as yours—they are old and warm; and they have a peculiar smell of their own."

"Yes, they're saturated with lamp-oil and clover," Bazarov replied with a yawn. "And the quantities of flies these dear little houses breed . . . Ugh!"

"Tell me," Arcady resumed after a short pause, "you were not badly treated as a child, were you?"

"You have seen my parents," Bazarov replied. "They are not very strict."

"Do you love them, Eugene?"

"Yes, I do, Arcady!"

"They love you greatly!"

Bazarov made no rejoinder for a while. "Do you know what I am thinking?" he asked at last, clasping his hands behind his head.

"No, I don't. What is it?"

"I'm thinking of the happy life they lead! At sixty father is always busy. He talks of 'palliative' measures, treats patients, is generous to the peasants—in short, he is making quite a spree of his old age; and mother has a good time too: her days are so crammed with all sorts of little jobs, sighs and groans, that she never has time to stop and think; but as for me . . ."

"As for you?"

"I keep racking my brains: now here I am lying under this hayrick. . . . The confined space I occupy is so minute when compared with the rest of the universe, where I am not and have no business to be; and the fraction of time I shall live is so infinitesimal when contrasted with eternity, in which I have never been and never shall be. . . . And yet here, in this atom of myself, in this mathematical point, blood circulates, the brain is active, aspiring to something too. . . . What a monstrous thing! How absurd it seems!"

"Allow me to point out," Arcady retorted, "that what you say applies generally to all men . . . "

"Quite right," Bazarov interrupted him. "All I wanted to say was that they, my parents, that is, have their minds occupied and do not worry about their own insignificance. It does not stink in their nostrils . . . while I . . . I feel only bored and angry."

"Angry? Why angry?"

"Why? Why need you ask me? Have you forgotten?"

"I remember everything, but, at the same time, I do not admit that you have the right to be angry. You are unhappy, I agree, but . . ."

"Ah! I can see, Arcady, that your idea of love is no different from that of all the other young men of the new generation: 'Cluck, cluck, cluck, my little hen,' you all exclaim, but when the 'little hen' begins to strut towards you, then you all take to your heels! I am not made like that. But enough. It's a shame to chatter about what can't be helped." He turned over on his side. "Aha! There's a lusty fellow of an ant dragging a dying fly. Drag it along, brother, drag it along! Take notice of her resistance, take every advantage of the fact that, as an insect, you have the right to feel no compassion—unlike us, poor self-divided brethren!"

"You can hardly call yourself that, Eugene!" Arcady exclaimed. "When did you become 'divided'?"

Bazarov raised his head.

"That's the one thing I'm really proud of. I am not 'divided' and no female can break me either. Amen! Full stop! I shan't refer to the subject again."

The friends lay for a while in silence.

"Yes," Bazarov began, "man is a strange creature. When you observe in a detached sort of way the remote life these 'old folk' lead here, it could not seem better. It's eat, drink and be sure you do the right thing in the right way. But it's not really like that; one would only get bored if it were. There is also the need we feel for bothering about other people, even if we do no more than swear at them or suffer them to importune us."

"Life should be so arranged that every moment of it can

be packed with significance," Arcady remarked thoughtfully.

"That's all very well! Significance is sweet, even though
it may be false; but we can also come to terms with the
insignificant. . . . But all this tittle-tattle, all this petty
wrangling, that's the trouble."

"All this wrangling would stop if men refused to admit it."

"H'm . . . you have just uttered an *inverted platitude.*"

"What?" Arcady cried out. "What do you mean?"

"Just this: to say, for example that education is useful is
a platitude; but to say that education is harmful is an inverted platitude. It sounds more dashing, but in essence it
comes to the same thing."

"But where is truth? On which side?"

"Where? Like an echo, I shall answer where?"

"What a despondent mood you're in to-day, Eugene."

"You don't say so? I've been out in the sun too long, and
shouldn't have eaten so many raspberries."

"In that case, it wouldn't be a bad idea to have a nap,"
Arcady remarked.

"Maybe. But don't stare at me, we all look silly when
asleep."

"And do you mind what people think of you?"

"I don't quite know what to reply. A real man does not
worry about that; for people do not need to have opinions
about a real man; he must either be obeyed or hated."

"Very strange! I don't hate anyone," Arcady replied after
a moment's reflection.

"And I hate lots of people. You have a tender wishy-
washy heart. Hatred is not in your line. . . . You're timid
and have no confidence in yourself. . . ."

"And you?" Arcady interrupted him. "Have you confidence in yourself? Have you such a high opinion of yourself?"

Bazarov remained silent.

"When I meet a man who will not wilt before me," he
said with measured deliberation, "then my opinion of myself
will change. Hatred! Now here is an example: this morning
when you passed the house of Philip, the village bailiff, you
remarked: 'What a pleasant, neat-looking house.' And you
went on to say: 'Russia will reach perfection when every
peasant will own a house like that, and each of us must help
to that end. . . .' But I've developed a hatred for that 'every

peasant,' that Philip or Sidor, for whose sake I must crawl out of my skin and who will not even thank me for it. . . . And why do I need his thanks? Well, just imagine him living in his neat-looking house while I shall be sprouting weeds. What comes after?"

"Don't go on like that, Eugene. . . . To hear you talking to-day leaves me no alternative but to agree with those who reproach us for having no principles."

"You're talking just like your uncle. There are no principles in general—you haven't tumbled to that yet! There are only sensations. Everything depends on them."

"How's that?"

"Just so. Now take me, for example: my negative attitude is the result of my sensations. If I find pleasure in denying, it's because my brain is so constructed—and that is all there is to it! Why do *I* like chemistry? Why do *you* like apples? Precisely because of our particular sensations. There is a connexion between them. And mankind will never succeed in probing deeper than that. It isn't everyone could tell you that, and next time I shan't tell you as much."

"Not tell me? And is honesty a sensation too?"

"Obviously!"

"Eugene!" Arcady exclaimed sorrowfully. . . .

"Well? What is it? Not to your taste, eh?" Bazarov interrupted him. "No, brother! Once you have made up your mind to scythe, why, you must scythe your very feet from under you! . . . However, we have philosophized quite enough. As Pushkin said, 'Nature wafts upon us the silence of sleep.'"

"He never said anything of the sort," Arcady retorted.

"Well, even if he didn't, as a poet he might and should have said it. Incidentally, he must have served in the army."

"Pushkin was never in the army!"

"Really? But on every page he has, 'Into battle, into battle! For the honour of Russia!'"

"That's pure invention on your part! A downright slander!"

"Slander? As if that mattered! What a word you've picked on to frighten me! However much slander you may heap on a person, he really deserves twenty times as much."

"We'd better have a snooze!" Arcady replied sadly.

"With the greatest of pleasure," Bazarov replied. But neither of them felt like sleeping. A feeling of hostility almost seethed in the young men's hearts. Within five minutes they opened their eyes and exchanged silent glances.

"Look!" Arcady suddenly exclaimed. "A withered maple leaf has left its branch and is falling to the ground; its movements resemble those of a butterfly in flight. Isn't it strange? The saddest and deadest of all things is yet so like the gayest and most vital of creatures."

"Oh, my dearest friend Arcady!" Bazarov cried. "One thing I entreat you; don't talk so beautifully."

"I talk as best I can. . . . Why, that's sheer despotism. If a thought occurs to me, why shouldn't I express it?"

"That's so. But why shouldn't I express my thoughts too? In my opinion, it's indecent to talk beautifully."

"What is decent then? To abuse people?"

"Oho! I can see you're determined to follow in your uncle's footsteps. How that idiot would rejoice if he heard you!"

"What did you call Uncle Paul?"

"I called him an idiot, as was fitting."

"But this is becoming unbearable!" Arcady exclaimed.

"Aha! Your family feelings are manifesting themselves," Bazarov remarked calmly. "I have noticed how very firmly they are embedded in people. Man seems ready to reject everything, to give up every prejudice; but he cannot bear to admit, for instance, that a brother of his, who steals other people's handkerchiefs, is a thief. And let's face it, we do find it incredible, don't we, that any brother of mine, that my brother, should turn out to be no genius?"

"I spoke from a sense of justice and out of no family feeling," Arcady protested hotly. "But since you do not understand that feeling, since you lack that *sensation,* you are incapable of judging it."

"In other words, Arcady Kirsanov is too elevated for my understanding: I am to bow to him and keep mum."

"Shut up, Eugene, please; or we shall end by quarrelling."

"Ah, Arcady! Do me a favour, let's quarrel thoroughly —go the full hog, to the point of annihilation. . . ."

"If we go on like this, we may end up by . . ."

"By fighting?" Bazarov interjected. "What of it? Here, in the hay, in these idyllic surroundings, far from the world and the ken of people—it wouldn't be too bad. But you wouldn't be able to stand up to me. . . . Just wait till I get a grip on your throat. . . ."

Bazarov stretched out his long, tough fingers. . . . Arcady turned round and got ready, as though in fun, to defend himself. . . . But in his friend's face he surprised such a malevolent expression, in his crookedly smiling lips and glinting eyes such a serious threat, that he instinctively felt uneasy. . . .

"Ah, that's where you've got to!" Vassily Ivanich's voice rang out at that instant, and the old army doctor presented himself before the young men, in a homespun linen jacket and a straw hat, also of home-make. "I've been looking for you everywhere, everywhere. . . . But you have picked on an excellent spot and are engaged in a fine occupation. 'Lying on the ground, gazing at the sky. . . .' Do you know —there is something particularly significant in that!"

"I only look at the sky when I feel like sneezing," Bazarov growled and, turning to Arcady, he added in a low voice: "A pity he interfered."

"Shut up," Arcady whispered back, pressing his friend's hand stealthily. "No friendship could bear such strain for long."

"When I look at you, my young friends," Vassily Ivanich said, shaking his head and leaning forward with hands clasped on a cunningly wrought stick of his own handiwork, with the figure of a Turk carved on it by way of a knob, "when I look at you, I can't help admiring you. What strength and flowering youth! How many abilities and talents! Why, the two of you might be . . . Castor and Pollux!"

"There you go—plunging into mythology again!" his son exclaimed. "One can tell at once that you were a Latin scholar in your day! Why, if I remember rightly, you were awarded a silver medal for a Latin composition, weren't you?"

"The *Dioscuri,* the *Dioscuri!*" Vassily Ivanich repeated.

"Enough, father. Don't be sentimental."

"I can allow myself this every once in a while," the old man muttered. "However, gentlemen, I did not seek you out in order to pay you compliments, but, firstly, to announce to you that dinner will soon be ready, and secondly, to warn you, Eugene. . . . You are a man of the world and a judge of people, and you know women too . . . so you must be charitable. . . . Your mother wishes to have a thanksgiving mass celebrated on the occasion of your arrival. Don't imagine that I'm asking you to assist at the mass—it's already over; but Father Alexei . . ."

"Oh, the ecclesiastic?"

"Well, yes, the priest; he is going to be . . . at dinner. . . . I did not expect it and even advised against it . . . but somehow or other that's the way it's happened . . . he would not take the hint. . . . Well, and there was your mother too. . . . And besides, he is a very good and reasonable man."

"I presume he won't eat my portion of the dinner, will he?" Bazarov asked.

"Heavens, what a thing to say!" Vassily Ivanich laughed.

"That's all I ask. I am quite prepared to sit at table with any man."

Vassily Ivanich set his hat straight.

"I was sure in advance," he said, "that you were above prejudice. And here am I—an old man, still alive in my sixty-second year, and I haven't any prejudices either" (Bazarov's father did not dare to admit that he also had wished to have the mass celebrated. . . . He was not a whit less devout than his wife). "And Father Alexei very much wants to make your acquaintance. You will like him, you'll see. He is not against playing a game of cards either, and he is even . . . but let this go no further . . . he is even not averse from smoking a pipe."

"Well, in that case, we'll settle down to a game of whist after dinner, and I'll trounce him."

"Ha, ha, ha! We shall see! Two can play at that game!"

"You don't mean you're going to have a fling as you were in the habit of doing once?"

A blush of confusion spread over Vassily Ivanich's bronzed cheeks.

"Shame on you, Eugene. . . . Let sleeping dogs lie. Well, I am quite ready to confess in front of your friend that I was addicted to that passion in my youth—indeed, I was; and didn't I have to pay for it! However, how hot it is. May I sit down beside you? I'm not in the way, am I?"

"Of course not," Arcady replied.

With creaking limbs, Vassily Ivanich sank down into the hay.

"Your present billet, my dear sirs," he began, "reminds me of my camping days in the army; the field hospitals were also pitched near some hayrick, and that was something to thank God for." He sighed. "I have had a great deal of experience, a very great deal of it in my time. Thus, for instance, let me tell you, if you will allow, a very curious episode during the plague in Bessarabia."

"For which you were awarded the order of St. Vladimir?" Bazarov interposed. "We know, we know. . . . Incidentally, why do you never wear it?"

"But I told you that I have no prejudices," Vassily Ivanich muttered (only the day before he had given orders for the red ribbon to be removed from his jacket). Then he began to describe the episode of the plague. "Why, he's fallen asleep," he suddenly whispered, with a kindly wink, pointing to his son.

"Eugene! Get up," he added loudly. "It's time for dinner. . . ."

Father Alexei, a stout and imposing personage with thick, carefully brushed hair and an embroidered sash girding his mauve silk cassock, turned out to be a very adroit and resourceful man. He took the initiative in hastening to shake hands with both Arcady and Bazarov, comprehending in advance that they had no need of his blessing, and in general he conducted himself without any reserve. Never betraying himself, he managed also to avoid treading on other people's toes; at the right moment he made a joke about Latin as taught in the seminaries and said a word in favour of his bishop; he drank two glasses of wine, but declined a third; he accepted a cigar from Arcady, but abstained from smoking it, saying that he would take it home with him. His only none-too-pleasant feature was the slow and careful gesture he made with his hand when he tried to catch the flies that settled on his face, in the process sometimes crushing them. He took his seat at the green baize table with a moderate show of pleasure, but ended by winning two roubles and fifty kopecks in currency notes from Bazarov: in Arina Vlassyevna's house they had not yet learnt how to reckon in silver. . . .

As usual, she sat near Bazarov (she did not play cards herself), with her fist as ever propping her cheek; she got up only when it was necessary to give an order for some fresh delicacy to be served. She was afraid of showing her fondness for Bazarov, and he did not encourage her to do so; he did not seek endearments from her, and as a result the father had advised her not to "disturb" their son too much. "Young men are not very keen on that sort of thing," he kept repeating to her. There is no need to enlarge on the sort of dinner that was served that day: Timofeyich had employed himself personally at daybreak to drive off in search of some extra special Circassian beef; the steward had driven off elsewhere for turbot, perch and crayfish; for the mushrooms alone the peasant women raked in forty-two kopecks in copper. But Arina Vlassyevna's eyes, which she could not tear away from her son, wore an expression not only of tenderness and devotion; one could also spy in them a shade of sorrow mingled with curiosity and fear; and there lurked, too, a look of resigned reproach.

However, Bazarov was in no mood to probe the signifi-cance of his mother's expression; he addressed her but rarely, and then only to ask some brief question. Once he asked her to give him her hand "for luck"; quietly she slipped her soft little hand into his rough and broad palm.

"Well," she inquired after a while, "did it not help?"

"I had worse luck than ever," he replied with a careless smile.

Meanwhile the game of whist was in progress.

"What big risks they do take!" Father Alexei exclaimed in a tone of feigned regret, stroking his handsome beard.

"It's the Napoleonic rule, Father, the Napoleonic rule," Vassily Ivanich interjected, slamming down an ace.

"It brought him to St. Helena," Father Alexei retorted, playing a trump.

"Would you like a little black-currant juice, Enyushicka?" Arina Vlassyevna asked her son.

But he merely shrugged his shoulders.

"No!" he said to Arcady next day. "To-morrow I shall leave this place. I'm bored. I feel like work but I can't work here. I shall go to your part of the country again; I left all my equipment there. In your house I can at least lock myself in. But here, although my father keeps assuring me, 'My study is at your disposal—no one will interrupt you,' he will dog my steps. And I get an uneasy conscience when I lock myself in from him. And mother too. I can hear her sighing next door, and whenever I go out to her, I find I have nothing to say."

"She will be very upset," Arcady replied, "and he too."

"But I shall come back to them."

"When?"

"Oh, on my way to Petersburg."

"I am particularly sorry for your mother."

"Why? Has she won you over with her raspberries and black-currants?"

Arcady looked down at his feet.

"You don't know your mother, Eugene. She's not only a fine character, but also really intelligent. This morning she talked to me for half an hour, and all she said was both interesting and to the point."

"No doubt she was enlarging about me all the time?"

"You were not the only subject of conversation."

"Maybe. As a detached observer you can see more clearly. It's a good sign when a woman can keep up a conversation for half an hour. But I shall depart all the same."

"It won't be so easy for you to break the news to them. They are still discussing plans for us a fortnight ahead."

"I know it won't be easy. Some devil prompted me to tease my father this morning: he gave orders a few days ago to have one of his rent-bound peasants flogged—and an excellent thing too. Yes, yes, don't look at me with such horror—an excellent thing too, because the peasant in question is a most frightful thief and drunkard; but father did not expect that I, as they say, should become acquainted with the facts. It threw him into great confusion, and now I must give him another shock. . . . It can't be helped! Anyway, the wound will heal in time!"

Although Bazarov had said, "It can't be helped!" a whole day passed before he made up his mind to inform his father of his intention. Finally, as he was bidding him good night in his study, he said with a drawn-out yawn:

"Yes . . . I almost forgot to tell you. . . . Will you order our horses to be sent to Fedot's as relays?"

Vassily Ivanich was astounded.

"Is Mr. Kirsanov leaving us then?"

"Yes, and I am going with him."

The old man was completely nonplussed.

"You are going away?" he stuttered.

"Yes. . . . I must go. Will you please see to the horses?"

"Very well. . . ." The old man quavered. "For the relay . . . very well . . . only . . . only . . . Why must you?"

"I must visit the Kirsanovs for a short while. And then I shall come back again."

"Yes! For a short while. . . . Very well." Vassily Ivanich

pulled out his handkerchief and, after blowing his nose,
bowed down almost to the ground. "Well? That . . . all
that will come to pass. I thought you would stay with us
. . . a little longer. Three days. . . . After three years that's
. . . that's very little, very little, Eugene!"

"But I assure you that I shall be back very soon. It's
essential for me to go."

"Essential. . . . Well? One must do one's duty, first of
all. . . . So, we'll have to send the horses? Very well. Your
mother and I, of course, did not expect this. She has just
procured some fresh flowers, to make your room brighter."
(His father did not mention that, as soon as it was light, he
had got up barefoot in his slippers, to take counsel with
Timofeyich and, pulling out with shaking hands one ragged
banknote after another, had instructed him what purchases
to make, laying stress particularly on the food and red
wines which, as far as he could observe, were most appre-
ciated by the young men.)

"Freedom's the important thing," he went on. "That has
always been my rule . . . one must never be an obstacle . . .
one must never . . ."

Suddenly, he stopped talking and made for the door.

"We'll see each other very soon, father, I assure you."

But without turning round, Vassily Ivanich merely made
a gesture with his hand and went out. Back in the bedroom,
he found his wife already in bed, and he began to say his
prayers in a whisper so as not to wake her. However, she
did wake.

"Is that you, Vassily Ivanich?" she asked.

"It's me, my soul!"

"Have you just come from Yenusha? Do you know, I'm
worried if he can sleep comfortably on the sofa. I told
Anfisushka to lay your camp mattress on it and the new
pillows; I'd gladly give him our feather mattress, but I
seem to remember that he does not like too soft a bed."

"Never mind, my dear, don't worry now," her husband
replied. "He's comfortable enough. The Lord have mercy
on us, poor sinners," he went on saying his prayers in a
low voice. He had pity on his old wife; he did not wish
to tell her overnight of the sorrow that was in store for her.

Bazarov and Arcady drove off the next day. From early
morning an atmosphere of dejection had reigned in the
house; the plates dropped out of Anfisushka's hands; even

Fedka was in a state of perplexity, and ended by taking off his boots. Vassily Ivanich fussed about more than ever; he was obviously trying to put a good face on things, talked loudly and stamped his feet, but his face looked drawn and he consistently avoided looking at his son. Arina Vlassyevna sobbed quietly; she would have broken down altogether and lost control of herself had not her husband spent a whole two hours in the morning consoling her. When Bazarov, after repeated promises to return not later than in a month's time, at last tore himself away from their clinging embraces, and took his seat in the tarantass; when the horses moved off, the bells tinkled, and the wheels spun round—when nothing more was left to gaze at, the dust had settled, and Timofeyich, all bent and tottering, had made his way back to his tiny room; when the old folk were alone in the house, which now looked suddenly shrunken and decrepit; the Vassily Ivanich who, only a few instants before, had bravely waved his handkerchief as he stood on the porch, slumped into a chair and let drop his head on his chest.

"He has abandoned us, abandoned us," he quavered. "He has left us; he found us boring. He's all alone now, alone like this finger!" he repeated several times, and each time he thrust out his hand with the forefinger pointing away from the rest.

Then Arina Vlassyevna came to his side and, pressing her grey head to his, said: "It can't be helped, Vasya. A son is like a lopped-off branch. As a falcon he comes when he wills and goes where he lists; but you and I are like mushrooms growing in a hollow tree. Here we sit side by side without budging. But I shall stay with you for ever and unalterably, just as you will stay with me."

Vassily Ivanich removed his hands from his face and embraced his wife, his constant companion, with a warmth greater than he had ever shown her in his youth; she had consoled him in his grief.

XXII

In silence, exchanging only a few trivial remarks now and then, our friends finally drove up to Fedot's. Bazarov was not quite satisfied with himself. Arcady was disappointed in him. Moreover, his heart was full of that inexplicable nostalgia which is familiar only to the very young. The coachman harnessed a fresh relay of horses and, clambering up on his seat, asked them: "Am I to turn right or left?"

Arcady gave a start. The road to the right led to town and then homewards: the road to the left led to Anna Odintzov's.

He glanced at Bazarov.

"Eugene," he asked, "shall we turn left?"

Bazarov looked away.

"What foolishness is this?" he muttered.

"I know it's foolish," Arcady pursued. . . ."But what of it? It's not the first time."

Bazarov pulled his cap over his forehead.

"As you like," he said at last.

"Turn left," Arcady shouted.

The tarantass rolled off in the direction of Nicolskoye. But having resolved to be *foolish,* the friends relapsed into still more obdurate silence, and they even looked sulky.

Judging by the way the butler received them in the porch of the Odintzov house, the friends got an inkling that they had acted unwisely in thus giving way to a sudden impulse. They were obviously not expected. Looking sheepish, they waited for a long time in the drawing-room. Finally, Madame Odintzov came out to see them. She greeted them with her usual courtesy, but expressed surprise at their rapid return and, to judge by her hesitant gestures and speech, she did not seem too pleased. They hastened to declare that they had only dropped in on the way and would set out again in about four hours in the direction of the town. She confined herself to a faint exclamation, asked Arcady to pay her respects to his father, and then sent for her aunt. The princess came in, sleepy-eyed, and this made her wrinkled old face look even more spiteful. Katya, who was feeling unwell, stayed in her room. Arcady suddenly felt that he wanted to see Katya at least as much as Anna Sergeyevna. The four hours were spent in small talk; Anna Sergeyevna listened and chatted without smiling at all. Only when they came to take leave, did she look as if her former friendliness had warmed her heart again.

"I'm suffering from an attack of spleen just now," she confessed. "So don't pay any attention to me and do come back again—I mean this for both of you—in a little while."

Arcady and Bazarov replied with silent bows. Taking their places in the tarantass and without halting on the way, they set off home to Maryino, where they arrived safely on the evening of the following day. During the whole of the journey neither of them so much as mentioned Madame Odintzov's name; Bazarov, in particular, hardly opened his mouth and persisted in keeping his eyes off the roadway, an expression of sour concentration on his face.

At Maryino everyone was extremely glad to see them. The continued absence of his son had begun to disquiet Nicholas Petrovich; throwing up his legs in the air and bouncing up and down on the sofa, he let out a shout when Fenichka ran in and with radiant eyes informed him of the "young gentlemen's" arrival. As to Paul Petrovich, he experienced a certain pleasurable excitement and smiled condescendingly as he shook hands with the returning wanderers. They began to talk and ask questions; Arcady chattered most of all, especially at supper, which was prolonged till well past midnight. Nicholas Petrovich ordered several bottles of port, just fresh from Moscow, to be brought out, and set the pace so fast that his cheeks flushed a raspberry colour, and he laughed in a way that was either childish or nervous. The general gaiety spread to the servants' quarters too. Dunyasha ran to and fro like one possessed, and kept banging the doors; as to Peter, he was still trying to strum a Cossack waltz on a guitar at three o'clock in the morning. The night air resounded with the strumming of plaintive and pleasurable notes; but with the exception of a few short preliminary flourishes, the cultured butler failed to obtain any other effects: nature had denied him an aptitude for music as it had for everything else.

In the meantime, life at Maryino had not been follow-

ing a smooth pattern, and poor Nicholas Petrovich was
having a bad time. Each day the "farm" brought increasing
worries—and they were cheerless, stupid worries. The complications with the hired labourers were becoming unbearable. Some of them had insisted on being paid off or on
having their wages increased, others had pocketed their advance and decamped. The horses fell sick; the harness
simply wore away; the work in the fields had been badly
done; the threshing machine ordered specially from Moscow
proved too heavy and unusable; another such machine
broke down as soon as it was tried; half the cowsheds were
burnt out because a short-sighted old woman had gone out
on a windy day to fumigate her cow with a burning brand.
. . . This old woman later insisted that the disaster had been
caused by her master's taking it into his head to start manu-
facturing "foreign" cheeses and dairy products. The steward
grew lazy and began to get stout, as every Russian will
when he has his "bread buttered." Whenever he caught
sight of Nicholas Kirsanov in the distance, he gave evidence
of his energy by throwing a stick at some trotting porkling
within reach or by waving his fist threateningly at some
half-naked urchin, but for the most part he slumbered. The
peasants, who were now supposed to pay rent, were never
prompt to meet their obligations and filched their landlord's timber; almost every night the watchman would
catch or be obliged to confiscate by force the peasant nags
that he found grazing on the meadows of the "farm."
Nicholas Kirsanov attempted to institute a system of fines
for such encroachments, but the matter usually ended by
the master feeding the horses at his own expense before
returning them to their owners a day later.

The climax came when the peasants started to squabble
among themselves: brothers demanded that the holdings
should be split up among them individually and their wives
refused to live together under the same roof. Fights boiled
up of a sudden and, as though at a word of command, a
whole crowd of them would be up on their feet, swarming
round the entrance to the office, importuning their master,
their faces quite often bruised and bloody and they themselves in a state of inebriation, clamouring for justice and
retribution; in an uproar of howling voices, the women's
shrill whining would mingle with the men's raucous swearing. Kirsanov did his best to separate the adversaries, shout-

ing till he was hoarse but knowing in advance that it was impossible, in any case, to arrive at any reasonable solution. There was a shortage of hands for harvesting: a neighbouring freeholder, who looked a decent enough fellow, had undertaken to provide reapers at a commission of two roubles per acre and had then cheated Kirsanov in the most shameless fashion. The peasant women on his own estate began to demand extortionate wages and, in the meantime, the corn was going to seed. To make matters worse, while they were still behindhand with the reaping, the local council started to issue threats and to demand full payment of the interest due. . . .

"I simply can't go on like this!" Nicholas Petrovich had exclaimed despairingly more than once. "It's impossible for me to fight them on my own and my principles forbid me to send for the police; yet nothing can be done without the threat of penalties!"

"Du calme, du calme," his brother Paul counselled, purring, frowning and tugging at his moustaches.

Bazarov held himself aloof from these domestic "wrangles"; nor was it his business as a guest to interfere in matters which did not concern him. The day following his arrival at Maryino he became engrossed in his frogs, his infusoria, and his chemical compounds, and spent all his time over them. Arcady, on the other hand, considered it his duty, if not to assist his father, at least to appear ready to help him. He listened to him patiently and, on one occasion, even ventured to give him some advice, not so much in the hope of its being taken to heart as in order to demonstrate his interest. He felt no repugnance for farming: he even found pleasure in thinking of agriculture as a possible occupation for himself, but at this time his head was still full of other projects. To his own amazement, Arcady found himself constantly thinking of Nicolskoye. Formerly he would merely have shrugged his shoulders if anyone had suggested that he would feel at a loose end under the same roof as Bazarov, and what a roof too!—that of his own parents; but he now felt bored and attracted elsewhere. He decided that he must try and work off his tedium by indulging in long and exhausting walks, but that did not help either.

One day, while talking to his father, he found out that Nicholas Petrovich had in his possession a few letters of

some interest, written once upon a time to his late wife by
Anna, Madame Odintzov's mother. Arcady did not leave
his father in peace until he was shown these letters, for
which Nicholas Petrovich was obliged to rummage in twenty different boxes and trunks. On getting possession of
these partly mouldering sheets of paper, Arcady seemed
to calm down, as though he had set himself some definite
goal. "I mean this for both of you," he whispered often to
himself, recalling Anna Sergeyevna's phrase. "She added
that herself. I'll go, I will, and the devil take the conse-
quences!" But then, remembering their last visit, the cool
reception and the ensuing embarrassment, he was overcome with hesitation. The "dare and venture" of youth, the
secret desire to try his luck, to measure his strength all by
himself, without any patronage, finally prevailed.

Ten days had not passed since his arrival in Maryino,
when, on the pretext of studying the Sunday-schools, he
was off at a gallop again to town and, from there, to Nicolskoye. Ceaselessly urging on his driver, he rushed to his
destination, like a young subaltern into battle: he felt at
once terrified and gay, and was devoured with impatience.
"But above all—I must not worry about it!" he kept repeating. His driver turned out to be a dashing fellow; pulling
up at a roadside inn, he would say: "One for the road?" or
"Shall we have one?" But once *having had one*, he did not
spare the horses. Then, at last, the high roof of the familiar
house came into view. . . . "What am I doing?" flashed of
a sudden through Arcady's head. "Hadn't I better turn
back?" But the troika sped smoothly on; the driver was
encouraging the horses and whistling at them. Already the
bridge was thundering under the hooves and the wheels,
already the alley of trimmed fir trees was running forward
to meet him. . . . A lady's rose-coloured dress gleamed
among the dark foliage, and a young face peeped from
under the light fringe of a parasol. . . . He recognized Katya,
and she recognized him. Arcady ordered the driver to halt
the galloping horses and, jumping out of the carriage, went
to meet her.

"It's you!" she exclaimed, a blush gradually suffusing her
face. "Let's go and find my sister, she's here in the garden;
she will be very pleased to see you."

Katya conducted Arcady through the garden. Their meeting struck him as a particularly happy omen; so delighted

was he to see her that she might have been a close relative. Everything had turned out so well: there had been no formalities, no butler to announce him. At the turning of the path, he caught sight of Anna Sergeyevna. She was standing with her back to him. On hearing their steps, she slowly turned her head.

Arcady was on the point of feeling embarrassed again, but her very first words immediately reassured him.

"Good day to you, fugitive!" she said in her calm, affectionate voice, coming forward to meet him, smiling and screwing up her eyes from the sun and wind. "Where did you unearth him, Katya?"

"I have brought you something, Anna Sergeyevna," he began, "something you were far from expecting . . ."

"You have brought yourself—and that is the best you could do."

XXIII

After seeing Arcady off with mocking solicitude, letting him understand that he was not in the least deceived as to the real purpose of his journey, Bazarov isolated himself completely and feverishly fell to work. He avoided arguments with Paul Petrovich, particularly as the latter now assumed an excessively aristocratic air in his presence and gave vent to his opinions in grunts rather than words. On one occasion, however, Paul Petrovich did venture to engage in controversy with the Nihilist on the then fashionable topic of the rights of the Baltic Barons, but he soon thought better of it and, pausing suddenly in the middle of his discourse, remarked with frigid politeness: "But what's the use? We fail to understand each other; or, at least, I have not the honour to understand you."

"No wonder!" Bazarov exclaimed. "Man is capable of understanding everything—the vibration of ether and the radiation of the sun; but he can never comprehend why another person should blow his nose in a manner different from his own."

"What? Are you trying to be witty?" Paul Petrovich re-marked questioningly and walked away.

However, he did sometimes ask Bazarov's permission to watch his experiments, and once he even moved his gen-erously scented face, washed with the finest of soaps, close to the microscope to observe a transparent protozoon swal-low a green speck of dust and fussily masticate it with the help of some very dexterous, fist-like organs attached to its throat. Nicholas Petrovich dropped in to see Bazarov more frequently than his brother; he would have come every day "to school himself," as he put it, if the management of his estate had not made such great demands on his time. He did not disturb the young naturalist: he would sit down somewhere in a corner and watch him attentively, asking a cautious question now and then. At table, he did his best to turn the conversation to physics, geology or chemistry, for every other topic, even farming, to say nothing of politics, might have led to a clash if not to mutual recrimination. Nicholas Petrovich divined that his brother's hatred of Bazarov had in no way diminished. A trifling incident, one of many, confirmed this hypothesis. Here and there in the neighbourhood, cholera had broken out, and had even "weeded out" a couple of inhabitants from Maryino. One night Paul Petrovich felt violently indisposed. But he bore his pains until the morning without resorting to Bazarov's medical skill—and, when he saw him on the following day, pale as he still was, but with his hair carefully groomed and his cheeks clean-shaven, he retorted to Bazarov's question, "Why didn't you send for me?" by saying, "But I seem to recall your saying that you have no faith in medicine." So the days passed. Bazarov applied himself to his work stead-ily and grimly . . . and yet there was a person in Nicholas Petrovich's household with whom, though he did not open his heart fully, he at least enjoyed chatting. . . . That person was Fenichka.

He usually met her early in the morning, in the garden or the courtyard: he never ventured to visit her room, and, for her part, she only once went as far as his door, to inquire if she should bathe Mitya or not. Not only was she not afraid of him and had every confidence in him, but she also felt less constrained and more able to talk in his presence than in that of Nicholas Petrovich. It is hard to explain why this was so; perhaps because she sensed unconsciously that Bazarov was quite free from aristocratic prejudice, from that consciousness of superiority which is both alluring and intimidating. In her eyes he was an excellent doctor and a forthright man. She felt no shame at nursing her baby in his presence, and on one occasion, when she suddenly felt faint and developed a splitting headache, she accepted a spoonful of medicine from his hands. When Nicholas Petrovich was about, she seemed to avoid Bazarov —out of no duplicity but simply from a sense of decency. More than ever she was apprehensive of Paul Petrovich: of late he had begun to keep an eye on her; and he would suddenly confront her, as though he had sprung out of the ground behind her back, in an English-cut suit, his face set and suspicious, and his hands in his pockets.

"It's like having a cold shower," Fenichka complained to Dunyasha, while the latter only sighed and let her mind stray to another "heartless man." Without suspecting it, Bazarov had become the "ruthless tyrant" of Dunyasha's soul.

Fenichka liked Bazarov, and he liked her. Even the expression of his face seemed to change when he talked to her: it grew brighter, almost assuming a look of good-nature, and his manner, ordinarily so casual, became playful and considerate. Fenichka looked prettier every day. There comes a period in the life of young women when, of a sudden, they begin to flower and blossom like summer roses; such a time had come for Fenichka. Everything contributed to this, even the sultry heat of July, which was then raging. Wearing a flimsy white dress, she looked whiter and more diaphanous than ever: the sun had not tanned her, but the heat, from which she could not shield herself, had made her cheeks and ears go a faint pink and, infusing her whole body with gentle languor, was reflected in the dreamy torpor of her bewitching eyes. She could barely get on with her work; her hands kept slipping to her knees. She could hardly take a step, and kept moaning and complaining with an amusing show of helplessness.

"You should bathe more often," Nicholas Petrovich would say to her. He had rigged up a large bathing-tent over one of the ponds which had not yet dried up.

"Oh, Nicholas Petrovich! But I'd die before I ever got there, and I'd die again on the way back. There is no shade at all in the garden."

"You are quite right, there is no shade," Nicholas Petrovich would reply, mopping his forehead.

One day, as Bazarov was returning from a stroll at about seven in the morning, he came across Fenichka in the lilac arbour, which had stopped flowering long ago but was still thickly covered with green leaves. She was sitting on a bench and, as usual, wore a white kerchief on her head; beside her lay a large bunch of red and white roses still sprinkled with dew. He bid her good morning.

"Ah, Mr. Bazarov!" she exclaimed and, in order to see him, raised the edge of her kerchief a trifle, baring her arm to the elbow as she did so.

"What are you doing here?" Bazarov inquired, sitting down beside her. "Are you making a bouquet?"

"Yes, for the lunch table. Nicholas Petrovich is fond of flowers."

"We have plenty of time before breakfast. What a lot of flowers!"

"I have just picked them, before it was too hot for walking. Now is the only time I can breathe. This heat makes me sick. I'm afraid of falling ill."

"That's sheer fantasy! Let me feel your pulse." Bazarov took her hand, felt her evenly throbbing pulse and did not even bother to count the beats. "You'll live to be a hundred," he said, letting drop her hand.

"Ah, God forbid!" she exclaimed.

"Why not? Don't you want to live a long life?"

"Yes, but not a hundred years! We had a granny of eighty-five—and what a martyr she was! Black as soot, deaf, hunchbacked, coughing all the time; she was only a burden to herself. What sort of a life is that!"

"So it's better to be young?"

"But of course."

"Why should it be better? Tell me!"

"Why? Oh, because being young, I can do anything—I can come and go, and carry things, and I don't have to rely on anyone. . . . What could be better?"

"But I don't mind whether I am young or old."

"How can you say that—'I don't mind?' I simply don't believe you."

"But judge for yourself. What need have I of youth? I live all alone, have no ties. . . ."

"It all depends on yourself."

"That's just the point—it doesn't! If only I could find someone to take pity on me."

Fenichka looked sideways at Bazarov, but made no rejoinder. "What is the book?" she inquired after a short pause.

"This? It's about science, a very learned book."

"And you study all the time? Don't you get tired of it? I expect you must know everything by now."

"Evidently not. Just try and read a few pages of this."

"Why, I shouldn't understand anything. Is it in Russian?" Fenichka asked, picking up the heavily bound volume in both hands. "What an enormous book!"

"It's in Russian."

"All the same, I shan't understand anything."

"I didn't give it to you that you might understand it. I only want to watch you as you read. When you read, the tip of your nose twitches most endearingly."

Fenichka, who was about to construe in a low voice an article "On Creosote," which she happened to turn up, burst out laughing and threw the book down . . . it slipped from the bench and fell to the ground.

"I like you also when you laugh," Bazarov pursued.

"Don't say things like that."

"I like you when you talk. It reminds me of a babbling brook."

Fenichka turned away her head.

"What a man you are!" she exclaimed, fingering the flowers. "Why do you bother to listen to me? You are accustomed to very bright ladies."

"Ah, Fenichka, do believe me: all the brightest ladies in the world are not worth your little elbow."

"What a fancy you have!" Fenichka whispered, clasping her hands.

Bazarov picked the book up from the ground.

"This is a medical book. Why do you throw it about?"

"A medical book?" Fenichka repeated, turning to face him. "Do you know? Why, ever since you gave me those drops for Mitya, do you remember, he's been sleeping ever so soundly! I don't know how to thank you; you are so very kind, really you are."

"Doctors usually charge a fee, you know," Bazarov remarked with a smile. "As you are aware, doctors are quite a greedy crowd."

Fenichka raised her eyes: they looked even darker in the dazzling light which was reflected on the upper part of her face. She was not quite sure if he were joking or not.

"If you like, we will gladly . . . I shall have to ask Nicholas. . . ."

"So you think I want money?" Bazarov interrupted her. "No, it's not money I want from you."

"What then?" Fenichka asked.

"What?" Bazarov repeated. "Try and guess."

"I'm not much good at guessing!"

"Well, let me tell you then; I want . . . one of those roses."

Fenichka laughed again and threw up her hands, so amused she was at Bazarov's wish. But though she was laughing, she also felt flattered. Bazarov stared closely at her.

"By all means, by all means," she brought out at last and, stooping over the bench, began to sift the roses. "Which do you prefer? Red or white?"

"A red one, and not too large."

"Here, take this," she said, sitting up. Then jerking back her outstretched hand and biting her lips, she peered at the entrance of the arbour, straining her ears.

"What's the matter?" Bazarov inquired. "Is it Nicholas Petrovich? . . ."

"No. . . . He's out on the farm . . . and anyhow I'm not afraid of him . . . but there's Paul Petrovich. . . . It seemed to me . . ."

"What?"

"He seems to be prowling about. No. . . . There's no one there. Now, please take it," Fenichka said, giving Bazarov a rose.

"And why should you be afraid of Paul?"

"He frightens me. It's not that he says anything—he doesn't, but he keeps staring at me in such a knowing way. You don't like him either. Do you remember how you always used to argue with him? I had no idea what it was about, but I could see that you were twisting him round your little finger. . . ."

Fenichka illustrated with her hands how she thought Bazarov dealt with Paul Petrovich.

Bazarov smiled.

"And what would you have done if he had begun to get

the better of me?" he asked. "Would you have taken my side?"

"Who am I to meddle? No. No one could get the better of you."

"You think so? But I know a little finger that could topple me over like a feather if it wanted."

"Whose finger?"

"You pretend not to know? What a wonderful scent this rose has. Just smell it."

Fenichka stretched her slender neck forward and put her face close to the flower. . . . The kerchief fell from her head upon her shoulders, disclosing a wavy mass of black, glossy and slightly rumpled hair.

"Just a minute. I want to smell it too," Bazarov exclaimed, and, stooping forward, kissed her warmly on her parted lips.

She quivered, pressing both her hands against his chest, but her pressure was feeble, and he was able to renew and prolong the kiss.

There was a sound of a dry cough behind the lilac shrubs. Fenichka instantly edged away to the other end of the bench. Paul Petrovich showed himself, made a slight bow, and, exclaiming in a sort of jaundiced and dejected tone, "So that's where you are!" walked away. Fenichka at once gathered up all the roses and fled from the arbour.

"How could you!" she whispered as she departed. Her whisper conveyed a note of sincere reproach.

Bazarov recalled another recent scene: his conscience pricked him and he experienced a feeling of contempt mingled with regret. But he immediately shook his head, congratulated himself sardonically on his "own formal entry into the ranks of the gay Lotharios," and marched off to his room.

In the meantime, Paul Petrovich had left the garden and walked as far as the copse. He remained there for quite a while. When he came back for breakfast, his face looked so clouded that Nicholas Petrovich inquired with solicitude if he was feeling quite well.

"As you know, I am sometimes subject to bilious attacks," was Paul Petrovich's calm reply.

XXIV

Two hours later he knocked at Bazarov's door.

"Pardon me for interrupting your scientific researches," he began, sitting down on a chair by the window and leaning with both hands on a handsome cane with an ivory knob (he usually did not carry a cane), "but I have to ask you to spare me five minutes of your time . . . no more."

"My time is at your disposal," replied Bazarov, whose face had twitched as soon as Paul Petrovich crossed the threshold.

"Five minutes will be ample. I have come to put a question to you."

"A question? What is it?"

"I shall explain if you will be good enough to listen. In the early days of your stay in my brother's house, before I denied myself the pleasure of talking with you, I had occasion to hear you express opinions on many subjects; but, as far as I can remember, you have never made any reference to single combats or duelling in general, either in conversation with me or in my presence. May I inquire what your views are on this subject?"

Bazarov, who had risen to receive Paul Petrovich, sat down on the edge of a table and crossed his arms.

"This is what I think," he replied. "From the theoretical point of view duelling is stupid; but from the practical point of view—well, that's another question."

"That is to say, you mean, if I understand you correctly, that in practice, whatever your theoretical view of duelling may be, you would not suffer yourself to be insulted without demanding satisfaction!"

"You have fully grasped my meaning."

"Very well. I am pleased to hear you say so. Your words have rescued me from a dilemma."

"From indecision, you mean."

"As you like. I am trying to express myself in a way you will understand; I . . . I am no seminary rat. What you say will spare me from resorting to a certain unfortunate necessity. I have decided to fight you."

154

Bazarov stared at him round-eyed.

"To fight me?"

"Precisely."

"And for what reason, may I inquire?"

"I could explain," Paul Petrovich began. "But I would prefer not. I think you are in the way here. I cannot stand you, I despise you, and if that is not enough for you . . ."

Paul Petrovich's eyes flashed. . . . Bazarov's glinted too.

"Very well then," he articulated slowly. "Further explanations are superfluous. You have succumbed to the fantasy of testing your chivalrous spirit on me. I could have denied you that pleasure, but I shall let you have your way!"

"I am most grateful to you," Paul Petrovich replied. "I hope that you will now accept my challenge without forcing me to resort to compulsory measures."

"That is to say, if we dispense with allegory, you would resort to that cane?" Bazarov coolly remarked. "You are quite right. There is no need for you to affront me. Nor would that have been without some peril to you. You may remain a gentleman. . . . I also accept your challenge like a gentleman."

"That's fine," Paul Petrovich exclaimed, putting his cane into a corner. "It now remains for us to discuss the conditions of the duel; but, first of all, I should like to know whether you consider it necessary for us to have recourse to the formality of a slight dispute which might serve as an excuse for my challenge?"

"No, we had better dispense with the formalities."

"I am of that opinion myself. I also assume that it would be out of place to probe into the real reasons for our encounter. We just can't bear each other. Isn't that enough?"

"Isn't that enough?" Bazarov echoed him ironically.

"As to the conditions of the duel, we shall be without seconds . . . for where can we procure them?"

"Exactly. Where can we procure them?"

"I have the honour to suggest the following: let us fight early to-morrow morning, at six o'clock, behind the copse, with pistols, at ten paces on each side of the barrier. . . ."

"At ten paces? All right. Let that be the distance over which we shall hate each other."

"We can make it eight," Paul Petrovich remarked.

"We can. Why not?"

"We shall fire two shots and, as a precaution, each of us

must put a letter in his pocket, holding himself responsible
for his own demise."

"I don't altogether agree with that," Bazarov replied.
"It's beginning to smell rather like a French romance, a bit
improbable."

"Perhaps. However, you will agree that it would be
unpleasant to be suspected of murder?"

"I agree. But there is a way of avoiding that depressing
approach. We have no seconds, but we can have a witness."

"May I inquire who it will be?"

"Why, Peter."

"Which Peter?"

"Your brother's valet. He is quite up to the standards of
contemporary culture, and would play his part, and all it
entailed in these circumstances, quite *comme il faut.*"

"I have the impression that you are joking, my dear sir."

"Not at all. If you will ponder on my suggestion, you
will conclude that it is full of common sense and simplicity.
Murder will out, but I shall take it on myself to coach
Peter in a befitting manner and to deliver him on to the
battlefield."

"You like joking," Paul Petrovich said, rising from his
chair. "But after the amiable readiness you have displayed,
I have no right to insist further. . . . So everything is in
order. . . . By the way, have you any pistols?"

"How should I have pistols? I am no warrior."

"In that case I shall have to offer you a set of mine. You
may rest assured that I have not used them these five years."

"That is very comforting news."

Paul Petrovich picked up his cane. . . .

"To conclude, my dear sir, it only remains for me to
thank you and to allow you to resume your studies. I have
the honour to take leave of you."

"Until I have the pleasure of meeting you again, my
dear sir," Bazarov said as he conducted his visitor to the
door.

Paul Petrovich went out, leaving Bazarov standing at the
door. The latter suddenly exclaimed: "The devil take it!
How beautiful and how stupid! What a farce we have
thumped through! Circus dogs could not have done their
turn any better. And there was no getting out of it; he
would have hit me at the slightest provocation, and
then . . ." (At the very thought Bazarov turned pale; all his

pride reared up within him.) "Then I should have had to strangle him as I might a kitten." He went back to his microscope, but his heart had been stirred, and he now lacked the composure essential for precise observation. "He must have seen me with Fenichka this morning," he thought. "But is it for his brother's sake that he intervened in this fashion? And is a kiss so very important? There must be something else behind it. Bah! Perhaps he is in love with her himself? Of course, he is in love; it's as clear as daylight. What a complication, just imagine! . . . What a mess!" he decided at last. "It's a mess from whichever angle one may look at it. In the first place, I shall have to risk my own head, and then I shall have to go away anyhow; and there is also Arcady . . . and that angelic Nicholas Petrovich. It's a mess, a holy mess."

The rest of the day passed somehow, uneventfully and limply. Fenichka might never have existed; she kept to her room like a mouse to its hole. Nicholas Petrovich looked worried. He had received a report that a blight had set in among the wheat crop on which he had set so much store. Paul Petrovich's icy politeness had a crushing effect on everyone, including even Prokofyich. Bazarov began to write a letter to his father, but tore it up and threw it under the table. "If I die," he thought, "they will hear of it; but I shall not die. No, I shall be about for a long time yet." He ordered Peter to present himself next morning as soon as it was light on a matter of some urgency. For some reason, Peter had got it into his head that Bazarov wished to take him to Petersburg. Bazarov went to bed late, and throughout the night was a prey to confused dreams. . . . Madame Odintzov kept looming before him: she assumed the likeness of his mother and was followed by a kitten with black whiskers; the kitten turned out to be Fenichka; and Paul Petrovich merged into a dense forest, which he nevertheless had to fight. At four o'clock Peter woke him; he dressed at once and went out with him.

It was a glorious, fresh morning; tiny mottled clouds stood out, like fleecy lambs, in the transparent azure of the sky; fine beads of dew lay sprinkled over the leaves and grasses, glittering like silver among the cobwebs; the rosy tints of dawn still seemed to cling to the moist dark earth; from the depths of the sky larks showered their songs. Bazarov reached the copse, sat down on the edge of it in the shade, and only then divulged to Peter what service he expected of him. The cultured valet was scared to death; but Bazarov calmed his fears by assuring him that he would have nothing to do except stand at a distance and look on, and that he would incur no responsibility. "And yet," he added, "just think of the important part you will have to play!" Peter threw up his hands, stared at his feet and, all green with fright, leaned back for support against a birch tree.

The road from Maryino skirted the copse; a light dust lay on it, undisturbed by wheel or foot since the previous day. Bazarov could not help glancing down the road, plucking as he did so tufts of grass, and chewing them, repeating to himself, "This is sheer idiocy!" The early morning chill made him shudder a couple of times. . . . Peter glanced at him dismally, but Bazarov only grinned back at him; he was showing himself no coward.

A thud of hooves could be heard in the wood. From behind the trees a peasant emerged. In front of him he was driving a couple of horses hobbled together and, as he went past Bazarov, he stared at him in a strange sort of way without doffing his cap—a circumstance which Peter evidently interpreted as a bad omen. "That fellow is up early too," Bazarov thought, "but at least he is up on business, while we . . . ?"

"They seem to be coming," Peter whispered of a sudden.

Bazarov raised his head and caught sight of Paul Petrovich. Wearing a light check jacket and snow-white trousers, he strode rapidly down the road; under his arm he carried a box wrapped in green cloth.

"I'm so sorry. I believe I have kept you waiting," he said, bowing first to Bazarov and then to Peter, in whose person he for an instant respected something in the nature of a second. "I did not want to wake my valet."

"It doesn't matter," Bazarov replied. "We have just arrived ourselves."

"Ah! so much the better!" Paul Petrovich looked round him. "There is no one about, no one to disturb us. . . . Shall we proceed?"

"By all means."

"I assume that you require no further explanations?"

"I don't."

"Would you like to load the pistols?" Paul Petrovich inquired, taking them out of the box.

"No! You had better do that. I shall measure out the paces. I have longer legs," Bazarov added with a smile. "One, two, three . . ."

"Mr. Bazarov, sir," Peter stammered with difficulty (he was shaking as in a fever), "by your will, I shall now stand aside."

"Four . . . five . . . Yes, stand aside, my good man, stand aside, you may even stand behind a tree and stop your ears, only don't shut your eyes; and if anyone falls, run forward and help them up. Six . . . seven . . . eight . . ." Bazarov came to a halt. "Is that enough?" he asked, turning to Paul Petrovich, "or shall I throw in a couple more paces?"

"As you like," the other replied, stuffing in the second bullet.

"All right, we'll make it two more." Bazarov drew a line on the ground with the toe of his boot. "There's the barrier. By the way, how many paces shall we stand away from it? That's important. We did not discuss it yesterday."

"Ten I should think," Paul Petrovich replied, handing both pistols to Bazarov. "Will you deign to make your choice?"

"I will deign. But you must agree, Paul Petrovich, that our single combat is extraordinary to the point of being comic. Just have a look at our second's physiognomy."

"You are still bent on joking," Paul Petrovich replied. "I do not deny the strange circumstances of our duel, but I consider it my duty to warn you that I intend to fight seriously. *A bon entendeur, salut!*"

"Oh, I don't doubt for a moment that we are both resolved to annihilate each other; but why shouldn't we laugh, too, and combine *utile dulci*? Let's do it: you will address me in French, and I shall reply in Latin."

"I mean to fight quite seriously," Paul Petrovich repeated, taking up his position. Bazarov, for his part, counted off ten paces from the barrier and then came to a stop.

"Are you ready?" Paul Petrovich asked.

"Yes, I am."

"Let us begin."

Bazarov moved forward slowly while Paul Petrovich advanced towards him, his left hand in his pocket and his right gradually raising the pistol. . . . "He is aiming straight at my nose," Bazarov thought to himself, "and how carefully he's aiming too, the bandit! What a horrible sensation. I shall fix my eyes on his watch chain. . . ." Something hissed close to Bazarov's ear, and at that very moment a shot rang out. "I heard it, so I must be all right then." The thought had just time to flash through his head. He took another step and, without aiming, pressed the trigger.

Paul Petrovich gave a slight start and his hand went to his thigh. A trickle of blood flowed down his white trousers.

Bazarov threw away his pistol and approached his adversary. "Are you wounded?" he inquired.

"You had the right to summon me to the barrier," Paul Petrovich said. "This is only a scratch. According to the conditions, each of us has another shot."

"You must excuse me, but that will have to wait till next time," Bazarov replied, putting his arm round Paul Petrovich who was beginning to grow pale. "Now I am no duellist but a doctor, and I must begin by inspecting your wound. Peter! Come here, Peter! Where have you got to?"

"That's sheer nonsense. . . . I don't need any help," Paul Petrovich said, spacing out his words, "and . . . we must . . . again . . ." He was about to tug at his moustache, but his arm sagged, his eyes rolled back, and he lost consciousness.

"Here's a novelty! A swoon! As though there were cause!" Bazarov involuntarily exclaimed, letting Paul Petrovich sink to the ground. "Let's see the damage." He pulled out his handkerchief, wiped the blood, and probed all round the wound. . . . "The bone's intact," he muttered through his teeth. "The bullet has gone through but quite near the surface; one of the muscles, the *vastus externus*, must have been grazed. You will be dancing within three weeks if you feel like it! . . . Ah, a swoon! Ugh, what weak nerves these people have! Just look, how thin-skinned he is!"

"Is he killed?" Peter's quavering voice came fluttering behind his back.

Bazarov looked round.

"Go along quickly and fetch some water, my man. As for him, he'll survive both of us."

But the highly cultured servant did not seem to grasp

his words and remained rooted to the spot. Paul Petrovich slowly opened his eyes.

"It's the end of him!" Peter whispered, making the sign of the cross.

"You're quite right. . . . What an idiotic face!" the wounded gentleman exclaimed, forcing a smile.

"Go and fetch some water, you devil!" Bazarov yelled.

"There's no need. . . . It was only a momentary vertigo. . . . Will you help me to sit up? . . . like that. . . . This scratch only needs a bandage. I can walk home, or the droshky can be fetched. If you are agreeable, we will not renew the duel. You have conducted yourself very nobly . . . to-day, you must note."

"There's no need to dwell on the past," Bazarov replied. "As to the future, it's not worth while racking your brains over it, for it is my intention to depart at once. Now you must allow me to bandage your leg; your wound is not dangerous, but it would be advisable to stop the bleeding. But first of all we must revive this poor mortal."

Bazarov shook Peter by his collar and sent him off to fetch the droshky.

"Take care and don't alarm my brother," Paul Petrovich instructed him. "Don't you dare to say a word to him about this."

Peter rushed off. While he was seeking the droshky, the adversaries sat on the ground without exchanging a word. Paul Petrovich tried to avoid looking at Bazarov; he was reluctant to make peace with him; he was ashamed of his own arrogance, of his failure; he was ashamed of what he had done, although he felt that the incident could not have ended more propitiously. "At least he will not stick round here any longer," he consoled himself, "and that is something to be grateful for." The heavy, awkward silence persisted. They both felt embarrassed. Each of them realized that the other read his thoughts. Such awareness is agreeable between friends, but most disagreeable between enemies, especially when it is impossible for them to thrash it out or to part.

"Have I bandaged your leg too tightly?" Bazarov inquired at last.

"No, it's all right, perfect," Paul Petrovich replied, adding after a while: "We shan't be able to hide this from my brother. We shall have to tell him that we fell out over politics."

"Very well," Bazarov agreed. "You can tell him that I was abusing all Anglomaniacs."

"Excellent. Now what do you suppose that fellow is thinking about us?" Paul Petrovich went on, pointing to the peasant who had driven his hobbled horses past Bazarov a few minutes before the duel and who, as he was now trudging back along the road, played up at the sight of the gentry and doffed his cap.

"Who can tell!" Bazarov replied. "Very likely he is not thinking at all. The Russian peasant is in truth that mysterious Unknown, about whom Mrs. Radcliffe talked so much once upon a time. Who can understand him? He does not understand himself."

"Ah, so that's what you think!" Paul Petrovich began, but suddenly exclaimed: "Look what that idiot, Peter, has done! There's my brother coming at full speed!"

Bazarov turned round and perceived Nicholas Petrovich sitting pale-faced in the droshky. Before it had time to pull up, he leapt out and rushed towards his brother.

"What's the meaning of this?" he cried in an agitated voice. "Eugene Vassilich, I ask you, what does it mean?"

"It's nothing," Paul Petrovich replied. "A pity you were disturbed. Mr. Bazarov and I had a slight altercation, and I have paid slightly for it."

"For heaven's sake! What was it all about?"

"How am I to explain? Mr. Bazarov referred disrespectfully to Sir Robert Peel. I hasten to add I alone am to blame for all that has happened, and Mr. Bazarov has conducted himself perfectly. It was I who challenged him."

"But you are bleeding, my dear!"

"And did you suppose that I had water in my veins? This blood-letting might even do me some good. Isn't that so, doctor? Now help me to get into this droshky and don't look so gloomy. I shall be quite recovered by to-morrow. Fine! Off we go, coachman!"

Nicholas Petrovich followed the droshky on foot; Bazarov was on the point of staying behind. . . .

"I must ask you to attend to my brother," Nicholas Petrovich said to him, "until we fetch another doctor from town."

Bazarov silently nodded.

An hour later Paul Petrovich lay stretched out in bed

with a skilfully bandaged leg. The whole household was in a state of panic. Fenichka had fainted. Nicholas Petrovich wrung his hands in silence while Paul Petrovich continued to laugh and joke, especially with Bazarov; he had donned a fine cambric shirt, a fashionable morning jacket and a smoking-cap, and, forbidding the blinds to be pulled down, jokingly complained of having to abstain from food.

By night-time he had developed a temperature and his head ached. Then the town doctor arrived. Nicholas Petrovich had paid no heed to his brother, nor had Bazarov wished him to do so; the latter sat about in his room all day, looking bilious and angry, and only went in to see the invalid for a moment every now and then. He happened to run into Fenichka a couple of times, but she jumped out of his way in horror. The new doctor recommended cooling drinks and, incidentally, confirmed Bazarov's diagnosis that there was no danger of complications. Nicholas Petrovich told him that his brother had been careless and had wounded himself. To this the doctor had replied, "H'm!" but on receiving there and then twenty-five roubles in silver exclaimed: "You don't say so! That happens often enough. Exactly so!"

No one in the house undressed or went to bed. Nicholas Petrovich kept tiptoeing into his brother's room and tiptoeing out again; Paul Petrovich would doze off, groan gently, or say to him in French, *"Couchez-vous,"* and then ask for a drink. Once Nicholas Petrovich made Fenichka take him a glass of lemonade; Paul Petrovich stared at her fixedly as he emptied the glass. By morning the fever had become a little more pronounced and a slight delirium had set in. At first Paul Petrovich talked wildly; then he suddenly opened his eyes and, seeing his brother standing by the bed and stooping anxiously over him, said, "Isn't it true, Nicholas, that Fenichka has something in common with Nelly?"

"Which Nelly, Paul?"

"Why do you ask? With Princess R. of course. The top part of her face especially. *C'est de la même famille.*"

Nicholas Petrovich made no reply, but inwardly he wondered at the persistent vitality of his elderly brother's sentiments. "So this is how it has all come back," he thought to himself.

"Ah, how I love that worthless creature!" Paul Petrovich

moaned, dejectedly clasping his hands behind his head. "I will suffer no upstart to touch . . ." he muttered a few moments later.

Nicholas Petrovich only sighed; he had no suspicion to whom these words might refer.

Next morning, at about eight o'clock, Bazarov came to see him. He had already had time to pack his belongings and to set at liberty all his frogs, insects and birds.

"You have come to take leave of me?" Nicholas Petrovich asked, rising up to meet him.

"That is so."

"I understand you and fully approve what you are doing. My poor brother is, of course, to blame; he has been punished for it. He told me himself that he had made it impossible for you to act otherwise. I am ready to believe that you could not avoid this duel, which . . . which to a certain extent was undoubtedly due to the persistent antagonism between our mutual outlooks." (Nicholas Petrovich was getting entangled in his words.) "My brother is a man of the old school, hot-tempered and heady. . . . Thank God, the matter ended no worse. I have taken all the necessary steps to avoid publicity. . . ."

"I shall leave my address with you in case of any unpleasant developments," Bazarov remarked casually.

"I hope there will be none. . . . I very much regret that your stay in my house has ended . . . in this fashion. I feel all the more aggrieved, since Arcady . . ."

"No doubt I shall be seeing him," said Bazarov, whom every sort of "explanation" and "protestation" never failed to irritate. "If I don't, I beg you to give him my greetings and to ask him to accept my regrets."

"And I beg . . ." Nicholas Petrovich replied with a bow. But Bazarov had gone out without waiting for him to finish his sentence.

On learning that Bazarov was about to depart, Paul Petrovich expressed the wish to see him and shook hands with him. But even on this occasion Bazarov remained as cold as ice; he realized that Paul Petrovich wished to appear magnanimous. He did not succeed in bidding farewell to Fenichka: he was only able to exchange a few glances with her through a window. Her face looked very sad to him. "A lost soul most likely," he said to himself. . . . "Yet she may scramble out of it somehow!" Peter, on the other hand, was so moved that he wept on his shoulder until Bazarov cooled his ardour by asking him whether "his eyes were not in a damp spot." Dunyasha was obliged to take refuge in the copse in order to conceal her feelings. The man responsible for all this grief clambered into a cart, lit a cigar, and when, as the road branched off after the fourth mile, he saw for the last time the Kirsanovs' domain and the new manor house spread out in a straight line, he spat and muttered to himself, as he wrapped his over- • coat more closely round him, •

"These damned gentry!"

Very soon Paul Petrovich's condition had improved for the better; but he was obliged to keep to his bed for another week. He bore his "imprisonment," as he called it, philo-sophically, but he fussed about his toilet overmuch and had all his articles of apparel sprinkled with eau-de-Cologne. Nicholas Petrovich read the papers to him; Fenichka at-tended to him as before, bringing him chicken broth, lemon-ade, soft-boiled eggs and tea; but a secret terror gripped her each time she entered his room. Paul Petrovich's unexpect-ed action had frightened all the folk in the house and her above all; only Prokofyich did not lose his presence of mind and argued that, in his day, the gentry used to duel— "the gentry only amongst themselves, while they had the like of them outsiders thrashed in the stables for their in-solence."

Fenichka felt almost no twinges of conscience; but she was tortured at times when she pondered on the real cause of the dispute; and Paul Petrovich, too, was in the habit of staring at her so strangely . . . that, even when her back was turned, she could feel his eyes upon her. Her state of continuous inward alarm had made her grow thinner, though, as is often the case, she looked even prettier.

One day—it was morning—Paul Petrovich felt much better and moved from his bed to the sofa. After inquiring about his health, Nicholas had gone off to the threshing-floor. Then Fenichka came in with a cup of tea and, setting it down on the table, was about to leave the room. Paul Petrovich detained her.

"Why are you in such a hurry, Fenichka?" he began. "Have you things to do?"

"No. . . . I must pour out the tea."

"Dunyasha can do that without you; come and sit for

a while with an invalid. By the way, I should like to have
a chat with you."

Fenichka sat down without a word on the edge of an
arm-chair.

"Listen," Paul Petrovich said, tugging at his moustaches.
"I have long wanted to ask you a question. Are you frightened of me?"

"I? ..."

"Yes, you. You never look me straight in the face. It's
as though you were not clear of conscience."

Fenichka blushed, but glanced at Paul Petrovich. He
seemed very strange to her, and her heart quivered gently.

"But your conscience is clear?" he asked her.

"Why shouldn't it be?" she whispered.

"Who knows? However, who is there you could have
offended? Me? That is improbable. Other people in the
house? That's also unlikely. My brother, perhaps? But you
love him, don't you?"

"Yes, I do."

"With all your soul? With all your heart?"

"I love Nicholas Petrovich with all my heart."

"You really mean it? Look at me, Fenichka" (it was the
first time he called her by that name). "You know, lying is
a major sin!"

"I am not lying. If I did not love Nicholas, I would have
nothing to live for."

"And you would not exchange him for anybody?"

"For whom could I exchange him?"

"One never knows! For the gentleman who has just left,
for example?"

Fenichka got up.

"Great Heavens, why do you torment me? What have
I done to you? How can you say such things? ..."

"Fenichka," Paul Petrovich said in a lugubrious voice, "I
saw everything. ..."

"What did you see?"

"Why, over there ... in the summer-house."

Fenichka blushed crimson to the roots of her hair and
the tips of her ears.

"But how was I to blame?" she asked with difficulty.

Paul Petrovitch sat up.

"You are not to blame? No? Not at all?"

"Nicholas Petrovich is the only person I love in the

whole wide world, and I shall love him for ever!" she
burst out with unexpected force, while sobs rose to her
throat. "And as to what you saw, on the Day of Judgment
I shall myself be able to say that I did no wrong; and I
would rather die at once rather than be suspected of such a
thing, of such behaviour behind my benefactor's back, your
brother's back. . . ."

But at this point her voice failed her, and she felt Paul's
hand gripping and pressing hers. . . . She looked at him
and turned to stone. He had grown paler than ever; his
eyes glittered, and what was even more astonishing, a
lonely, heavy tear rolled down his cheek.

"Fenichka!" he gasped in a sort of wondering whisper.
"Love him, do love my brother! He is so very kind and
good! Don't betray him for anyone in the world. Don't
heed anyone else! Just think! What could be more terrible than love unrequited! Never forsake my poor dear
Nicholas!"

Fenichka's eyes had dried and her fear had passed—so
great was her amazement. But imagine her feelings when
Paul Petrovich himself pressed her hand to his lips, and
kept it there, without kissing it but only sighing feverishly. . . .

"Oh, Lord," she thought, "has he had a fit?"

At that instant the whole of his wasted life quivered inside him.

The stairs creaked beneath rapid footsteps. . . . He
pushed her aside, and fell back on the pillow. The door
opened, and Nicholas, cheerful, fresh and rosy-cheeked,
appeared. Mitya, fresh and rosy-cheeked as his father, was
jumping up and down in his arms in only a shirt, while his
bare feet clutched at the large buttons of his father's country
overcoat.

Fenichka threw herself at Nicholas Petrovich and, clasping her arms round him and their son, let her head drop on
his shoulder. Nicholas Petrovich was surprised: the shy
and modest Fenichka normally never showed her affection
in the presence of a third person.

"Is anything the matter?" he asked and, glancing at his
brother, handed Mitya over to her. "You're not feeling
worse, are you?" he inquired, going up to Paul Petrovich.

The latter hid his face in a cambric handkerchief.

"No . . . it's all right . . . it's nothing. . . . On the contrary, I feel much better."

"A pity you were in such a hurry to change over to the sofa. Where are you going now?" Nicholas Petrovich added, turning to Fenichka; but she had already banged the door behind her. "I was going to show you my little champion; he wanted to see his uncle. Why did she take him away? But tell me, what's the matter? Did anything happen between you, tell me?"

"Brother!" Paul Petrovich said solemnly.

Nicholas Petrovich started. He felt pained, he knew not why.

"Brother," Paul Petrovich repeated, "give me your word that you will fulfil a certain request of mine."

"What request? Tell me."

"A most important one. As I see it, your whole happiness depends upon it. I have pondered a great deal on what I am now going to say to you. . . . Brother, you must do your duty, that of an honest and noble man; you must put an end to the temptation and bad example you are setting —you, the best of men!"

"What are you driving at, Paul?"

"Marry Fenichka . . . she loves you; she is—the mother of your son."

Nicholas Petrovich stepped back and threw up his hands.

"Is it you, Paul, I hear saying this? You, whom I always regarded as a resolute opponent of such marriages! And now you recommend it! But don't you realize, it was only out of respect for you that I have not long ago fulfilled what you have now very justly described as my duty?"

"A pity you respected my judgment in this case," Paul Petrovich answered with a wan smile. "I'm beginning to think that Bazarov was right after all in reproaching me for my aristocratic outlook. No, my dear brother, enough of cutting capers and thinking of etiquette: we are already elderly, peaceful folk; it's high time we put aside all pretensions. So be it, as you say, let us fulfil our duty; I am sure we shall also find happiness."

Nicholas Petrovich rushed to embrace his brother.

"At last you have opened my eyes!" he exclaimed. "I wasn't wrong to maintain that you were the kindest and wisest of men; but now I realize that you are as reasonable as you are generous."

"Calm yourself, calm yourself," Paul Petrovich inter-rupted him. "Be careful now and don't press on my leg—the leg of your reasonable brother, who fought a duel, like any lieutenant, when on the verge of fifty. And so, we have settled the matter; Fenichka will be my . . . *belle sœur.*"

"My dear Paul! But what will Arcady say?"

"Arcady? Why, he'll be simply delighted! Marriage is not a principle he upholds, but his feeling of equality will be flattered. Yes, indeed, why have we still got all these castes *au dix-neuvième siècle?*"

"Ah, Paul, Paul! Let me kiss you again. Don't be alarmed about your leg, I shall be very careful."

The brothers embraced.

"Now what do you think? Should we not inform her at once of your intention?" Paul Petrovich asked.

"Why hurry?" Nicholas Petrovich retorted. "Why? Have you already discussed it?"

"Discussed it? *Quelle idée!*"

"Well, everything is in order then. First you must get better; we shall not overlook this, we must think it over, consider it. . . ."

"But you have already decided?"

"Of course I have, and I thank you from the bottom of my heart. But now I must leave you; you must rest; all this excitement is bad for you. . . . We shall talk it over very soon. Now go to sleep, my dear, and may God grant you health!"

"Why does he thank me?" Paul Petrovich thought when left alone. "Doesn't it depend entirely on him? As for myself, I shall go off somewhere as soon as he gets married, as far as possible, to Dresden or Florence, and there I shall stay till I fade away."

Paul Petrovich moistened his forehead with eau-de-Cologne and closed his eyes. In the radiant light of day, his handsome, wasted head reclined on the white pillow like the head of a corpse. . . . Indeed, he was a corpse.

XXV

IN the shade of a lofty ash tree, Katya and Arcady were sitting on a turf bench in the garden at Nicolskoye; allowing her elongated body to assume an elegant posture known to sportsmen as the "Hare's stance," Fifi had chosen a spot for herself on the ground nearby. Arcady and Katya were both silent; in his hands he held a half-open book, and she was engaged in picking crumbs from the bottom of her basket and throwing them to a small family of sparrows which, with the cowardly persistence characteristic of them, hopped about and chirped right under her feet. A faint rustling breeze among the foliage of the ash tree was shifting pale-gold patches of sunlight back and forth over the shadowy path and over Fifi's tawny back; Arcady and Katya were both immersed in unrelieved shadow: only now and then did a bright gleam of sunshine illumine her hair. They were both silent; but their very silence and the way they sat together spoke eloquently of their confiding intimacy; each looked unmindful of the other and yet full of an inward joy at being so close together. The expressions on their faces had altered, too, since we had last seen them; Arcady appeared more collected, Katya more lively and enterprising.

"Don't you think," Arcady began, "the Russians have been right to name the ash tree *yasen, yasen*—lucent? No tree is as lucent when the sun shines."

Katya looked up and said, "Yes," and Arcady thought, "She at least does not reproach me for using beautiful language."

"I don't like Heine," Katya said, with her eyes indicating the book in Arcady's hands, "when he is either sarcastic or plaintive. I prefer his pensive and nostalgic moods."

"And I prefer his gibing tone," Arcady remarked.

"That's the residue of your sardonic turn of mind."

("Residue!" Arcady thought. "If only Bazarov could hear that!")

"You just wait," Katya went on, "we shall transform you."

"Who will transform me? You?"

"Who? Why, my sister, and Porfiry Platonich, with whom you have now stopped quarrelling, and auntie, whom you accompanied to church the day before yesterday."

"I couldn't very well refuse! And as for Anna Sergeyevna, you must remember that she agrees with Eugene on many points."

"My sister was under his influence then, just as you were."

"As I *was*! Why? Have you noticed any signs of my breaking away from that influence?"

Katya made no reply.

"I know," Arcady went on, "you never took to him."

"I am not in a position to judge him."

"Do you know what, Catherine Sergeyevna? Every time I hear you say that, I disbelieve you. . . . There is no man living who is not capable of being judged by any of us! You are merely quibbling."

"Very well, then let me tell you that he . . . it's not that I don't like him, but I have no contact with him. It's as though I had nothing in common with him . . . just as you haven't either."

"Why do you think that?"

"How am I to explain? . . . He's like a wild beast, we're just domestic animals."

"Am I a domestic animal too?"

Katya nodded her head. Arcady scratched behind his ear.

"Now listen, Catherine Sergeyevna. You are really being very offensive."

"Why? Would you prefer to be a wild beast?"

"Not wild, but strong and energetic."

"You can't just wish that. . . . Your friend does not *wish* it, he *is* like that."

"H'm! So you assume that he has exercised a great influence on Anna Sergeyevna?"

"Yes. But no one can dominate her for long," Katya added softly.

"Why do you think so?"

"She is very proud. . . . I didn't mean that. . . . I meant that she sets great store by her independence."

"Who doesn't?" Arcady asked, while the thought flashed through his mind, "What's he got to do with it?" "What's she got to do with it?" was the thought that also occurred to Katya. The same ideas tend to occur simultaneously to young people who are in the habit of seeing each other often and of being on terms of intimacy.

Arcady smiled, and coming a little closer to Katya whispered to her:

"Now confess, you are a bit frightened of *her*."

"Of whom?"

"*Her*," Arcady repeated significantly.

"And you?" Katya asked him in her turn.

"I also. You will note I said 'I also.' "

Katya wagged a finger at him.

"I'm surprised at you," she began. "My sister has never been so well disposed to you as just now; a great deal more so than when you first arrived."

"You don't mean it!"

"And you haven't noticed it? Aren't you pleased?"

Arcady reflected for a moment.

"What have I done to win Anna Sergeyevna's favour? Perhaps it's because I brought her your mother's letters?"

"That may be one reason; but there are others which I shan't tell you."

"Why won't you?"

"I won't."

"Oh, I know how stubborn you are."

"I am stubborn."

"And observant."

Katya glanced sideways at Arcady.

"Perhaps you find that irritating? What are you thinking about now?"

"I was wondering how you had acquired that acute sense of observation which is so much a part of you. You are so shy and distrustful; you keep everyone at bay. . . ."

"I have lived so much alone, and willy-nilly that stimulates the imagination. But do I keep everyone at bay?"

Arcady cast a grateful glance at Katya.

"That is all very fine," he continued, "but people in your position, I mean persons of your means, have this gift but rarely; it's as hard for them to see the truth as for a Tsar."

"But I'm not rich."

Arcady was astonished and failed to grasp at once what Katya had said.

Then it dawned on him. "The property is really her sister's," he thought, and the idea did not displease him.

"How well you put it!" he exclaimed.

"What do you mean?"

"You put it so well—quite simply, without any embarrassment or undue emphasis. Incidentally, I imagine that there must be something distinctive, a sort of feeling of pride in a person who realizes and acknowledges his poverty."

"Thanks to my sister, I have been spared the experience of poverty; I referred to my situation only because it cropped up in the conversation."

"So be it! But you must admit that you have just a particle of the pride I referred to a moment ago."

"For instance?"

"For instance—excuse me for asking the question—but you would not consent to marry a rich man, would you?"

"If I loved him very much. . . . No, maybe, even then I wouldn't accept him."

"Ah, you see!" Arcady exclaimed, adding after a while: "And why wouldn't you accept him?"

"Because even folk-songs tell one that such a marriage does not make a happy pair."

"Perhaps it's your ambition to dominate or . . ."

"Oh, no! Why do you say that? On the contrary, I am ready to yield, I can understand that; that is happiness, but a life of utter submission. . . . No, I've had my fill of it, as it is."

"Your fill of it, as it is," Arcady repeated. "Yes, yes," he went on, "I can see you're of the same stock as Anna Sergeyevna; you are quite as independent as she is, but more secretive. . . . I am positive that you would never be the first to declare your feelings, however overpowering and holy they may be. . . ."

"How could it be otherwise?" Katya inquired.

"You are quite as intelligent; you have as much character, if not more than she. . . ."

"Please don't draw comparisons between me and my sister," Katya hurriedly interrupted him, "I stand to lose. You have evidently forgotten that my sister is beautiful as well as intelligent, and . . . you especially, Arcady, should not say such things, with such an assumed air of seriousness into the bargain."

"What do you mean by 'you especially'? And why do you suppose that I am not serious?"

"Of course you are not serious."

"You think so? And what if I do believe in what I am saying? If I feel that I have not even expressed myself forcibly enough?"

"I don't quite understand you."

"Really? Well, it's as clear as daylight now: to be precise, I find that I praised your sense of observation too highly."

"What do you mean?"

Arcady turned away without replying, while Katya found a few more crumbs in the basket and began to throw them to the sparrows; but she jerked her arm too violently, and the sparrows flew off in alarm before they had time to peck at the crumbs.

"Catherine Sergeyevna!" Arcady exclaimed of a sudden. "It may be all the same to you, but I should like to state that, far from having any preference for your sister, I wouldn't exchange you for anyone else in the world."

As though frightened of the words that had just burst from his lips, he got up and quickly walked away. Katya let drop both her hands and the basket into her lap, and for a while sat with drooping head, gazing after Arcady. Gradually her cheeks were suffused with scarlet; but her lips remained unsmiling, and her dark eyes shone with perplexity and another as yet nameless feeling.

"Are you alone?" Anna Sergeyevna's voice rang out close by. "I thought you went into the garden with Arcady."

Katya showed no haste as she looked round at her sister (dressed elegantly and with careful taste, Anna stood on the path, tickling Fifi's ears with the point of her open parasol), and with deliberation said: "I am alone."

"I can see that," the other replied, laughing. "Then he must have gone in."

"Yes."

"Were you reading together?"

"Yes."

Anna Sergeyevna took Katya under the chin and raised her face.

"You did not quarrel, I hope?"

"No," Katya replied, gently disengaging herself from her sister's hand.

"What a solemn answer! I expected to find him here and was going to ask him to take a stroll with me. He has begged me so often to go for a walk with him. By the way, your new boots have just arrived from town, go and try them on: I noticed yesterday that your old pair were quite worn out. In general, you don't pay enough attention to your footwear and you have such pretty little feet! And you have such lovely hands too—only they are a trifle too large; so you must make the most of your feet. But you are no coquette."

Anna Sergeyevna went down the path, her attractive dress making a slight rustling sound; Katya rose from the bench and, picking up the volume of Heine, went her way too—but not to try on her boots.

"Pretty little feet," she thought to herself as she slowly and lightly mounted the stone steps of the terrace, which was scorching in the sun. "Pretty little feet, you say. . . . Well, he will find himself kneeling at those very feet."

But at once she felt ashamed of herself, and nimbly ran upstairs.

As Arcady was walking down the corridor towards his room, the butler caught up with him and announced that Mr. Bazarov was waiting for him.

"Eugene!" Arcady muttered almost apprehensively. "How long has he been here?"

"He has just arrived. He ordered me not to announce him to madame, but to take him straight to your room."

"Can anything have happened at home?" was Arcady's first thought as he ran hurriedly upstairs and flung open the door of his room. On seeing Bazarov, he was reassured, although a more experienced eye would probably have discerned many signs of an inward perturbation in the unexpected visitor's normally energetic but somewhat sunken face. He was sitting on the window-sill, a dusty overcoat slung over his shoulders and a cap pulled over his eyes; he did not get up even when Arcady, with noisy exclamations, flung his arms round his neck.

"How unexpected! What fates bring you here?" he kept repeating as he fussed about the room, like a person who imagines that he is delighted and wishes to demonstrate the fact. "There's nothing wrong at home, is there? Everyone's well, I suppose?"

"Everything is all right at home, but not everyone is well," Bazarov replied. "Now don't be such a chatterbox, but tell them to bring me a drink of *kvas*. Sit down and listen to what I have to tell you very briefly but, I hope, forcibly."

Arcady calmed down and heard Bazarov describe his duel with Paul Petrovich. Arcady was greatly astonished and even depressed; but he did not think it necessary to disclose this; he contented himself with inquiring whether his uncle's wound was really a slight one. On being assured that the wound was extremely interesting in every respect except the medical one, he forced a smile in spite of a feeling of anguish and shame. Bazarov seemed to have an inkling of this.

"Yes, brother," he said, "that's what comes of living among these feudal barons. You are liable to become like them and to join in their knightly tourneys. Well, I'm off to visit my pater," Bazarov concluded, "and I just dropped in to see you on the way . . . 'in order to inform you of all this' I might have said, if I did not think it stupid to tell useless lies. No, I dropped in here—the devil alone knows why! You see, sometimes it pays a man to grab himself by a tuft of hair and jerk himself out as one might pull a radish from its bed. A few days ago I succeeded in doing this. But I was overcome with a desire to have one more peep at what I was leaving behind—at the bed in which I was rooted."

"I hope these words don't apply to me," Arcady protested with emotion. "I hope you do not intend to cut yourself off *from me*."

Bazarov stared at him fixedly, almost piercingly.

"And would that upset you very much? My impression is that *you* have already cut yourself off from me. How fresh and spruce you look. . . . Your affairs with Anna Sergeyevna must be making excellent progress."

"What affairs of mine with Anna Sergeyevna?"

"Wasn't it for her sake that you left town and came here, my little warbler? Incidentally, how are those Sundayschools getting on? Aren't you in love with her? Or do you want to appear modest now?"

"Eugene, you know I have always been frank with you; I assure you, I swear you are mistaken."

"H'm! That's a new one," Bazarov exclaimed under his breath. "But you mustn't excite yourself, I don't care a jot. A romantic might say, 'I feel our ways are beginning to diverge,' but I tell you quite plainly that we have palled on each other."

"Eugene . . ."

"My dear, that's no misfortune; the world is full of things that pall on one. And now I wonder whether it isn't time for us to say farewell. Ever since I've been here, I have felt sick, as though surfeited by too much reading of Gogol's letters to the wife of the Governor of Kaluga. Incidentally, I gave orders for the horses not to be unharnessed."

"But look here, this is impossible!"

"Why?"

"Quite apart from me, it would show a great lack of respect for Anna Sergeyevna, who would certainly wish to see you."

"Well, you're mistaken there."

"On the contrary, I am convinced that I am right," Arcady protested.

"Why pretend? And since we have come to that point, didn't you call in here for her sake?"

"The observation may be just, but you are nevertheless mistaken."

But Arcady was right. Anna Sergeyevna did want to see Bazarov, and she sent the butler to ask him to call on her. Bazarov changed his clothes before seeing her: as it turned out, he had packed his new suit in such a way as to have it handy.

Anna Sergeyevna received him in the drawing-room and not in the study where he had so unexpectedly confessed his love for her. She graciously extended the tips of her fingers to him, but her face showed signs of uncontrollable tension.

"Anna Sergeyevna," Bazarov hastened to say, "I must begin by reassuring you. You see before you a simple mortal, who has already recovered his senses and who hopes that others, too, have forgotten his foolishness. I am now going away for a considerable period and, as you will agree, though I am no tenderfoot, the idea that you may still remember me with disgust would be an unhappy one for me to carry away."

Anna Sergeyevna gave a deep sigh, such as a climber might utter on reaching at last a high mountain peak, and then a smile lit up her face. For a second time she extended her hand to Bazarov and returned the pressure of his own.

"Let sleeping dogs lie," she replied, "especially as, to be quite frank, I was also to blame, if not by being coquettish, then in some other fashion. In short, let us be friends as before. The past was a dream, wasn't it? And who ever remembers dreams?"

"Who indeed? And, besides, love . . . Why, it's merely an imaginary feeling."

"You don't say so? I'm very glad to hear it."

So spoke Anna Sergeyevna, and so spoke Bazarov. They both believed that they spoke the truth. But did their words really contain truth, complete truth? They could not be sure of that, nor could the author. But their conversation sounded as if they understood each other perfectly.

In the course of it, Anna Sergeyevna inquired what Bazarov had been doing at the Kirsanovs'. He was on the point of telling her about his duel with Paul Petrovich, but restrained himself at the thought that she might think he was trying to show off, and told her instead that he had been working all the time.

"And I had a fit of depression, Heaven knows why," Anna Sergeyevna said. "Then I recovered; your friend Arcady arrived, and I fell into my groove again, the part that suits me."

"And what is that part, may I ask?"

"That of an aunt, governess, mother, call it what you like. By the way, you know, I had never previously fathomed your close friendship with Arcady; I used to attach very little significance to him. But now I know him better and am convinced of his intelligence. . . . But, above all, he is young, young . . . not like you and me, Eugene Vassilich."

"Is he as shy as ever in your company?" Bazarov inquired.

"Why? Was he . . ." Anna Sergeyevna started to say but, after a moment of reflection, added: "He is more confiding now, he talks to me. Formerly he used to avoid me. However, I did not seek his company either. He's more friendly with Katya." A feeling of gloom came over Bazarov. "Women can't help lying!" he thought to himself. "You were saying that he avoided you," he exclaimed with a chilly smile, "but it was probably no secret from you that he was in love with you?"

"What? He too?" burst from Anna Sergeyevna's lips.

"He too," Bazarov repeated with a meek bow. "You don't mean to say that you hadn't realized it, that I am telling you something new?"

Anna Sergeyevna lowered her eyes.

"You are mistaken, Eugene Vassilich."

"I don't think so. But perhaps I should not have broached the subject." "Now don't lie in the future," he added to himself.

"Why should you not have broached it? But I think that even here you attach too much significance to a momentary impression. I am beginning to suspect that you are inclined to exaggerate."

"Let's drop the subject, Anna Sergeyevna."

"Why should we?" she retorted, while at the same time changing the topic. She still felt ill at ease with Bazarov, although she had told him, and had assured herself, that the past had been forgotten. She experienced a slight pressure of fear when engaged in the simplest conversation with him or even when joking with him. Such is often the case with people who are travelling in a ship at sea: they talk and laugh heedlessly just as they would on solid ground; but at the slightest stoppage, the least sign of anything out of order, their faces will at once reflect a feeling of extraordinary alarm, thus showing their persistent awareness of a persistent danger.

Anna Sergeyevna's talk with Bazarov did not last very long. She grew thoughtful, made vague replies, and at last suggested that they should pass into the drawing-room where they found the princess and Katya. "And where is Arcady Nicolaievich?" the lady of the house inquired. On learning that he had not been seen for over an hour, she sent a servant to look for him. He was not easily to be found: he had penetrated into the very depths of the garden and, with his head propped on his folded hands, sat there plunged in thought. His reflections were profound and grave, but not despondent. He knew that Anna Sergeyevna was closeted alone with Bazarov, but he felt less jealous than before; on the contrary, his face looked calm and radiant; his features betrayed amazement and joy, as though he had come to some decision.

XXVI

THE late Mr. Odintzov had disapproved of innovations, but had tolerated a "certain display of noble taste"; as a consequence he had built something in the nature of a Greek portico, constructed of Russian brick, on a spot in his garden between the hothouse and the pond. On the blind, back wall of this portico six niches had been prepared for the statues which Odintzov had intended to order from abroad. These statues were intended to represent Solitude, Silence, Meditation, Melancholy, Modesty and Sensibility. One of these statues, that of the goddess of Silence with a finger held to her mouth, was actually delivered and set up. But the very same day her nose was chipped off by some of the farm lads and, although the local plasterer had offered to take it upon himself to patch up a nose "twice as good as her old one," Odintzov had had her stored away, and the goddess found herself relegated to a corner of the threshing-barn, where she remained standing for many years, exciting the superstitious awe of the peasant women. The façade of the portico had long overgrown with thick shrubbery: only the capitals of the columns could be perceived jutting out above the tangle of foliage. Inside the portico itself it was cool even in the midday heat. Anna Sergeyevna had avoided the spot ever since she had come across a hedgehog there, but Katya made frequent use of it and often sat on the roomy stone bench under one of the niches. Here, in the cool shade, she read and worked, or surrendered herself to that sensation of perfect peace with which we are all presumably familiar and whose charm lies in a barely conscious and silent observation of the sweeping wave of life that for ever rolls all round us as well as within us.

On the day following Bazarov's arrival, Katya was seated on her favourite bench while Arcady sat beside her. He had persuaded her to accompany him to the portico.

There was still an hour to go before breakfast; the dewy morning had already surrendered to the heat of day. Ar-

cady's face wore the same expression as on the previous
day, but Katya's showed signs of worry. Immediately after
morning tea, her sister had called her into the study and,
following that preliminary display of affection which invariably alarmed Katya a little, had counselled her to be
more guarded in her manner towards Arcady and, in particular, to avoid those solitary talks with him which, according to her, had already been remarked on by her aunt and
the whole of the household. Moreover, Anna Sergeyevna
had already felt out of sorts the previous evening; and Katya
herself felt ill at ease, as though conscious of her own guilt.
Thus, when she had acceded to Arcady's fresh request, she
promised to herself that this would be the last time.

"Catherine Sergeyevna," he began with a certain bashful
fluency, "ever since I have had the good fortune to stay
in the same house as yourself, I have had occasion to discuss many topics with you, and yet there is an important
. . . question I have not yet broached. Yesterday, you remarked that I had altered since my stay here," he added,
catching but at the same time avoiding the questioning look
that Katya had fixed upon him. "I have indeed altered in
a great many respects, and you yourself know that better
than anyone else—you know it, for it is really to you I owe
this transformation."

"I? . . . To me?" Katya stammered.

"I am no longer the cocksure youth I was when I first
arrived here," Arcady went on. "It's not for nothing I have
just turned twenty-three. As before, I have every wish to
lead a useful life, and I still want to devote all my energies
to the pursuit of truth; but I can no longer seek my ideal
where I did before; I can perceive it now . . . much closer
to hand. Until recently I failed to understand myself, I set
myself tasks above my capacity. But quite recently my eyes
were opened, thanks to a certain emotion. . . . I know I am
not expressing myself very clearly, but I hope you will
understand me. . . ."

Katya made no reply, but she stopped looking at Arcady.

"I assume," he continued with greater emotion, while a
chaffinch, perched in the foliage above his head, poured out
its enraptured song, "I assume it is the duty of every honest
man to be quite frank with those . . . with those who . . .
in a word, with those whom he holds dear, and so I . . . I
intend . . ."

But at this point Arcady's eloquence betrayed him; he stammered, grew confused, and was obliged to stop for a while; Katya still kept her eyes lowered. She looked as if she failed to understand where all this was leading and waited to be enlightened.

"I can see that I am going to surprise you," Arcady resumed, gathering strength, "all the more so, since this emotion of mine has some bearing . . . some bearing, you will note, on you. I seem to remember your reproaching me yesterday with a lack of seriousness," Arcady pursued, looking like a man who had just plunged into a bog and feels himself sinking deeper and deeper with each step he takes, but who nevertheless presses on in the hope of getting across more quickly. "That reproach is often levelled . . . is often applied to young people even when they no longer merit it; and if I had more confidence . . ." ("Help me now, why don't you help me!" Arcady inwardly exclaimed in desperation, but Katya sat on as before without even turning her head.) "If I might hope . . ."

"If I were only convinced of the truth of what you say," Anna Sergeyevna's clear voice rang out at that moment.

Arcady at once stopped talking, and Katya grew pale. A path ran past the shrubbery which concealed the portico. Along it Anna Sergeyevna was strolling with Bazarov. Katya and Arcady could not see them, but they could hear each word they uttered, the rustling of their dress and the sound of their breathing. They advanced a few steps and then, as though deliberately, came to a halt right in front of the portico.

"Now you see," Anna Sergeyevna went on, "we both made a mistake; we are no longer young, either of us, and I in particular; we have experienced much and are tired; we are, both of us—why be modest?—intelligent: we became interested in each other, our curiosity was roused . . . and then . . ."

"And I went stale," Bazarov interjected.

"You know very well that was not the reason why we parted. But whatever it might have been, we felt no absolute need of each other, and that was the main reason. . . . We were . . . how shall I put it? . . . too alike. We failed to recognize that at once. On the other hand, Arcady . . ."

"You feel the need of him?" Bazarov asked.

"Don't talk like that, Eugene Vassilich. You told me

yourself that he was not indifferent to me, and I myself
have always had the impression. I realize that I am old
enough to be his aunt, but I have no wish to conceal from
you that he has been in my thoughts more often. I find his
fresh and youthful sentiments quite delightful. . . ."

" 'Enchanting' is the word more commonly used in such
contexts," Bazarov interrupted her; a trace of anger could
be detected in his calm but hollow voice. "Yesterday
Arcady was secretive with me; he did not mention either
you or your sister. . . . A revealing symptom that."

"He treats Katya like a brother," Anna Sergeyevna said.
"And that is what I like about him, though perhaps I
shouldn't allow them to be so intimate."

"Are you speaking as . . . a sister?" Bazarov drawled.

"Of course . . . but why are we standing here? Let's walk
on. What a strange conversation we're having, don't you
think? Could I ever have expected to speak to you in this
way? You, I am afraid of you . . . and yet at the same time,
I trust you, because fundamentally you are very kind."

"In the first place, I am not at all kind; and in the second,
I don't mean anything to you now, and that's why you think
me kind. . . . It's like placing a wreath at a corpse's head."

"Eugene Vassilich, it isn't in our power . . ." Anna
Sergeyevna began to say; but a breeze rustled among the
foliage and wafted her words away.

"Of course, you are free," Bazarov was heard to say after
a while. But the rest was lost, the steps faded away . . . and
silence supervened.

Arcady turned to face Katya. She was sitting in the same
position as before, only her head had sunk even lower.

"Catherine Sergeyevna," he said in a trembling voice,
clenching his fists, "I love you for ever, irrevocably, and I
love only you. I wish to tell you this, to learn what you
think, and to ask your hand; I am not rich, but I am prepared to make every sacrifice. . . . Why don't you reply?
Do you believe me? Do you think I am speaking lightly?
But just remember these last few days! Aren't you convinced that everything else—yes, everything else, has long
ago melted into thin air? Look at me now, just say one
word . . . I love . . . I love you . . . you must believe me!"

Katya's eyes looked grave and radiant as she glanced up
at Arcady and, after reflecting for an instant, she replied
with barely a smile, "Yes."

Arcady leapt from the bench.

"Yes! You said 'yes,' Catherine Sergeyevna! But what do you mean? That I love you? That you believe me? . . . Or . . . or . . . I dare not say it. . . ."

"Yes," Katya repeated, and this time he understood her. He grasped her long, lovely hands and, breathless with joy, pressed them to his heart. He could hardly stand on his feet and kept repeating, "Katya, Katya . . . ," while she, in her perfect innocence burst out crying, laughing the while at her own tears. Who has not seen such tears in the eyes of his beloved has never experienced the degree of terrestrial happiness of which man is capable when stunned with gratitude and overcome with shyness.

Early next morning Anna Sergeyevna gave orders for Bazarov to be summoned to her study and, with a forced laugh, handed him a folded letter. It was from Arcady: in it he asked for her sister's hand.

Bazarov quickly scanned the letter and made an effort to hide the feeling of spiteful pleasure which momentarily flared up in his breast.

"So that's it," he exclaimed. "And as recently as yesterday you assumed that he had only a brotherly regard for Catherine Sergeyevna. What will you do now?"

"What do *you* advise me to do?" Anna Sergeyevna asked him, continuing to laugh.

"I assume," Bazarov replied, also with a laugh, although, like Anna, he felt anything but gay and far from amused. "I assume that we must give the young couple our blessing. It's a good match in every way; Kirsanov is quite well off, an only son, and his father is decent enough—he's not likely to offer any objections."

Anna Sergeyevna paced up and down the room, her face alternately going white and red.

"You think so?" she said. "Well, I see no obstacles. . . . I'm glad for Katya's sake . . . and Arcady Nicolaievich's. Naturally, I shall wait for the father's reply. I shall send Arcady in person to parley with him. As it happens, I was right yesterday when I told you that we were growing old, both of us. . . . How was it I noticed nothing? I'm surprised at myself!"

Anna Sergeyevna laughed again, and then at once turned away.

"Young folk are very wily these days," Bazarov remarked, laughing also. "Well, good-bye," he started to say after a pause. "I hope you will bring this affair to a very happy conclusion. I shall show my joy from afar."

Madame Odintzov turned quickly to face him.

"Are you going away? Why not stay *now*? Do stay . . . you are such an amusing conversationalist. . . . Talking to you is like walking on the edge of a precipice. At first one is frightened, then one picks up courage. Do stay."

"Thank you for suggesting it, Anna Sergeyevna, and also for your flattering opinion of my conversational talent. But I find that I have been mixing too long already in company alien to me. Flying-fish can stay in the air for a while, but very soon they must dive back into the water; with your permission I must also plunge back into my real element."

Madame Odintzov stared at Bazarov. A bitter smile twisted her pale face. "This man loved me once," she thought—and a feeling of compassion for him swept over her as, with every token of sympathy, she offered him her hand.

But he saw through it. "No!" he exclaimed, stepping back. "I may be poor, but till now I have never accepted charity. Good-bye, and look after yourself."

"I am positive this is not our last meeting," Anna Sergeyevna replied as he bowed and left the room.

"So you have taken it into your head to make yourself a nest," he said that day to Arcady, squatting on the floor and packing his valise. "Well? It's a good thing. Only you shouldn't have been so crafty. I expected you to pursue a different line. Or, maybe, you were yourself staggered by it all."

"I was not exactly expecting this outcome when I took leave of you," Arcady replied. "But why are you being so crafty yourself and saying, 'It's a good thing,' when I know perfectly well your opinion of the engagement?"

"Ah, dear friend, how you do express yourself!" Bazarov exclaimed. "Just look at what I am doing: just because there's room in the valise here am I stuffing it with hay: it's the same with our life's valise: we pack it full of anything that comes to hand, just to avoid leaving an empty space. Don't be offended, please: you will probably remember the opinion I have always entertained of Catherine Sergeyevna. Some young ladies have the reputation of being clever because they sigh cleverly: but your young lady can look after herself, and do it so well that she will look after you too—well, that's how it should be." He banged down the lid of the valise and rose from the floor. "And now, in parting, let me tell you again—there is no point in deceiving ourselves—that we are parting for good, and you know that yourself . . . you have acted wisely; you were not made for our bitter, harsh and unsettled life. You have only youth, ardour and passion, but no arrogance or vehemence; and for the ends we pursue, that is quite useless. Your fellow noblemen cannot get much further than well-bred resignation or well-bred indignation, and that's just trivial. For instance, the likes of you won't stand up and fight—and yet you imagine you're heroes—but we insist on fighting. Yes, that's the trouble! The dust of us would bite your eyes out, the dirt of us would soil you, and anyhow you haven't reached our stature yet; unconsciously you admire yourselves, you find pleasure in railing against yourselves; but we find all that boring—give us fresh victims! We are made to break other men! You may be a good lad; but you're too soft, a liberal gentleman—*ay volla too,* as my father would say."

"Is this our final farewell, Eugene?" Arcady mournfully asked. "And have you nothing more to say to me?"

Bazarov scratched the back of his head.

"Yes, I have," he exclaimed. "I have other things to say to you, but I shan't say them now because that would be sheer romanticism: it would be too sugary. Get married as quickly as you can; start a nest of your own, and beget plenty of children. They are bound to have brains, if only because they will be born in the right age—not as we were. Ah! The horses are ready, I see, time to be off! I have said good-bye to everyone. Well? Shall we embrace?"

Arcady threw his arms round the neck of his former mentor and friend, and the tears flooded to his eyes.

"What it is to be young!" Bazarov said calmly. "I have every confidence in Catherine Sergeyevna. Just you wait, she will console you soon enough."

"Farewell, brother!" he said to Arcady after climbing into the cart and, pointing to a pair of jackdaws sitting side by side on the stable roof, added: "There's a fine example for you! Take it to heart!"

"What do you mean?" Arcady asked.

"What? Are you so weak in natural history? Or have you forgotten that the jackdaw is the most respectable of family birds? Let him be your model! . . . Farewell, *signor*."

With a rattle the cart rolled away.

Bazarov had spoken the truth. While conversing with Katya that evening, Arcady became completely oblivious of his former mentor. He was already beginning to submit to her, and Katya sensed this without being surprised. Next day he had to drive to Maryino to see his father. Anna showed no desire to disturb the young people, and it was only for the sake of decorum that she did not leave them alone for too long. The news of the impending wedding had plunged the princess into a state of terrible rage, and very considerately Anna Sergeyevna kept her out of the way. At first, she was afraid lest the spectacle of their happiness might not prove a trifle painful; but, as it turned out, the opposite was true: far from paining her, their happiness engrossed and finally won her over completely. This made Anna Sergeyevna rejoice in spite of her depression. "Bazarov was evidently right," she thought, "it was curiosity, mere curiosity, a partiality for a quiet life, and egoism . . ."

"Children!" she exclaimed aloud. "Tell me, is love an imaginary feeling?"

But neither Katya nor Arcady grasped what she meant. They fought shy of her; they could not forget the conversation which they had inadvertently overheard. However, very soon Anna Sergeyevna was destined to reassure them; nor did it prove difficult for her, for she had recovered her peace of mind.

XXVII

BAZAROV'S old parents were all the more overjoyed at their son's arrival as they had hardly expected him. Arina Vlassyevna was so excited and fussed so much about the house that Vassily Ivanovich promptly likened her to a partridge: the tuft of her short blouse really did give her a bird-like air. He contented himself with a few vague grunts and with chewing the amber mouthpiece of his pipe; gripping the back of his neck, he swivelled his head round as though trying to verify that it was well screwed on, opened his mouth wide and guffawed noiselessly.

"I have come to stay for a whole six weeks, old chap," Bazarov informed him. "I want to work, so please don't be in my way."

"You'll forget the look of my face, that's how I shall be in your way!" Vassily Ivanovich retorted.

He fulfilled his promise. After lodging his son in the study as before, he not only kept out of the way but also restrained his wife from any superfluous displays of tender emotion. "Last time, we got a little on Yeniushka's nerves, my dear," he said to her. "We must be more prudent now." The old lady agreed with her husband, but derived very little benefit from it, for now she saw her son only at table and was much too intimidated to talk to him. "Yeniushinka!" she would call out every now and then—but before he had time to look round, she would pick at the tassels of her handbag and murmur: "Oh, it's nothing, nothing at all, just an exclamation!" And then she would go to her husband and, putting her hand under her chin, say: "My dear, how can I find out what Yeniushka would like for dinner? Cabbage or beetroot soup?" "Why didn't you ask him yourself?" "Oh, I'd only annoy him!" However, very soon Bazarov stopped locking himself in: the fever of work dropped away from him, and gave way to gloomy nostalgia and aching restlessness. A strange fatigue was apparent in all he did; even his normally firm and impetuously resolute stride had altered. He stopped taking long walks and began to look round for distraction; he now took his tea in the drawing-room, sauntered about the orchard with his father and had "silent smokes" with him; once he even asked after Father Alexei. At first, his father was delighted at this change, but his joy was short-lived.

"Yeniushka is breaking my heart," he confided dolefully to his wife. "It's not that he is dissatisfied or angry, that wouldn't matter so much, but he seems upset and sad—that is what's so dreadful. He keeps mum all the time; I'd rather he lost his temper with us. He's losing weight, and the colour of his face is none too healthy."

"Oh Lord, Oh Lord!" the old woman whispered. "I'd

hang a holy charm round his neck, but he wouldn't let me."

With great discretion, Vassily Ivanovich tried several times to question Bazarov about his work, his health, and about Arcady. . . . But Bazarov's replies were reluctant and casual and, once, observing that his father was gradually trying to worm something out of him in conversation, he said with chagrin: "Why do you always tiptoe after me? It's worse than ever."

"Never mind, I didn't mean it!" the wretched father hastily replied. So his politic approach bore no fruit.

One day, in the hope of stirring his son's sympathy, he broached the subject of the imminent emancipation of the serfs and of progress; but the latter only answered indifferently: "As I was walking yesterday by the side of a fence, I heard some local lads bawling, instead of some old song, this new refrain:

> The appointed hour is drawing nigh,
> And love comes welling to the heart. . . .

That's progress for you."

Occasionally, Bazarov went for a stroll to the village and, in his usual bantering tone, engaged some peasant in conversation.

"Well, old man," he would say to him, "tell me about your notions of life. They say that the whole power and future of Russia depends on you folk, and that you will open a new period of history—you will give us a real language and laws." Thus addressed, the peasant would either make no reply at all, or would answer somewhat in this strain: "That we might . . . also, it depends . . . more or less on the limitations imposed on us."

"Now you must explain to me the foundations of your world," Bazarov would interrupt him. "Is your world the same as rests on three fishes?"

"It's the earth, master, that is stood on three fishes," the peasant would explain reassuringly, in a good-natured patriarchal, sing-song voice. "But as against our, so to say, world there is set up, as we well know, the will of the gentry; that is why you are our fathers. And the more exacting the master, the better is the peasant pleased."

After hearing a peasant deliver himself thus, Bazarov on one occasion shrugged his shoulders contemptuously and turned his back on him, and the peasant went on his way.

"What were you palavering about?" another peasant asked him, a middle-aged man of sulky mien, who, as he stood on the porch of his cottage, had followed from a distance his encounter with Bazarov. "Was it about the arrears you were talking?"

"It wasn't about the arrears, mate!" the first peasant replied in a voice which had already shed all trace of patriarchal sing-song, and had, on the contrary, assumed a note of harsh independence.

"I was just having a few words with him; my tongue needed loosening a bit. A master's always a master, we know that; they ain't got much understanding."

"How could they!" the other peasant replied and, tilting back their caps and loosening their belts, they began to discuss their own affairs and needs. Alas! This self-assured Bazarov, who had shrugged his shoulders so contemptuously, this Bazarov who prided himself on being able to talk to peasants (as he had boasted when arguing with Paul Petrovich), had no suspicion that in their eyes he was something in the nature of a mere jack-pudding.

However, at last he did find something to preoccupy him. One day, in his presence, his father was bandaging a peasant's injured leg, but the old man's hands shook so much that he had some difficulty in applying the bandages; his son came to his assistance, and from that day on helped him regularly with his patients, but he never ceased to mock at the remedies he suggested or at his father's eagerness to apply them. But Bazarov's mockery did not upset his father in the least; they even brought him some comfort. With two fingers gripping his soiled dressing-gown in the region of his belly, and puffing away at his pipe, he listened to Bazarov with evident enjoyment; the greater the venom of his son's quips, the more humour there was in the happy father's laughter, as he showed every one of his blackened teeth. Occasionally, he even began to repeat some of these obtuse and pointless sallies, like the one, for instance, which without rhyme or reason he repeated for several days on end: "Well, that's only the ninth degree!" He did so because his son had used the expression when he heard that he was in the habit of going to early mass.

"Thank God! He's shaken off his dejection!" he whispered to his wife. "The way he told me off to-day was a marvel!"

The idea of having his son as an assistant filled him with enthusiasm and brimmed him with pride. "Yes, yes," he would say to some peasant woman, in a long, loose-fitting peasant coat and horned head-dress, thrusting a bottle of Goulard water or a pot of madwort ointment into her hands, "you should praise the Lord every minute of the day, because my son is staying with me; do you realize that you are being treated according to the very latest scientific and modern methods? The Emperor of the French, Napoleon III himself, has no better doctor." The peasant woman who had come to complain of being "hoisted in the gripes" (she was unable, however, to explain the significance of these words), kept bowing low and fumbling in her bosom for the doctor's fee—the four eggs that lay there wrapped in an odd bit of linen.

One day Bazarov even extracted a tooth from an itinerant pedlar of gaudy fabrics, and, although this tooth was normal, the father preserved it as a rare specimen and, when showing it to Father Alexei, kept repeating over and over again:

"Just look at those roots! How strong Eugene must be! He jerked the pedlar right up into the air. . . . I believe he could pull up an oak tree! . . ."

"Excellent!" Father Alexei responded at last, at a loss what to reply or how to cope with the old man's ecstasy.

One day a peasant from a neighbouring village drove up, bringing a brother of his, who had contracted typhus. Lying on a heap of straw, the unfortunate man was on the point of death, his body was covered with purple patches, and he had long ago lost consciousness. Vassily Ivanich expressed regret that it had occurred to no one to seek medical advice sooner, and pronounced against any hope of recovery. As a matter of fact, the peasant failed to get his brother home— he died in the cart on the return journey.

Three days later, Bazarov walked into his father's room and asked him if he had any silver nitrate.

"I have some. What is it for?"

"I need it . . . to sterilize a cut."

"For whom?"

"For myself."

"What? For yourself! What's happened? What sort of a cut is it? Show me it."

"Here it is, on my finger. This morning I drove out to the village—you know the one from which the typhus patient was brought. For some reason, they were getting ready to perform an autopsy, and I thought I'd get some practice."

"Well?"

"So I got permission from the district doctor to do it, and then I cut myself."

Vassily Ivanich suddenly turned quite pale and, without a word, hurried into his study, returning immediately with a little silver nitrate. Bazarov was about to take it and go off.

"For God's sake!" Vassily Ivanich exclaimed. "Let me do it myself."

"You're a great one for practice," Bazarov replied with a smile.

"It's no joking matter, please. Show me your finger. It's not a big cut. Is it painful?"

"Press harder; don't be afraid."

Vassily Ivanich paused.

"What do you think, Eugene? Wouldn't it be better to sear it with a hot iron?"

"That should have been done before. Actually, even silver nitrate is useless now. If I'm infected, then it's already too late."

"What do you mean . . . too late?" The old man was barely able to utter these words.

"What do you expect! It's over four hours since it happened."

Vassily Ivanich burned the cut a little more.

"But hadn't the district doctor any caustic?"

"No, he hadn't."

"My God, how's that? A doctor—and yet without such an essential thing!"

"You should have seen his lancets," Bazarov said, and then went out.

Till late that evening, and all through the following day, Vassily Ivanich picked on every excuse to penetrate into his son's room and, though he made no reference to the cut and even attempted to chat quite casually with him on various topics, stared so persistently into his eyes and watched him so anxiously that Bazarov finally lost his patience and threatened to depart. Vassily Ivanich thereupon promised not to worry him, particularly as Arina Vlassyevna, from whom he naturally kept everything back, had already begun to ask him why he was sleeping so badly and what had come over him. For two whole days he held himself in check, although his son's appearance, which he kept under stealthy observation, was very far from satisfying him. . . . But on the third day, at dinner, he could contain himself no longer. Bazarov was sitting with eyes lowered and without tasting a single dish.

"Why don't you eat, Eugene?" he asked, assuming a casual expression. "The food seems well cooked."

"I don't feel like it, that's why."

"You have no appetite?" he asked, adding timidly: "And does your head ache?"

"It does. Why shouldn't it?"

Arina Vlassyevna sat up and took notice.

"Please don't be angry, Eugene," Vassily Ivanich went on, "but will you let me feel your pulse?"

Bazarov stood up.

"I can tell you, without your feeling it, that I have a temperature."

"And do you feel feverish too?"

"Yes, I do. I'd better go and lie down; will you send me up some lime tea? I must have caught a chill."

"That's why I heard you coughing last night," his mother said.

"I've got a chill," Bazarov repeated and went off.

While Arina Vlassyevna was preparing the lime tea, the old man strode into the next room and there silently tugged at his hair.

That day Bazarov did not get up again and passed the whole of the night in a state of half-conscious, heavy slumber. On opening his eyes with an effort at about one o'clock in the morning, he perceived his father's pallid face bent over him in the glimmer of the icon-lamp, and bade him go away; the latter complied, but was soon back on tiptoe, and partly concealing himself behind the door of a wardrobe, stood there, unable to tear his eyes away from his son. Arina Vlassyevna also did not go to bed and, opening the study door, would come in to hear "how Enyusha was breathing" and also to have a peep at her husband. She could only catch a glimpse of his hunched, motionless back, but this brought her some relief. Next morning, Bazarov made an attempt to get up, but felt giddy and his nose began to bleed; he went back to bed. Vassily Ivanich silently attended to his wants; Arina Vlassyevna came in now and then to ask how he felt. He would reply "Better," and turn his face to the wall. Vassily Ivanich would wave her away with both arms; biting her lips to hold back her tears, she would leave the room. It was as though sudden darkness had descended on the house; everyone's face looked drawn and everything was strangely still; a raucous cock had been removed from the yard and carried into the village; for a long time the bird remained perplexed at being treated in this fashion. Bazarov continued to lie in bed, his face tucked up to the wall. Vassily Ivanich attempted to ask him questions, but they only exhausted Bazarov, and the old man was reduced to sitting still in an arm-chair, now and then cracking his fingers. Off and on, he would go into the garden for an instant, stand for a while there, like a piece of statuary, stricken with unutterable amazement (this expression did not leave his face for a moment); then he would return to his son's room, avoiding as best he could his wife's anxious questioning on the way. At last, she managed to seize hold of his hand and ask him feverishly, almost menacingly: "What is the matter with him?" He managed to collect himself and to force a smile in reply; but to his horror, instead of a smile, a hollow laugh unexpectedly burst from his lips. Early next morning, he sent for a doctor. In case he might take umbrage, he thought it right to warn his son of this step.

Bazarov suddenly turned on the sofa, stared fixedly and dully at his father, and asked him for a drink of water. As he handed a glass of water to him, his father profited by the opportunity to feel his forehead. It was simply blazing.

"I'm in a bad way, old chap," Bazarov began. "I've caught the infection. In a few days, you will have to bury me."

Vassily Ivanich staggered as though he had been kicked on his legs.

"Eugene!" he whispered. "What do you mean? . . . God forbid! You've got a chill. . . ."

"That'll do," Bazarov interjected in a deliberate voice. "No doctor should talk like that. You know very well all the symptoms of the disease."

"Where are the symptoms . . . of the disease, Eugene?
. . . I ask you!"

"And what is this?" Bazarov said, pulling back the sleeve
of his shirt and showing his father the ominous red patches
which had burst out on his skin.

Vassily Ivanich gave a shudder and froze with fear.

"Assuming," he brought out at last, "assuming . . . that
. . . that this is something in the nature . . . of an infection . . ."

"Pyæmia," his son prompted.

"Well, yes . . . something . . . in the nature . . . of an
epidemic . . ."

"Of pyæmia," Bazarov repeated sternly and distinctly.
"Oh have you forgotten your lecture-notes?"

"All right, all right, as you wish . . . But we shall cure
you in any case."

"Stuff and nonsense," Bazarov retorted. "However, that's
not the point. I did not expect to have to die so soon; it
really is rather an unpleasant accident. Mother and you
must now make the best of your strong religious convictions; here is your chance to put them to trial." He took a
few more sips of water. "May I ask you to do something
for me . . . while I can still think clearly? To-morrow or the
day after, my brain, as you know, will hand in its resignation. Even now I'm not quite sure whether I am making
myself clear. When I was lying down, I seemed to see a
pack of red hounds frisking round me, and you were setting
them against me as if I were a woodcock. I feel drunk. Do
you understand me clearly?"

"Of course, Eugene. You are talking quite normally."

"So much the better. You told me that you had sent for
the doctor. . . . That brings you some comfort. . . . Now
comfort me too; send a messenger . . ."

"To Arcady," the old man picked him up.

"Who is Arcady?" Bazarov inquired as though reflecting.
. . . "Ah, yes! That fledgling! No, leave him in peace: he's
a jackdaw by now. Don't be astonished, this is no delirium.
But please send a messenger at once to Madame Odintzov,
Anna Sergeyevna, there's a lady landowner of that name.
. . . Have you heard of her?" (The old man nodded.)
" 'Bazarov sends his respects and wishes to inform her
that he is dying,' You will do that for me?"

"Of course I will. . . . But how can you die, Eugene?

. . . Judge for yourself! What will justice mean if that happens?"

"I don't know. But do send the messenger."

"This very minute. I'll write her a line myself."

"No, why should you? Tell her simply that I send my respects, that's all that is needed. And now I shall return to my hounds again. How strange! I want to concentrate and think of death, but I can't even do that. I merely see a patch of sorts . . . and that's all."

He turned over again heavily facing the wall. On leaving the study, Vassily Ivanich got as far as his wife's bedroom and collapsed there on his knees in front of the icons.

"Pray, Arina, pray!" he moaned. "Our son is dying."

The doctor, the same district practitioner who could produce no caustic when it was required, came along and, after examining the patient, advised them to adopt a prophylactic treatment, and followed this up with a few words on the possibility of recovery.

"And did you ever happen to observe that anyone in my present condition has ever *failed* to reach the Elysian fields?" Bazarov asked and, suddenly gripping the foot of a heavy table next to the sofa, shook it and made it budge.

"My strength. . . . I still have some strength left, and yet I must die . . ." he said. "An old man, at least, has had time to become disenchanted with life, but I . . . Yes, just try and repudiate death. It repudiates you, and that's all there is to it! Who is that crying there?" he went on after a while. "Mother? Poor soul! For whom will she now make her wonderful broths? You also seem to be snivelling, Vassily Ivanich? Well, if Christianity is no help, at least try and be a philosopher, a stoic, maybe! Didn't you once boast to me that you were a philosopher?"

"A fine philosopher I am!" Vassily Ivanich sobbed as the tears streamed down his cheeks.

With every hour Bazarov grew worse; as normally happens in cases of surgical poisoning, the infection spread rapidly. But he had not yet lost consciousness and could grasp what was being said; he was still putting up a fight. "I refuse to be delirious," he whispered, clenching his fists. "How absurd!" And he would at once add: "Now, what is the balance, if we deduct ten from eight?" His father strode about the room like a madman, suggesting one remedy after another, and repeatedly covering his son's feet. "We must wrap him in cold sheets . . . give him an emetic . . . a mustard-plaster for his stomach . . . a bleeding," he would exclaim with great intensity. The doctor, who had stayed on at his request, agreed to all his suggestions, gave the patient lemonade, and for his own use wheedled now a pipe full of tobacco, now "something strong and warming," in short, a portion of vodka. The mother kept vigil on a low bench near the door and every now and again went off to say her prayers; a few days ago, a small hand-mirror had slipped from her grasp and splintered, and this she had always interpreted as a bad omen; even Anfisushka could find no words to console her. Timofeyich had departed with the message for Madame Odintzov.

Bazarov spent an uncomfortable night. . . . A relentless temperature tormented him. Morning brought some relief. He begged his mother to comb his hair, kissed her hand, and drank two mouthfuls of tea. His father felt slightly cheered.

"Thank God!" he repeated. "The moment of crisis has come . . . the crisis has come."

"Just imagine!" said Bazarov. "What does the word mean? It has just occurred to you: 'crisis' you say, and feel relieved. It's amazing the trust men still put in words. You may dub a man a 'fool' for instance, without laying hands on him, and yet he will feel out of sorts; but if you call him a 'brainy chap' and give him no money—then he will be simply delighted."

This little tirade, reminiscent of Bazarov's previous sallies, greatly moved his father.

"Bravo! Excellently spoken, splendid!" he exclaimed, pretending to clap his hands.

Bazarov smiled wryly.

"What do you think?" he asked. "Is the crisis past or just beginning?"

"You feel better, that's what I think. That's why I'm so glad," Vassily Ivanich replied.

"That's fine; there's no harm in rejoicing. And did you send the message to her, you remember? Did you send it?"

"Of course I did."

The turn for the better did not last long. The disease made headway again. Vassily Ivanich spent all his time at his son's bedside. He looked himself as if he were the victim of extraordinary tortures. Several times he was on the point of saying something—but the words stuck in his throat.

"Eugene!" he gasped at last. "My son, my dear, dear son."

This unexpected form of address affected Bazarov. He turned his head slightly and, apparently trying to throw off the pressure weighing down upon him, called out: "What is it, father?"

"Eugene," Vassily Ivanich continued, sinking on his knees by the bed, although Bazarov had not opened his eyes and could see nothing. "Eugene, you are better now; by God's grace you will recover; but make the most of this moment, give your mother and myself some consolation, do your duty as a Christian! It's terrible for me to have to say this to you; but more dreadful still . . . it will be for eternity, Eugene . . . just think what that means. . . ."

The old man's voice trailed off as a strange expression flitted over his son's face, while he continued to lie there with eyes closed.

"I have no objection if that will help to console you," he replied at last. "But there seems no point in hurrying yet. You said yourself that my condition had improved."

"It has, Eugene, it has: but who knows, it's all in God's power, but if you do your duty . . ."

"No, I prefer to wait," Bazarov interrupted him. "I agree, the crisis has set in. But if we are both mistaken, it won't matter! Extreme unction can be administered even to the unconscious."

"Don't say that, Eugene. . . ."

"I'll wait. But now I want to sleep. Please leave me alone."

And he put his head back in the former position.

Rising from his knees, the old man sat down in the armchair and, holding his chin, began to bite his fingers. . . .

Suddenly his ears caught the rumble of a sprung carriage, a rumble that can be heard very clearly in the fastness of the country. Nearer and nearer the light wheels rolled; very soon the snorting of horses could also be heard. . . . The father jumped up and rushed to the window. A barouche, drawn by four horses, drove into the courtyard of the small house. Without understanding clearly the significance of what was happening, he ran out on to the steps,

brimming over with senseless joy. . . . A footman in livery
was opening the carriage door; a lady in a black veil and
black mantilla stepped down. . . .

"I am Madame Odintzov," she said. "Is Eugene Vassilich
still alive? Are you his father? I have brought my doctor
with me."

"Benefactress!" Vassily Ivanich exclaimed and, seizing
her hands, pressed his lips feverishly to them, while the
doctor, whom Anna Odintzov had brought, a squat man
in glasses and with a German face, was climbing out of the
barouche without any sign of haste.

"He is still alive, my Eugene is alive, and now he will be
saved! Wife! Wife! . . . A heavenly angel has . . ."

"Oh Lord, what is it?" the old lady stuttered, running
out of the drawing-room. Failing to understand anything,
she threw herself at once at Anna Sergeyevna's feet and,
like a crazy woman, began to kiss her dress.

"What is this! What are you doing!" Anna Sergeyevna
kept exclaiming; but Arina Vlassyevna paid no heed to
her, and Vassily Ivanich went on repeating: "Angel!
Angel!"

"*Wo ist der Kranke?* And the pashient is where?" the
doctor inquired at last not without a touch of indignation.

Vassily Ivanich collected himself.

"Here, here, please follow me, *würdigster Herr Kollege*,"
he added, drawing on his memories of the past.

"Eh!" the German said with a sour look.

Vassily Ivanich led him into the study.

"Here is the doctor whom Anna Sergeyevna Odintzov
has brought," he said, bending down to his son's ear. "And
she is here herself."

Bazarov suddenly opened his eyes.

"What did you say?" he asked.

"I said that Madame Odintzov has arrived and has
brought this gentleman—a doctor."

Bazarov looked round.

"So she's here. . . . I want to see her," he said.

"You will see her, Eugene, but, first of all, you must have
a word with the doctor. Our own doctor is no longer here,
so I must tell him the whole history of your illness, and
then we shall consult together."

Bazarov glanced at the German.

"Well, get on with it then, only don't spout Latin. I know quite well the meaning of *jam moritur*."

"Der Herr scheint des Deutschen mächtig zu sein," the new successor of Æsculapius started off, turning to Vassily Ivanich.

"Ich . . . habe . . . No, we had better talk Russian," the old man replied lamely.

"Ah, ah! Zo dat iz how it iz. . . . Pleeze. . . ." And so the consultation began.

Half an hour later, in the company of Vassily Ivanich, Anna Sergeyevna entered the study. Her doctor had already told her in a whisper that there was no hope for the patient's recovery.

Her eyes sought Bazarov . . . and she stopped in the doorway, taken aback by his feverish and, at the same time, deathly pale face, and by the turbid eyes that were now fixed upon her. She was really alarmed, overcome by a chilly and haunting fear: then it instantly occurred to her that she would have behaved very differently if she had really loved Bazarov.

"Thank you," Bazarov pronounced with an effort. "I did not expect it. It is a good deed. We meet again, as you foretold."

"Anna Sergeyevna was so kind . . ." his father began to say.

"Father, leave us," his son interrupted him. "Anna, you don't mind, do you? Now that . . ."

He nodded his head at his powerless, supine body.

Vassily Ivanich went out.

"Well, I must thank you," Bazarov repeated. "It was a royal gesture. They say kings visit the dying."

"Eugene, I hope that . . ."

"Ah, Anna Sergeyevna, let us speak the unvarnished truth. I'm done for. The wheel has run over me. As it turns out, there was no point in worrying about the future. Death is an old jester, but every man sees him in a fresh guise. Up to now, I have felt no fear. . . . Soon I shall lose consciousness, and then the lid will be clamped down!" (He waved his arms feebly.) "Well, what shall I say to you? . . . I was in love with you! That made little sense before, even less now. Love has a body, and my particular body is already disintegrating. It would be better if I told you—what a glorious woman you are! How beautiful you look standing there, so lovely. . . ."

Anna Sergeyevna involuntarily shuddered.

"No, don't be alarmed. . . . Just sit down over there. . . . But don't come near me—the disease is infectious."

Anna Sergeyevna quickly crossed the room and sat down in an arm-chair by the sofa on which Bazarov was lying.

"Great-heart!" he whispered. "Oh, how close you are, how young, and fresh, and pure . . . here in the middle of this sick-ridden room! . . . Well, we must say our farewells now! May you live long, that's the best of all things, and make the most of it while there's time. Take a good look at this ghastly sight, at this still writhing worm, crushed and yet glaring at you. And yet once he also dreamt of all the things he might accomplish, and believed he was immortal. Why should he die? He used to think 'I have a task to perform, I am a giant!' And now this giant's only task is to die a decent death, and that is no one else's business. . . . All the same, I shan't put my tail between my legs now."

Bazarov was silent and began to grope for his glass. Without taking off her gloves and breathing apprehensively Anna handed him a glass of water.

"You will soon forget me," he began again. "A dead man is no companion to the living. My father may tell you what a loss I shall be to Russia. . . . That's bosh, but don't disillusion the old man. A child must find something to console it, you know that. And be kind to my mother. You will not find the like of them in all the whole great world, in daylight even, and with the help of a lamp. . . . Does Russia need me? No, clearly she doesn't. Whom does she need? She might need a cobbler, a tailor too, a butcher . . . he sells meat . . . a butcher . . . wait a moment, I'm becoming involved. . . . I can see a forest here. . . ."

Bazarov put his hand to his forehead.

Anna Sergeyevna bent over him.

"Eugene, I am here."

He at once took her hand and raised himself.

"Farewell!" he exclaimed with unexpected force, and his eyes flashed a last gleam. "Farewell. . . . Listen. . . . I never kissed you then. . . . Ah, breathe on the dying flame, let it go out. . . ."

Anna Sergeyevna pressed her lips to his forehead.

"Enough!" he exclaimed, and sank back on the pillow. "Now ... darkness...."

Anna Sergeyevna tiptoed out of the room.

"Well?" The father asked her in a whisper.

"He's fallen asleep," she replied barely audibly.

Bazarov was fated to wake no more. By evening he sank into a state of complete coma, and died on the following day. . . . Father Alexei performed the last rites. When extreme unction was being administered and the holy oil touched his breast, one of his eyes opened: and it seemed as though at the sight of the priest in his vestments, the smoking censer, and the candles in front of the icon, something like a shudder of horror was momentarily reflected in his pallid face.

When at last he had sighed his last sigh, and the house became filled with general lamentation, Vassily Ivanich suddenly had a fit of frenzy.

"I said I'd rebel," he shouted hoarsely, his face all burning and distorted, waving his clenched fist in the air as though threatening someone. "I will rebel," he shouted, "I will!" But all in tears, Arina Vlassyevna clasped her arms round his neck, and they both fell prone on the ground. "And so," as Anfisushka related afterwards in the servants' quarters, "they bowed their dear heads, like lambs at noonday."

But the noonday blaze dies away, and is succeeded by the evening and then the night; and returning there, in that peaceful retreat, the tormented and the weary find their sweetest sleep.

XXVIII

SIX months passed. White winter was at its height, with its relentless silence of cloudless frosts, firm crunching snow, rosy hoar-rimed trees, pale emerald skies, curls of smoke above the chimneys, puffs of steam from doors quickly opened and shut again, glowing frost-bitten faces, and the jerky trotting of nags chilled to the marrow of their bones. The January day was already drawing to a close;

more and more firmly the evening chill compressed the con-
gealed air, and the blood-red sunset rapidly dwindled. In
the house at Maryino, the lights were being lit. In a black
tailed coat and white gloves, Prokofyich was laying the
table for seven with unwonted ceremony. A week ago, in
a small parish church, two weddings had been celebrated
without fuss and almost without witnesses—those of Arcady and Katya, Nicholas Petrovich and Fenichka: and,
this day, Nicholas Petrovich was giving a farewell dinner
for his brother Paul, who was setting out to Moscow on
business. Anna Sergeyevna was already in Moscow: having
generously endowed the young couple, she had gone there
immediately after the wedding.

Punctually at three o'clock they all gathered round the
table. Mitya had his place among them too, and could now
boast of a nanny in a showy head-dress. Paul Petrovich
was throning it between Katya and Fenichka: the "hus-
bands" had found a nook for themselves beside their wives.
Of late a change had come over our old friends; they appeared to have grown more handsome and mature. Paul
alone looked leaner and this, incidentally, gave an air of
great elegance, of the "grand seigneur," to his expressive
features. . . . Fenichka too had altered. Wearing a refreshing silk dress, a wide velvet bandeau round her hair, a gold
chain on her neck, she sat still and respectful, full of solicitude towards herself, towards everyone round her, and kept
smiling as though she wished to say: "Pardon me, it's not
my fault." But she was not the only person to smile—they
all smiled, and they all looked apologetic; they felt a little
awkward, a trifle sad, but at bottom very happy. They
attended to each other's wants with an air of amusing con-
sideration as though they had conspired to act in some
good-natured comedy. Of them all, Katya was most at
ease: she glanced about her with a trusting air, and it was
noticeable that Nicholas Petrovich had already become
devotedly attached to her. Towards the end of the meal he
rose and, raising his wine-glass, turned to Paul Petrovich.

"You are forsaking us . . . forsaking us, dear brother," he
began. "Of course, it will not be for long, but still I cannot
but express to you what I . . . what we . . . how much I . . .
how much we . . . But the trouble is I'm not very good at
making speeches! Arcady, you'd better do the rest."

"I can't, daddy; I'm not prepared."

"As if I was prepared! Well, brother, allow me then quite simply to embrace you, to wish you all the best, and do come back to us as soon as you can!"

Paul Petrovich embraced them all, Mitya of course included; moreover, he kissed Fenichka's hand, which she had not yet learnt to hold out properly. Drinking out of the glass that had been refilled with wine, he exclaimed with a deep sigh, "May you all be very happy, dear friends! *Farewell!*" This tail-phrase in English passed unnoticed, but all present showed signs of emotion.

"To Bazarov's memory," whispered Katya into her husband's ear as she clinked glasses with him. By way of a reply Arcady squeezed her hand warmly, but did not venture to propose the toast aloud.

This seems to be the end. But perhaps some of our readers would like to learn what each of the characters we have portrayed is doing now at this very moment. We are ready to oblige.

Recently Anna Sergeyevna married, out of conviction rather than love, a man who promises to be one of Russia's leading figures, a very able lawyer of a vigorous and practical turn of mind, resolute will and remarkable gifts of eloquence—a man still young and generous, but also cold as ice. They live in the greatest harmony and may one day achieve happiness or even love. Princess K died, forgotten by all on her deathbed. The Kirsanovs, father and son, have settled down at Maryino. . . . Their affairs have taken a turn for the better. Arcady has become passionately engrossed in estate-management, and the "farm" is already bringing in a considerable income. Nicholas Petrovich has become an arbitrator on land reforms and is hard at work; he is constantly touring his district; he indulges in long speeches (he is of the school that believes that peasants should receive "instruction," that is to say, that they must be worn down by frequent repetition of one and the same phrase). But to speak the truth, he fails to give complete satisfaction either to the cultured gentry, who now talk flauntingly, now despondently, about 'mancipation (giving the *an* a nasal French twist), or to the uncultured ones, who unceremoniously vituperate against "this 'mancipation." He is too soft for either camp. Katya has given birth to a son, Kolya, while Mitya is already a sturdy scampering boy and prattles away loquaciously. Next to her husband and Mitya, Fenichka adores no one more than her daughter-in-law, and whenever Katya sits down at the piano she is only too delighted to spend the whole day in her company. We must say a word about Peter. He is grown quite starchy with stupidity and self-importance, and drawls out all his o's likes au's: *"Nau* I shall *gau,"* he says. But he has also married and, together with his bride, has appropriated to himself quite a decent dowry. His wife is the daughter of a city market-gardener: she had previously turned down two eligible suitors for no other reason than their lack of a watch; Peter could not only boast of a watch, he even had a pair of patent leather boots.

On the Brühl terrace at Dresden, between two and four o'clock in the afternoon, at the most fashionable hour for promenading, you may come across a gentleman of some fifty years of age, already quite grey and apparently suffering from gout, but still handsome, elegantly dressed, and having that air of distinction which a man can only acquire as a result of long intercourse with the higher ranks of society. Paul Petrovich, the gentleman in question, had left Moscow and gone abroad for the sake of his health, and then stayed on in Dresden, where he frequents chiefly English people and Russian visitors. His manner with the English is simple, almost modest, but not undignified: they find him a bit of a bore, but respect him as *"a perfect gentleman."* He is less inhibited with Russians, unburdens his spleen to them, jests at his own expense and theirs, but he does all this with a certain air of charm, ease and breeding. He is a Slavophil in outlook: as we are well aware, this is considered *très distingué* in higher society. He reads nothing Russian, but keeps on his writing-desk an ashtray in the form of a peasant bast-shoe. Our tourists frequent him a great deal. While "temporarily in the opposition," Matvey Kolyazin paid a magisterial visit to him as he passed through Dresden on his way to the Bohemian watering-places; and the local inhabitants, whom he frequents but little, almost venerate him. No one is more successful than the Herr Baron von Kirsanov in obtaining easily and expeditiously tickets for the court choir, the theatre, and such places. He continues to do good works, within his capacity; he still causes a stir in a small way; it was not in vain that he had been a social lion once upon a time; but life seems to weigh

heavily on him . . . more heavily than he himself will admit.
. . . A mere glimpse of him in the Russian Church confirms
this, as he leans in some corner against the wall, immersed
in thought and remaining motionless for long periods with
tightly drawn lips, before he starts up of a sudden and begins almost imperceptibly to make the sign of the cross. . . .

Madame Kukshin also found herself abroad. She is now
in Heidelberg, a student no longer of the natural sciences
but of architecture, in which, as she declares, she has discovered some new laws. She is as friendly with students as
ever, especially with young Russian physicists and chemists,
who crowd Heidelberg and at first astonish the naïve
German professors by their sober outlook on the world,
only to amaze them subsequently by their complete inactivity and absolute sluggishness. In the company of two or
three such students of chemistry, who cannot distinguish
between hydrogen and nitrogen, though they bubble over
with critical negation and self-importance, and in the company also of the great Elyseyevich, Sitnikov, who is aiming
at greatness, gads about Petersburg and, as he assures us, is
engaged in furthering Bazarov's "cause." Rumour has it
that he recently received a drubbing, but came out of it
quits: in an obscure little article, tucked away in an obscure
little periodical, he hinted that the person who had assaulted
him was a coward. This he calls irony. His father still em-
ploys him on errands, and his wife treats him like a fool . . .
and a *littérateur*.

In one of the far corners of Russia stands a small village
graveyard. Like most of our graveyards it looks dismal:
weeds have long overgrown the ditches round it, the drab
wooden crosses sag and rot beneath their once freshly
painted gables; the tombstones are all askew, as though
someone were pushing them from below; two or three
scanty fir trees barely afford some meagre shade; sheep
wander at will over the graves. . . . But in their midst stands
a grave untouched by any human being, untrampled by any
animal: only the birds at dawn perch and sing on it. An
iron railing fences it in; two fir trees have been planted
there, one at each end; in that grave Eugene Bazarov lies
buried. Often from a nearby village a tottering old couple,
man and wife, make their way here. Supporting each other,
they walk with heavy steps; on reaching the railing, they
fall down upon their knees, and long and bitterly they

weep, and long and yearningly they gaze at the mute tomb-
stone beneath which their son is lying; exchanging a brief
word, they brush the dust from the stone, set a branch of a
fir tree right, and then resume their prayers, unable to tear
themselves away from this spot where they feel themselves
so close to their son and their memories of him. . . . Can
it be that their prayers, their tears, will remain unanswered?
Can it be that love, sacred and devoted love, is not omnip-
otent? Oh, no! However passionate, sinful and rebellious
the heart wrapped away in that grave, the flowers that blossom there peep at us tranquilly with innocent eyes: they
speak to us not only of all-embracing peace, of the vast repose of "indifferent" nature; they tell us also of everlasting
reconciliation and life without end. . . .

SELECTED READING LIST

Other Books by IVAN TURGENEV

The Hunting Sketches, 1852
Rudin, 1856 Novel
A Nest of Gentlefolk, 1858 Novel
On the Eve, 1860 Novel
First Love, 1860 Novel
Smoke, 1867 Novel
The Torrents of Spring, 1871 Novel
Virgin Soil, 1877 Novel

Selected Biography and Criticism

Freeborn, Richard. *Turgenev: The Novelist's Novelist*. New York and London: Oxford University Press, 1960.

Gettmann, R. A. *Turgenev in England and America*. Urbana, Illinois: University of Illinois Press, 1941.

Magarshack, David. *Turgenev: A Life*. New York: Grove Press; London: Faber & Faber, Ltd., 1954.

Yarmolinsky, Avrahm. *Turgenev: The Man, His Art and His Age*. New York: The Orion Press, Inc., 1959; London: Andre Deutsch, Ltd., 1960.